DESPERATE MEASURES

As adrenaline pumped into his body, he took one second to look across at the apartment he had been watching; the bedroom window was wide open. The signal confirmed, he dashed for the door, yanked it open, and almost threw himself down the rear steps.

He collided hard with a man who was at that moment coming in: a powerful, burly man who grabbed him and slammed him down onto the concrete-floored entryway. "What the hell are you doing here?" he demanded.

Tallon had to fight for breath; the impact of his landing had forced most of the air out of his lungs. "Police," he managed to gasp. "Let me go!"

He ran across the open area, his side crying for respite, toward the open window. His mind was fixed with total determination on his objective; his aches and pains were thrust aside. He got close to the window at last; just as he did so, he heard his patrol car scream to a halt at the front of the building, its overhead lights biting into the blackness of the night. He braced himself, took a short run, and launched himself into a flat dive through the open window.

He didn't actually feel it when he hit, he only knew that he did and then rolled with his head tucked close in and his arms protecting his neck. Then he was on his feet, legs apart, his weapon almost automatically in his hand.

There was a dim bedside lamp on and beside it stood Mary Clancy, naked, the pink glow dramatically outlining her body. And there was a man, a man with a mask over his face, and a knife held in his outstretched hand. The man whirled and the face of the Frankenstein monster was ghastly in the pale light.

Books by John Ball

Virgil Tibbs Mysteries

Five Pieces of Jade
Eyes of the Buddha
Then Came Violence
Singapore

Chief Jack Tallon Crime Novels

Police Chief
Trouble for Tallon
Chief Tallon and the S.O.R.

POLICE CHIEF

A Chief Jack Tallon Crime Novel

John Ball

SPEAKING VOLUMES, LLC
NAPLES, FLORIDA
2013

Police Chief

ISBN 978-1-61232-984-0

For Carol Brandt

Author's Note

This work was made possible because of the extraordinary help and cooperation of Chief Jerome Gardner of the Cheney, Washington, Police Department. He, and everyone in his organization, supported this project from its inception and made many significant contributions. Mayor Jerry Blakeley of Cheney and City Manager Charles Earl also provided material assistance. Special thanks are also tendered to the very attractive Mrs. Patricia Gardner, whose hospitality is scintillating.

It is necessary to state, however, that what follows is not a portrait of Cheney or of any of its citizens, and no such relationship should be inferred.

J.B.

Chapter One

At a few minutes past one in the morning a silent form crossed the edge of the small private parking area behind the gun store and all but disappeared in the deep shadows of the building. His black knit shirt and slacks helped to make him invisible, so did the dark, rubber-soled shoes that he wore and the nylon stocking mask that was stretched across his face. He paused for a long ten seconds, looking about for any evidence that he had been seen; then he signaled.

He already knew exactly how he was going to get up onto the roof. The job had been expertly and professionally cased; every detail had been planned with meticulous care. For an operation of this size, that was essential.

He was on the roof, hidden behind the two-foot-high ledge that ran around all four sides, in less than a minute. There he lay still for another fifteen seconds, time enough for the other three to make sure he had not been spotted.

Everything seemed to be all right. He got to his feet and ran almost silently across the roof, bent well over to keep the angle low. As soon as he was fifteen feet from the edge, there was no place that anyone could stand and spot him—except on another roof, and that was a chance he had to take. He knew that the odds against being seen were close to nil, and he had taken risks before—sometimes big ones.

The trap door was relatively simple to open, since he already knew that it was bugged and with what kind of equipment. Four minutes work with the tools he had brought cut away enough of the wood and tar paper to reveal the carefully hidden magnet that was part of the alarm system. Less than half an inch from it its mate was securely fastened to the framing. If any idiot had lifted the door out of position, the signal would have gone off almost instantly.

From his tool kit he took out another magnet, that had been coated on one side with adhesive compound. He peeled off the tape that protected the sticky outer surface and with careful fingers pressed it against the fixed magnet so that the circuit would remain unbroken. Then, smoothly and neatly, he lifted the trap door away. Below him there was a false attic seven feet high. Underneath that was the store, one of the largest of its kind in the entire Los Angeles complex. There were hundreds upon hundreds of guns of every kind, from tiny .22's to Magnums that could blast a man three houses away by shooting through the intervening walls. There were shotguns, rifles with the highest precision optical equipment, and some special weapons that the visiting public never saw. And tens of thousands of rounds of ammunición, enough to equip an army.

The critical part of the plan was the truck. It was a bold stroke that at the same time was almost foolproof. Half an hour after the store had closed Andy had driven the truck in, turned it around, and parked it behind the rear loading door. Then he had simply locked it and walked away. The name lettered on the panels was false, but it suggested that the truck had a right to be there. Because it had been done so openly, in broad daylight, no one had questioned it. If Andy had been stopped, he would have said that he had been hired to leave the truck at that address and that he had followed his orders.

As a second man came onto the roof, the first one made his thin rope fast and lowered himself carefully into the store. There were no lights on inside and even someone trying to look in through the front windows would not have been able to see him.

As he passed through the opening between the false attic and the ceiling of the store, his body interrupted the totally invisible and well-concealed infrared beam that crossed it exactly in the center. Within milliseconds a brilliant red light blinked rapidly on the panel at the alarm company. The operator on duty saw it and immediately picked up the direct line phone to the police dispatcher.

Ordinarily he would have waited a minute or two; residential customers were always tripping their own alarms by mistake and then quickly phoning in to explain. But the gun store was a different matter: it was the most sensitive target in the whole of Pasadena and it would trigger a maximum response. He gave the information to the dispatcher and then wished to hell that he could be on hand to see the action that would follow.

Sergeant Jack Tallon was driving a white Matador patrol car when the 459 call came over the radio. He listened for the address; the moment he heard it he hit the gas pedal hard, spun the wheel, and skidded into a maximum performance reverse turn as the words "all available units respond" came over the air. Avoiding the use of his overhead lights and siren, he burned rubber on the dry pavement as he raced toward his destination.

He had been at the gun store the last time that the alarm had been tripped, some eighteen months before. That time there had been a fanatical black hidden in the toilet. The suspect had come charging out with a .45 blazing and only the grace of God had kept him from killing someone before he had been cut down. Twice before that the gun store had been hit, once with one fatality, the other time with three. As he took a corner with the tires screaming, Tallon knew that almost certainly within the next few minutes someone was going to die.

Every damn car in the city would be rolling, and South Pasadena would respond also because the gun store was close to the dividing line. If it got really bad, the Highway Patrol would come, and the sheriff's SWAT team. They could save some time by calling the coroner, too, while they were at it. There was enough firepower in that damn gun store to kill every soul in the entire city, and that would be for openers. Jack hated the place with a fury that sometimes almost got out of control. Perry Gilcrist had been shot and seriously wounded with a weapon that had been sold in that store less than an hour before he had been hit.

He made the run in well under a minute and a half, but already there were at least six other units on hand. Since he was the ranking man in the field, he would be in command unless the watch commander or another lieutenant took over. He pulled his car smartly to the curb, facing the wrong direction, grabbed up his walkie-talkie, and came out with it in his left hand.

The nine men already on the scene were well trained and had started of themselves to do the right things. Jack issued rapid orders, building and sealing a perimeter around the building. Two of the men were already in the back. He sent a third to join them with explicit instructions as two more units jerked up to the curb. Down the street South Pasadena had two units that were already blocking off all nonemergency traffic—a good example of professionalism in action; they had seen what had to be done and they had done it.

With his handset Jack reported himself on the scene and advised that the perimeter would be in position in another thirty seconds. After that, if anyone tried to get out of the gun store, no matter what armament he had, God help him.

He spotted Agent Rex Bird, who was positioned with his back against the front wall of the store, between the front door and the north show window. "Can you confirm anyone inside?" he asked from fifty feet away.

"No, but I've got a man on the roof and he reports the trap open."

Down the street the flashing lights of a big fire department unit were approaching fast; immediately behind it a smaller paramedic truck was also coming in. That was good; ladders would be needed.

"I want two more men on the roof—fast!" Tallon directed. "Back up the guy who's up there. Keep a shotgun on that opening and check any others. Any pedestrians sighted?"

A young patrolman answered. "One, a man about a block and a half away."

"Going or coming?"

"Going."

"Nab him!"

The patrolman jumped to obey. As he vaulted into his car, he remembered that no one walks away from a mounting scene of police action without an urgent reason; the attraction is too great. His partner jumped in as he hit the starter, but before he could pull away, four additional units coming in almost blocked the roadway. Using his head, the young patrolman put out a radio call for the man on foot. He was heard by a unit coming from that direction that had the pedestrian in sight. As the driver swung sharply to the curb the man turned and started to run. The driver's partner jumped out, gun drawn, and froze him.

The pedestrian offered no resistance. The driver of the unit reported him in custody; instructions came back to return to the station with the suspect.

By that time there were thirty men on the scene. Jack Tallon was looking for the gun shop owner; he was reported on the way, but apparently he was taking his time. He sold guns, but had no evident great desire to be on the scene when they were likely to be in use.

By then the perimeter was solid; the building that housed the gun shop was completely surrounded, there were men on the roof, and sharpshooters stationed at three strategic locations from which they could safely fire.

Jack picked up his car mike and spoke to the dispatcher once more. "Patch me through to the phone inside," he directed. "Let it ring."

The watch commander knew his business; the number had already been dug from the files and within fifteen seconds the phone inside the shop was ringing. Jack couldn't hear it, but Agent Bird, who was closest to the door, held up his hand to indicate that he could.

Jack used a bullhorn, pointing it toward the building. "This is the police," he said, his words booming out in the cool night air. "The building is completely surrounded. Answer the telephone—it's for you."

Then he prepared to wait—a minute, two minutes, or longer. Meanwhile the telephone would continue to ring.

"How about the truck in back?"

He glanced at the man who had asked the question; it was the first that he had heard of the truck. "Get it out of there! Be careful."

He looked at his watch. He estimated that it had been thirty seconds since the phone had started ringing. He would give it another three minutes, then he would call in the SWAT team.

Of course the building could be empty. There was a very good chance that someone had been on the roof, had seen the magnets that tripped the silent alarm system, and had been smart enough to get the hell away from there before he was caught. A good athletic burglar could be off the roof and gone in little more than half a minute if his life depended on it, and where the gun store was concerned, that could well be the case.

Tallon dared to hope that the store was empty, but the fact that it was completely silent inside meant nothing. The alarm had not short-circuited—the open hatch made that certain. Either someone was inside, or else the suspect had made his getaway before the first unit had arrived. That had been less than a minute after the alarm had been called in.

It had been almost four minutes since the phone inside had started to ring, and there had been no answer. He picked up the mike and pressed the button. "No response to the phone," he reported. "We have enough perimeter, and it's secure. Notify the watch commander that I need SWAT."

"The watch commander is on the way," the dispatcher told him in cool feminine tones. "ETA less than two minutes."

"Good enough. Out."

For the next sixty seconds he could stop and collect himself. He was not going to send his men into that shop under any circumstances; they could be blown to pieces. In California the penalty for murder, even a cop killing, had been reduced to an effective seven years—little different from armed robbery. Since it was virtually the same price either way, hard cases that were cornered usually tried to gun their way out—there were a lot of police widows who could attest to that.

Red lights flashing, another unit was approaching fast. It parked behind the fire truck that stood waiting for orders and the watch commander got out. He came directly to where Jack was standing to confer.

"The perimeter has been up and tight from about two minutes after the alarm," Jack reported. "We found a truck left in back—it's gone, or going right now. The roof is covered and the sharpshooters are positioned. No response to the bullhorn or the telephone."

"How about the owner? His name's Jacobson."

"Here," a man said. Tallon looked and saw that the gun shop proprietor was short, plump, and apparently not too concerned. Tallon hated his guts on general principles. "Don't go away, we'll need you," he said.

At that moment Agent Bird, who was still positioned beside the front door, raised his free arm and waved it silently. Then he jerked his head toward the inside of the shop.

"Give them one more shot with the bullhorn," the watch commander directed. "If they don't respond, I'll call in SWAT."

The Special Weapons and Tactics people were the ones to penetrate the building; they had the proper equipment, and they knew exactly how to do it.

Jack picked up the bullhorn once more. "This is the police," his voice boomed out. "We know that you're in there. You're completely surrounded and you can't get away. You've had it. If you want to stay alive, come out the front door, one at a time, with your hands on top of your heads. If you do, we won't shoot and you won't be hurt. There's no other out. You've got one minute; do it now."

There was no response—utter silence mocked his words.

"All right, I'll call in SWAT," the watch commander said. "Keep everyone on his toes. Whoever's inside will know what to expect, and may make a break for it any second. And they'll have enormous firepower if they know where to find it."

Jack turned toward the shop owner. "Mr. Jacobson, do you have any automatic, or semi-automatic, weapons in there—where they might be found?"

Jacobson was still apparently unmoved. "Sure—we do. For police use, of course. Law enforcement agencies."

Tallon knew damned well that no law enforcement organizations bought official equipment in that store, but he had no time to debate the matter and no taste for it. Instead he called a man over who was standing by unassigned. "Pass the word," he directed. "See that every man on the perimeter knows that there are definitely people inside—one anyway—and that the store stocks automatic weapons. Keep it low."

"Right." The man left on the half run. Then Tallon used his handset. "Sharpshooters," he said.

Three quick responses came back, one after another.

"Confirmed that someone is inside—number unknown. There are automatic weapons available to them—and ammo." He looked at Jacobson, who nodded confirmation. For the first time the shop owner seemed not quite so disinterested. Perhaps his insurance wouldn't cover what might happen next.

The dispatcher called; SWAT was responding.

That meant blood—there was hardly any way out. And not nice neat dying, the way they did it on TV. It would be masses of blood, pieces of torn flesh, brains oozing out of skulls of what had just been living men—perhaps policemen who had been there only because it had been their duty.

Within the next hour almost certainly someone would die, perhaps several people. Then, for the first time, Tallon remembered that it was his anniversary.

Chapter Two

The anniversary was a special time that he and Jennifer held inviolate to themselves. It had happened when they had returned to the apartment house where they both lived after the best evening they had ever spent together. When he had paused in front of her door, neither of them had been anxious to see it end. They had known each other for some time, but never before had they been so close.

During the rest of the night, while he had lain beside her, he had blessed the fates that had brought them together, even though he had not been in love with her at that stage. Not very long after that he discovered that he had found his wife.

Each year after that they had celebrated the anniversary of that first night. Jennifer was waiting for him at that moment, not knowing what had happened or that he would probably be hours late in coming home. He hoped to God that he would live out the night; he might not if the person or persons inside decided to burst out with guns blazing before SWAT could get there. They might try, because of the underlying death wish that so often surfaced in those who deliberately courted violence.

He picked up the mike in his car once more. "Tallon," he identified himself. "Can you call my wife and tell her that I'll be late?"

"I'll pass the word," the dispatcher promised. It was a minor violation, but under the circumstances nothing was likely to be said. No one else knew about the anniversary, of course, but it would be understood that he'd had sufficient reason.

A call came in for the watch commander: SWAT was on the way. ETA twenty minutes. With a potentially explosive situation less than a hundred feet away, that was a long time to wait, but SWAT teams were limited and the one from the sheriff's department had a considerable distance to come.

While the watch commander stood by the radio, Jack went down the blind side of the building to check on the coverage at the rear. The truck had been moved; it stood well away where it wasn't blocking access to the rear alley. It should have been checked for prints first, but there had been no time for such niceties. Using his portable set he called for an impounding rig to tow it away. That meant some additional risk in case the shooting started while it was being done, but the truck was evidence and he wanted it out of there regardless.

The back coverage was good. Six men were posted and a sharpshooter commanded the area from a garage rooftop across the alley. He spoke to the agent in charge. "Somebody's inside, that's firm. Probably more than one—it could be up to four or five."

"We're expecting three or four," the agent responded. He was tight-lipped and obviously tense. Tallon forgave him that; earlier the agent had told him that his wife was in the hospital, about to have their third child. "Any news yet?" he asked.

The agent shook his head. "Not so far." He didn't bother to explain that he had no way of getting any; the question had only been an expression of interest—a reminder that there was another world in addition to the tight, dangerous one that surrounded them at that moment.

Jack checked his watch; SWAT should be on hand in eleven minutes. He returned to the street to find the firemen sitting almost aimlessly on their rig, waiting for some action. So far there was no fire and therefore it wasn't their ball game. The paramedics had their equipment set out and were ready whenever they might be needed.

The watch commander tapped Tallon on the shoulder. "Listen," he said. "Those bastards inside know they're trapped and they'd have to be imbeciles not to know that this is a SWAT call-up. How does that add up for you?"

"They may come out of there the hard way, shooting, at any moment. With automatic weapons. They've got three choices: that, death, or the joint—no other alternatives."

The watch commander jerked a quick nod. "That's how I see it. It can all hit the fan anytime."

"The guys know," Tallon said. "I told them."

Another patrol car rolled in and Phil Barnes got out. He was the one SWAT-trained man in the department; he had been off duty and hadn't heard the radio. He didn't speak to anyone; he opened the trunk of his special unit and began to put on his body armor. He knew without being told that if something exploded before the team arrived, he would be the man who would have to try and get in. He checked his weapons and then came up, ready for orders.

The radio that had been carrying a steady pattern of routine traffic broke into it with a fresh report: SWAT was estimating arrival within the next five minutes. Jack took a quick, thankful breath. Within a half-mile radius a lot of citizens were asleep in their homes without the least knowledge of what was going on.

Time became leaden and the very stillness was stifling. There was no way that the watch commander was going to order a break-in unless the situation changed drastically. The bullhorn stood on the hood of his car, but he made no move to use it.

Four minutes.

Agent Rex Bird, who had been standing on guard beside the front door without moving for some time, was relieved and Barnes took his place. From the south end of the boulevard a car came up the street at a high rate of speed. "Cover!" Jack yelled. It could be a diversion car, ready to throw a bomb as it sped past and make a breakout possible. It was a wild, crazy idea, but outfits like the Weathermen tried things like that; if they could kill or maim a few policemen, they would count it a great victory.

The car, a VW with huge oversize tires, sped past at close to its top speed; behind it a South Pasadena unit, siren screaming, was in hot pursuit. Tallon had had one quick look at the occupants and they had seemed like kids. He started breathing again as soon as it was safely past. It was taking a small unnecessary chance, but he left his position to step out in the roadway for a moment to see what had happened. Far up the street the South Pasadena car was pulling the VW over and it was stopping.

That was all he needed to know; he went back quickly and passed the word to the watch commander. "It's under control," he said.

The quiet returned and hung in the air. Barnes had his ear against the front of the building, listening. It had been so still for so long. Jack wondered if by any chance Rex had been wrong and the place was actually empty. If it was, God be praised. If he wanted to see people shot dead, he could always watch the tube.

Three more cars were coming up the boulevard from the south. They were moving fast, but lights were blinking on their roofs, proof that they were official. The sirens were off. All three pulled smartly to the curb, where there was room, and a tall lieutenant in dark fatigues was out almost at once. SWAT had arrived.

Eleven men poured out of the three vehicles, opened the trunks, and began to don body armor. The lieutenant checked the perimeter visually as he came down the sidewalk; in three or four seconds he was satisfied. Using parked vehicles for cover he crossed in front of the gun shop and walked directly up to the watch commander. "What have we got?" he asked. Jack filled him in, painting the picture clearly and leaving out his own opinions. It took him less than twenty seconds.

Rex Bird joined them and so did Jacobson, the owner of the gun shop. Once more the man stood stockily still, his hands in his pockets, trying to appear composed and not succeeding. Jack introduced Bird and identified Jacobson; there were no formalities.

"How sure are you that someone is inside?" the lieutenant asked Bird.

"Either someone is inside," the agent answered, "or some kind of animal is in there and made a definite noise. I heard it clearly."

The lieutenant looked at Jacobson, who understood the implied question. "I don't keep any animals," he said. "And there ain't any rats in the building. It's concrete and kept clean."

"Do you own it?"

"Yes."

"I want a floor plan."

It took the shop owner three times longer than it should for him to diagram the inside layout. Even then his account was incomplete; he entirely omitted the false attic. Jack raised the point and Jacobson filled it in. By the time the conversation had been completed, the SWAT team, in dark-colored coveralls, had gathered around. In addition to the lieutenant there were two sergeants and nine other men. They all wore body armor and the weapons they were carrying were heavy, wicked, and lethal: they almost held the scent of death. Tallon had a sudden wrenching; he almost prayed that the people inside, no matter who they were, would give themselves up. He had already seen too much violent death.

The lieutenant took over. "We'll make the penetration through the roof opening first. Keep it silent; use voiceless throat mikes and earphones. I want a complete infrared periscope check of the attic area before anyone moves in. From there we'll scope the store. After we have them numbered and spotted, I'll direct the action."

Rapidly he assigned positions to his team members: four in front, three in back, four—including himself—on the roof. Then he turned to the watch commander. "From now on it's our party, so let us handle it. I don't want any of your people getting hurt."

The watch commander remained cool. "It's all yours," he conceded. "We'll handle the traffic barricades and hold a secondary perimeter. I have three of our best sharpshooters in position; do you want me to pull them out?"

The SWAT lieutenant saw the light. "Let's keep them where they are. But since we don't know how the suspects are dressed, tell your men to be careful. They might look like us."

The dispatcher called for the watch commander, which meant that something was urgent. The Pasadena lieutenant picked up his mike and answered. A very bad traffic accident had just taken place at the eastern end of the city: a busload of campers returning late from the high Sierra had turned over and injuries were reported.

"You take it, Jack," the watch commander ordered. "I'll get someone else down here."

Tallon jumped into his car, spun it around, and went into code three condition. He didn't like to use the siren late at night, since it disturbed too many people, but it couldn't be helped. He reached Colorado Boulevard and turned right, speeding eastward down the principal business street of the city. As he drove, he called the dispatcher for more information. She advised that two cars had already responded and that a paramedic unit was on the way. So far, no word of fire.

In eight minutes he was on the scene; he stopped his car in the middle of the street, leaving the overhead lights on. It was a bus all right, apparently an older one of the type usually built for hauling school-kids. It lay on its side in the middle of the intersection, but it hadn't simply tipped over; by all appearances it had rolled at least 270 degrees and perhaps more. The flat side that was uppermost was badly damaged. Young voices were screaming inside.

Tallon took a quick, hard look and then used his handset. "I need a crane, something that can turn a large bus over. Medical help and ambulances. Three or four more units for backup. And a pumper from the fire department; there's spilled gas."

He went forward on the run, blotting out of his consciousness the sounds that he heard, the things he tried not to see, as he took the most effective action that he could. He spotted four policemen on hand as sirens told of more coming. He waved toward a crowd that was gathering even at that hour. "Keep those people back! Block off the street. Two of you; help me get these people out."

A paramedic unit hit its brakes and stopped. The two men in it took a few seconds to grab equipment, then they came on as fast as they could.

"There must be thirty people in that bus," Tallon barked. "Let's get 'em out of there!" Using what had been a roof ventilator, he climbed up onto the top side of the bus and looked down through the windows, sweeping the inside with his flashlight. What he saw knotted his stomach and for a moment he thought that he was going to lose control of himself. Then he took a fresh grip and faced what he had to do.

There was a closed emergency door at the rear of the bus; the paramedics were working to get it open. One of them ran back to their truck and returned in seconds with a heavy prying bar. With Tallon's help they broke it open and swung it back, giving a clear passage inside. He heard the sound of electronic sirens, rising in volume, but he didn't have time even to look up and see what they were. One of the paramedics let himself down inside the bus, finding a place where he could put his feet without stepping on someone. "I'll pass them up," he shouted above the mounting noise. "You take them."

Four young men, civilians, broke through the thin police line and ran up to the bus. "We'll help," one of them called up.

The paramedic inside handed up a girl, thirteen or fourteen years old. She was apparently unconscious and therefore much harder to handle. With the help of the other paramedic Jack took her and passed her down to the volunteers on the ground.

Two more paramedics appeared and a major piece of fire equipment turned a floodlight onto the scene. Men in heavy slickers came running forward.

The paramedic inside the bus shouted up once more. "Don't move anything; leave the bus where it is until we get them all out."

Tallon understood. He stood up for a moment and looked around. There were more people gathering, more emergency vehicles, but as yet no ambulances. He saw another young girl being passed up out of the bus; one look at the position of her head and neck told him that she was probably dead. He used his radio. "Tallon. I've got at least one S-5 and multiple injuries. I'll need all the help I can get."

Another policeman scrambled up beside him. "How about the Caddy?" he asked.

"What Caddy?"

"Half a block up the hill. Rolled into a ball; at least one person inside."

"Do what you can," Tallon answered. He had all that he could handle and more; the screams were still coming up from underneath his feet. He saw two ambulance men bring in a gurney. For a bare moment he closed his eyes tightly and wished fervently that it would all go away. Six paramedics were on the scene, thank God, plus the four volunteers. Three volunteers; one of them was being sick on the pavement.

He climbed down off the bus and gave quick orders that it was not to be moved. Ambulances were arriving and two or three tow trucks, hoping for business.

He needed more police cars, but he knew that none were available. Some still had to remain on patrol in the city; otherwise there could be chaos. For the first time he saw a radio station sound truck pulled up and close to it a man was talking into a microphone. He motioned for Tallon to join him, but he didn't even bother to shake his head. The damn fool should have known better.

He caught a paramedic by the sleeve. "How many S-5's?" he asked.

"Four so far."

"There's a wrecked Cadillac."

"We know." There was no time for more.

Because he wasn't a doctor, or a trained paramedic, he could only stick to the things he could do. And until relieved, he was in command of the whole operation. He got on his handset once more. "We need some clergy up here," he advised. "We've got at least four dead and it could be more. The crowd is still growing and I don't have enough help."

"Some reserves are coming; we've already called them."

"Good. Notify the public affairs unit. Are the hospitals all alerted?"

"Hospitals are standing by. More ambulances are coming from Arcadia and Glendale to help out."

He went off the air without formality. He saw a policeman and asked, "Where's the Caddy?"

The man pointed. "Half a block," he said.

Tallon went, aware for the first time of the tiredness in his legs. He had an overpowering urge to sit down for five minutes, but that was the one thing he could not do. He hiked up the hill, forcing himself to ignore the protests of his body. He found the Cadillac; it was lying on its roof, smashed in on almost every side. There was a man inside behind the wheel, hanging perfectly still. He could have been in shock or he could have been dead. A woman was beside him, much younger, and carefully dressed. She hung upside down in her seat belt that mercifully had been fastened. If she was alive, she might owe it to that elementary precaution.

It had to have been a fearful impact to have the bus lying on its side almost half a block away. He used his flashlight to attract the attention of a paramedic and then directed the beam onto the car. The man nodded.

Tallon came back down the hill to the now brightly lit scene that he knew would haunt him for years. Someone in white intercepted him. "Need you," the man said.

The ambulance man led the way to where six bodies were laid out in a row. They had not yet been covered and together they made a ghastly sight. They were blood-soaked, broken, and distorted, and they gave another solid impact into the pit of his stomach. "We can't spare a doctor," the man in white said.

Then Tallon knew what was wanted, and all police officers of his rank or higher had the necessary authority. He forced himself to get down on one knee and to examine each of the smashed bodies that were on display before him. There was no doubt, but he asked anyway. "Have the paramedics verified that they're all S-5?"

"Yes, sir."

"All right," Tallon said. "I pronounce these six persons dead."

The man who had summoned him picked up a sheet and began to cover the bodies as a flash bulb went off. Tallon stood up, looked across the short open space toward the still gathering crowd, and into the shocked and horrified eyes of his wife.

Chapter Three

When he finally did reach home, it was already broad daylight. He let himself in with a profound sense of gratitude that the impossible night he had just lived through was at last over. He should have been comfortably in bed hours ago, but he had not chosen to become a nine-to-five office worker and therefore he could not expect those kind of slender benefits. He was bone weary, but before he could fall into bed, he had to do something first, a kind of purification ritual.

He got out of his uniform and underwear in a series of mechanical movements and disposed of everything but his shoes in the soiled clothes hamper. The soft carpeting comforted his bare feet as he crossed the room; seconds later the water had run hot and he was under the shower. He spent some time washing himself thoroughly twice over and shampooing his hair. When he had finished he toweled himself down and then carefully cleaned underneath his fingernails.

The only thing he could not attack with the soap and water was the parade of images that persisted in his mind. As a man and as a police officer he could handle that problem, but Jennifer had been there too and she had seen things that never should have intruded into her life.

When he came out of the bathroom, his robe had been laid across the foot of the bed. As he put it on he heard Jennifer behind him; he turned and saw her coming into the room with a cup of cocoa in one hand and a plate of toast in the other. "This is a little something for you before you go to sleep," she said, and carefully handed him what she had prepared.

He took it gratefully. "Just what I need," he told her. "It was a helluva night."

"I know. I shouldn't have come." She sat down carefully beside him. "But I began to get frightened and called in to find out where you were. I came to be with you because it was still our anniversary and I at least wanted to see you. And I did."

He wanted to tell her that the day would not pass until they chose to let it, but the bright daylight that was forcing itself into the room burned away every hope of illusion. Their anniversary had passed and for the first time they had been forced to break their mutual vow never to let it go uncelebrated. He felt the tiredness surge back and he had no heart to say anything more. Whatever he might attempt would probably be wrong; he recognized that he was on the ragged edge.

He spoke very simply. "May I sleep for a little while? I'm very tired."

"Yes—you must be."

He drank his cocoa and ate two of the half slices of toast. Then he handed her back the dishes and without apology climbed into their bed. Almost before she was out of the room he was asleep.

When he awoke in midafternoon he allowed himself a few minutes to lie still and absorb the comfort of the warm bed. Then he forced himself to take a deep breath and swing his feet down onto the carpeting.

He shaved, washed, and dressed in the best casual shirt and slacks combination that he owned. At thirty-four his hair was still full and dark. His waistline was still trim and his muscle tone was almost undamaged by the decade that had passed since he had been an accomplished athlete. He only hoped to God that Jennifer would see him as he was, and not as he had been twelve hours before.

When he came out of the bedroom, she had his breakfast ready. He very much wanted to know what had happened at the gun store, but he was for the moment unwilling to pick up a phone and transform himself back into the policeman who might still be too fresh in her memory. Instead he sat down, exchanged some meaningless small talk with her, and then began his breakfast. When he had finished, she was ready to talk to him.

"Just for openers," she said. "Have you ever thought about doing something else?"

"No," he answered her honestly. "That's not exactly true, of course, all of the guys at one time or another have ideas about something else that they might like. But the real pros hang in there because it's their life. I guess you could put me in that class."

She didn't dispute that. "Do you know an officer named Bird?"

He reacted, he couldn't help it. "Yes, of course. What about him?" As he asked the question a sick fear gripped him. Rex Bird, when he had last seen him, had been just outside the gun store, part of the perimeter.

"He's in the hospital; he was shot last night. And two men are dead."

He could not help himself. "Policemen?" he asked quickly.

"No, two men who were in the gun store. They had to call in SWAT—I presume you know that."

"Yes, I do. Please, what happened to Rex?"

"According to the radio, two men who were in the store tried to shoot their way out. They didn't make it, but Bird was in the line of fire. They didn't say where he was hit, but he's in Huntington Memorial Hospital in fair condition."

Jack got to his feet because he could no longer endure sitting still. He walked toward the phone and then changed his mind. He went into the bedroom, came back again, and this time he did pick up the telephone and call in. He carried on a brief conversation and then hung up. "He'll be all right," he said. "He got it in the shoulder, but it didn't hit a vital spot."

"I'm glad, very glad," Jennifer said. "Is he married?"

"Yes, a couple of kids." He didn't say anything about the marital problems he knew Rex had been having. That was all too common in the police community and he didn't want to remind her of it.

"Thank God, for them. A bullet in the shoulder isn't very far from the heart, is it?"

He didn't answer her because the question was rhetorical anyway. Instead he tried a calmer, quieter tone. "It isn't always like last night—in fact I never had one like that before. The odds are way against it."

"But you did go up against armed robbers a few weeks ago. The supermarket thing."

He tried to brush that one aside, and failed. "We had six units there in less than three minutes. There was more than enough backup."

Jennifer came and stood beside him. "I'm not trying to scare you," she said. "It's just that I don't want to lose you—ever. Is that good enough?"

He took her into his arms. "Of course it is," he reassured her. "I take pretty good care of myself, don't ever forget that."

Two hours later he left for headquarters; the report work he had ahead of him was staggering and he could help himself by making an early start. As he drove toward the station, he remembered two or three of the men he had known who had left the force to take up other work. One of them was head of plant security for a major manufacturer; he was supposed to be doing very well. One had left to enter the ministry.

But the thought kept prodding him that he was a cop and that was what he liked to do. He liked the authority of his badge, the position that it gave him, and he was equally proud of the fact that he had never abused it. He even refused free coffee when it was offered to him, unless he sensed that a refusal would be misunderstood. He was a good man and he knew it.

He pounded a manual typewriter, turning out page after page of his official report in the usual language and with the merciful abbreviations that made the work just a little easier. As he relived his experiences of the night before, he took satisfaction in the fact that he could tell the whole thing exactly as it had occurred and that he had no need to apologize for the way he had conducted himself. Up in the fourth-floor executive suite it would also be known that he had done a good job. When he left for home, he took a copy of the current issue of *Police Chief* with him. That simple act didn't signify a decision, because taking a magazine home implied nothing more than the fact that he intended to read it. And he did that every month.

POLICE CHIEF' Whitewater, Washington. Pleasant Pacific Northwest city, population 8,500. Annual budget $240,000, sworn officers number ten. Must have minimum of five years police experience with major department with at least two years at administrative or management level. Bachelor's degree in police science or the equivalent in experience plus outstanding qualifications. Send resume to R. A. Collins, City Manager, 242 West Elm St., Whitewater, Washington.

The job would be an obvious sinecure for some retiring lieutenant, probably someone from the East who had a strong yen for wider open spaces and some chances to go fishing. Up there there would be no street gangs, no narcotic DOA's, no ghetto problems or militant radicals. There would be a regular paycheck to supplement his pension income. In a way that kind of life had its compensations; Jennifer had come from such a place originally and she still liked to talk about it.

Arnold Petersen looked again at the small photograph before he leaned forward and passed it around the table. "He's a handsome devil," he said. Then he quietly sat back and waited to measure the reaction of the others.

Dick Collins studied the picture briefly and then offered a deduction. "Since he's thirty-four years old and looks like that, he can't be a boozer. At least it isn't likely, if this is a recent shot."

Otis Fenwell, the city attorney, unfurled his senior citizen status and his lawyer's frown. "That doesn't necessarily follow. And whenever a man wants to leave a job where he's doing well and is secure, the first thing I want to know is *why*."

Marion McNeil was not in the least intimidated, even though she was precisely half Fenwell's age and was the newest member of the city council. "He gave the answer to that," she said. She adjusted her glasses and reread the brief letter that had come with the almost equally brief résumé. "I quote: We are contemplating a change because my wife and I would much prefer to spend the next stage of our lives in a more rewarding atmosphere. That's as clear as you could ask for. Also I like the way that he says: 'my wife and I.'"

Collins offered another comment. "You notice how he put it positively: he said that they wanted a more rewarding atmosphere, not that they wanted to get away from where they were."

Arnold Petersen was still a relatively young man himself, but he had accumulated enough experience to be sound in most of his ideas. He drew three hundred and fifty dollars a month for his services as mayor and gave all of it to the library fund, which was his pet project.

"I think we've talked enough to come to a decision," he said. "It seems to be the consensus that of the nine applicants, Sergeant Tallon looks like the best bet. Do we agree on that?"

He waited for a good ten seconds.

"Then perhaps it would be a good idea to get him up here and take a look at him."

"Under those circumstances, we would be obligated to pay his fare both ways," Fenwell noted.

"That would be a damn sight better than making a serious mistake," Marion snapped back. She did not particularly care for the quibbling for which the veteran attorney was noted.

No one present had any other immediate comment. After a suitable pause, Dick Collins, the city manager, offered an alternate proposal. "We certainly need someone fairly fast, but obviously we don't want to make a mistake." He could have added "as we did last time," but he was careful not to out of respect for Otis Fenwell's feelings and the fact that he had to get along with the city attorney if he wanted to stay in his job. "How does this sound to you: I'll call Tallon up and talk to him for five or ten minutes, that should give us a good deal more information about him. Or I'll be glad to delegate that call to anyone else on the council."

When silence greeted that suggestion, he continued. "If after a conversation with Tallon, he still looks good, then Arnold can talk to him when he goes down to Los Angeles for that medical meeting on the seventeenth. As far as I'm concerned, if Arnold is favorably impressed, that will be good enough for me. Also it will give him a chance to meet Tallon's wife."

Bill Albrecht, the city treasurer, had been sitting silently for some time, listening through half-closed eyes as he did his mental arithmetic. Having reached a conclusion, he at last spoke, and was listened to. "It's certainly the cheapest way and it doesn't commit us. If we were to invite him up here, then it could be awkward if we had to turn him down."

"I've got complete faith in Arnold," Marion said crisply. "If Tallon sounds all right on a phone interview, and if Arnold likes him, I'll vote to support his decision."

"And if Arnold doesn't like him?" Otis asked.

"Then I'll certainly go along with what he thinks."

Arnold Petersen was the kind of man who likes to have everything clearly spelled out right from the beginning. "Let me be sure that I understand the will of the council," he said. "If Dick's telephone interview is favorable, I'm to look this man Tallon up while I'm in Los Angeles. And if I find him suitable, then am I authorized to offer him a year's contract? We can't expect a capable man to go for any less than that."

"That's the way I understand it," Albrecht said.

"Then let's have a formal vote for the record."

The seven persons present all gave their approval. The City Council of Whitewater usually managed to reach agreement on significant issues because the nature of the community demanded it.

On the way out of the council chamber, Otis Fenwell made it a point to speak to Marion McNeil. He wasn't that fond of her, but he had the uncomfortable feeling that she could command a great deal of popular support. "I have full confidence in Dick and Arnold," he told her. "If they approve of this man, then I'm for hiring him."

"I'm glad to hear you say that," Marion responded, "I think most of us feel that way."

"The question still in my mind," Otis continued, "isn't as easy to answer. If we bring this big city policeman up here, into this quiet little community, is it going to be possible for him to fit in?"

Chapter Four

For the second time in two years, the Whitewater Police Department was preparing itself to welcome a new chief.

Sergeant Smallins had already taken all of the necessary steps, well remembered from the last time. He had made sure that the report file was typed up and current; he had had the four vehicles serviced, and the limited physical plant put in good order. When he looked into the small day room to be sure that the usual accumulation of paper coffee cups had been cleared away, he encountered Gary Mason doing a last bit of tidying up. Smallins looked around and could find nothing to criticize. "Let's see your uniform," he directed.

Mason stood straight to be inspected. At twenty-three he was the youngest, and the newest, member of the department. He had a fresh clean look that had helped him to get the job. "I put it on clean this morning," he volunteered.

"I hope it's appreciated," Smallins said.

Mason caught the tone, but avoided a direct response. "Do you know anything about the new chief?" he asked.

"Nothing definite. He's supposed to be from Los Angeles—a homicide investigator of some sort."

"Then why would he want to come up here?"

Temptation surged upward in Smallins; with an effort he pushed it away. "I wouldn't know."

"Maybe the big city pressures were too much."

"Maybe."

Momentarily Gary forgot the twenty years that separated them. "I've heard that some of those guys have a drinking problem. Too much work load."

"Yes, I've heard that too."

Since the small jail behind them was empty, and there were no sounds from the corridor, Mason decided to bring it out into the open.

"Tell me, Sarg, why didn't you . . . you're the logical man. How long have you been with the department?"

"Eleven years," Smallins answered promptly, his voice distinct and clear. He remained silent for a few seconds, then the temptation overpowered him. "If they had wanted me, they knew where I was."

"Why didn't you ask for it? You should have!"

Smallins pressed his lips together and shook his head. "I shouldn't have to do that. If they don't know my qualifications by now, they never will."

Francie came down the hall, a bundle of agitation. "It's ten minutes to nine," she warned.

In response Gary checked the tips of his shoes once more, and Sergeant Smallins returned to his desk.

At ten minutes to nine Jack Tallon took a final look in the mirror, adjusted the knot in his tie once more, and then let himself out of the motel room. Dick Collins had offered to meet him and take him down to the police headquarters for the first time, but he had declined. He already knew where it was; he had found it easily during his brief inspection tour of the city the night before. At first he had been a little disappointed when he discovered how limited Whitewater actually was. As he got into his car, his first and greatest hope was that Jennifer would be happy here.

He was not overly impressed by the fact that he would be the chief of police—the puddle in which he would be splashing was too small for that. Before he had left Pasadena, he had had a fruitful private talk with his captain. It had been agreed that if the new appointment didn't work out, Jack would let the captain know. After that, they would play it by ear. Neither of them had doubted Jack's ability to do the job, but both had been concerned that the change of locale might be too drastic.

At two minutes to nine he pulled up to the curb across from the small police station, carefully locked the doors of his car, and then turned toward his new job and whatever future it was destined to bring.

He pushed open the glass door and walked in. In front of him there was a small counter and behind it a receptionist-typist who quickly got to her feet. She was forty, one way or the other, but she had kept a good figure and her fingers were nicely tapered.

"Good morning," he said. "I'm Chief Tallon." It was the first time that he had attached the title to his name.

"Oh yes, sir—we're expecting you." She wanted to do something with her hands, but the bare counter top gave her no opportunity. "I'm

Francie," she added. "I'll be your secretary. I'll show you where your office is."

She had been expecting a much older man; one with a complexion that reflected the hard life of the harassed big city policeman. She had fixed that image so thoroughly in her mind, the handsome, still young man who confronted her had her confused.

She opened the connecting door that separated the tiny lobby from the inner workings of the department. The first door off the hallway had a plain, screwed-on plaque that read *Chief*.

Francie opened the door. "Here you are, sir," she said.

The office was good-sized and tidy beyond the point of naturalness. A substantial unmarred desk stood in almost the exact center of the room; the chair behind it had been placed with mathematical precision. A single sheet of typed paper had been put where it would command his attention.

There were two windows, one of which looked out across the quiet street toward the trees opposite. Against one wall there was a bookcase holding a set of the statutes of the state of Washington. There were two chairs for visitors and another small bookcase that was conspicuously empty.

There were two telephones on the desk. Francie explained, "The one with the buttons is the general phone; all of the regular incoming calls are on it. The other is your private line. It's unlisted and I just had the number changed."

"Thank you," he said. "That was very thoughtful. Is there anything urgent this morning that needs my attention?"

Francie meshed her fingers and then separated them again. "I don't think so, sir—everything has been quiet. You might want to read the daily report sheet, that's it on your desk. Otherwise . . ." She was at a loss to continue, because she had no idea what was expected of her.

Tallon understood. "I'll read the report presently. Right now I'd like to see the rest of the facility, and meet whoever else is on duty."

Her anxiety eased a bit. "Ned is out in the car," she explained, "but I can have him come in right away. We usually have one car out on patrol all the time."

"Of course." He understood that she was trying to impress him with the department's diligence, but the idea of a patrol force consisting of a single car made him wince.

"Sergeant Smallins is on duty," Francie said. "I think he would be the right person to show you around."

"I'd like to meet him," Tallon told her. He had already been briefed that his force consisted of three sergeants, a detective, and five uniformed officers. He also knew that Sergeant Smallins was the senior man and that he had served under four different chiefs—Jack included. Beyond that he had been told very little.

Francie conducted him to the next office down the corridor; as he walked in Sergeant Smallins rose to greet him. Tallon surveyed him quickly: he was a middle-aged man who stood a comfortable six feet and who had kept himself in shape. His face revealed very little, obviously by intention.

"Sergeant Smallins, this is Chief Tallon," Francie said. Her hands gave her further trouble as she realized that it should have been the other way around.

Smallins offered a firm handshake and a dignified, restrained smile. "Welcome aboard, sir, we're all very glad to have you with us."

"Good morning," Jack responded. "I take it that you're the watch commander."

Smallins hesitated only briefly. "I've been trying to keep things going properly until you got here." He turned toward the other desk in the room and the man behind it, who was also on his feet. He was younger and in civilian clothes; as the attention turned toward him he offered a ready, slightly tight smile. "This is Ned Asher, our detective."

Tallon acknowledged and shook hands. "How's your case load right now?" he asked.

"Two or three things to check out today, nothing too important, Chief. I hope you're going to like it here."

"I expect to," Tallon told him. "Where did you get your training, at the Spokane academy?"

Asher flushed enough to tell Tallon that he had already made his first mistake. "No, sir, nothing like that. I was in uniform for three years and then Chief Burroughs moved me into his job. Sergeant Smallins has taught me a great deal."

Tallon covered himself by nodding implied approval and waiting for Smallins to carry on.

The sergeant took him further down the hall to the next small office that held two additional desks. As he walked in Gary Mason jumped to his feet. Tallon looked into the fresh young face, read the hopefulness there, and knew almost at once how he would deal with this man. As Smallins performed the introduction Tallon confined himself to a few conventional words of greeting. Then he followed the sergeant into the small day room, where he was shown the limited fingerprinting and photographic equipment. Smallins opened cupboards to show where forms were stored, doing his best to make the slim facility seem more impressive.

There were at least a dozen more things Tallon hoped to be shown, but there was no breathalyzer, no polygraph, and very little in the way of record files.

Sergeant Smallins took him a few feet more to the rear of the building. "This is our jail, sir," he said. "I'm afraid it isn't very inviting."

"I never saw a jail that was," Tallon responded. "I take it that this is principally a holding facility."

"That's right; no time is served here except some weekend sentences. Most of those come from the college."

"Do we have much trouble up there?"

"Not for the past two or three years. Usually it's pretty well behaved, not like the ones you have down in California. It has its own police department with three full-time men and some part-time student assistants."

When he had inspected the jail, Tallon realized that he had already seen the whole of his department. For a few seconds he wondered if he would be able to survive in such a compressed environment.

Francie came hurrying down the hall, hands fluttering. "Chief Tallon, Mayor Petersen is here to see you. I showed him into your office."

Tallon thanked her and went back up the short corridor. Petersen was waiting for him, still on his feet. "Well, how do you like the place?" the mayor asked.

"So far, fine. I haven't met everyone yet, but I'm impressed by those I have."

"Good; I hoped you would feel that way. If you can spare a little time, I'd like to take you over to the paper. We have a weekly here and they want to do a story on you."

Tallon looked at Francie. "If anything goes down, you'll know where to find me," he said.

"Oh yes, sir. I'll let you know if anything happens."

The newspaper office was a combination enterprise. The front third of the building was given over to a stationery store that also carried a selection of paperback books. At one side there was a convenient counter that was also used for transacting newspaper business. Behind the shop area there was a single office, after that the rest of the floor space was filled by the printing plant.

Petersen went directly to the office where a tall, thin, elderly man presided over a small desk that was piled with paper of all kinds: correspondence, proof sheets, stock samples, invoices, and a number of advertising pieces. As the mayor walked in without the formality of an invitation, the older man half rose to greet him. "Hello, Doc. Is this our new chief?" he asked.

"Harry Gilroy, Chief Tallon," Petersen pronounced. "Harry runs the paper and writes a syndicated column; it's picked up all over the state."

The publisher shook hands with surprising firmness. His palm had the hardness of a man who frequently works with his hands, and there was no infirmity in him. "Any time that we can help you, Chief, we'll do it," he said, the bluntness of his words softened by his friendly tone. "We're not a big crusading paper, but we do all right within our limits."

Tallon answered him in kind. "Thanks. I'm going to need support and when I do, I'll ask for it."

"I hear you loud and clear. Care to see the shop?"

Gilroy led him into the back without waiting for an answer. There was a good array of printing equipment that had been well placed, properly lighted, and was obviously carefully maintained. That told Tallon a good deal more about his host—a man he would have to have on his side all the way if he hoped to keep his job.

Gilroy was speaking. "Besides the paper, we do quite a bit of job printing. We even turned out a nice-looking book of verse by our local poet of the Northwest, Lucy Pavano. You can see that we've gone to phototype and we also do speedprinting, if you ever need anything in a hurry."

"I'll remember that," Jack said.

Gilroy motioned to a muscular young man who was plainly waiting to be introduced. "This is Bert Ziegler, you'll want to get to know him. He does it all around here: typesetting, makeready, and whatever. Not a bad writer either; he turns out a lot of our feature stuff. We use as much original material as we can put together and cut down the boiler plate to the minimum; it makes for a better, livelier paper."

Ziegler seized his opportunity. "Is it too soon to ask you how you like our city, Chief Tallon?"

"Yes, it is," Tallon answered. "But if I didn't think that I was going to like it, I wouldn't have come here."

"But it is a lot different from the life in a big city, isn't it? Especially in the law enforcement field."

Tallon knew he would have that hanging around his neck for the next several weeks, at least. "Of course it's different," he answered. "In some ways worse, in a good many ways better."

Ziegler had a pad of paper and a pencil in his hand. "I don't want to push the point, but won't you miss the basic excitement of the Los Angeles area?" He flushed. "I've never been there myself, but I imagine that police work there must be very challenging."

"It is, you're right about that, but I've had twelve years of it, and that's enough for one stretch."

"You could go back someday, then?"

That irritated Tallon, it was too much like a cub reporter trying to grill him like a wire service veteran. He drew breath to snap back, but he caught himself in time. As far ahead as he could see at that moment, Whitewater was his city, and he would have to stop thinking of it as a semi-buried small town. He rammed that lesson home in his mind; he was part of this place now and if he wanted to earn his paycheck, he would have to fit himself into its dimensions.

"I haven't any plans beyond doing the best that I can right here," he answered.

Gilroy came to his rescue. "Why don't you make an appointment with the chief for later," he suggested. "Then you can do an in-depth interview."

"Right," Ziegler answered.

When they had retreated from the press room, Gilroy offered an explanation. "Bert is still at the stage where he's sure that everything is better in the big city—and much more exciting. He hasn't quite learned yet to appreciate the local talent."

"Of which there is plenty," Petersen added. He smiled a little grimly. "Especially up around the college; they have co-ed housing there now. Incidently, while I think to mention it, there's a small campus police force, but in the event of anything serious you have overriding authority."

"Thank you," Jack said.

He spoke almost mechanically as he tried to overcome a sudden chill. He had not realized how much his background in the Los Angeles megalopolis might prove to be a handicap in his new job. Ziegler had shown him what might be the tip of an iceberg of unknown depth and size. It was one part of the drastic readjustment he had committed himself to make, and it would undoubtedly persist until Jennifer and he had both been fully accepted.

Jennifer, of course, would help greatly, because everyone would like her. There was no way that they could do otherwise.

He excused himself, went back to his office, sat down for the first time behind his new desk, and read the daily report. It was a collection of trivialities. He read it through twice and then pushed the intercom button on his main telephone in the hope that it would summon Francie. She appeared, flushed, a notebook and pencil in her restless hands. "Did you want me, sir?" she asked.

"Yes, Francie. I'd like to call a meeting, as soon as possible, of all the members of this department. What would be the most convenient time?"

"How about four-thirty, sir? That's when the shift will be changing and everyone will be in except for Wayne; he's the night man. I can call him and ask him to be here."

"Four-thirty it is," Tallon said. "Let me know if there's anyone who can't make it."

"Oh, don't worry—everyone will make it."

That step taken he scanned the mail that had been put on his desk. Apparently his predecessor had wanted to see everything that came in; there were routine ads and mailbox stuffers that should have been wastebasketed on delivery.

His private phone rang; it was Dick Collins, the city manager, inviting him for lunch the next day. He accepted, of course, and then summoned Francie once more. "Ask Sergeant Smallins to come in, if he isn't busy," he directed. He knew that he could have omitted the last four words, but he didn't want to sound like a martinet on his first morning.

During the next hour he went over the total inventory of equipment that his department had available with the man who was presumably his unofficial deputy. There was very little, but he wouldn't ask for something that wasn't available and thereby underline his big city background still further. Smallins was co-operative, he had to be, but there was a stiffness in the man who was many years older than his new chief. Tallon sensed it but didn't let it bother him; being the chief of police was not a popularity contest.

By the time he had finished it was well past noon and he broke for lunch. Ignoring his car, he walked to one of the four restaurants that the city of Whitewater could boast. The several cars parked outside testified that it was open, so he went inside.

The place was called *Hawaiian Gardens* in an apparent desperate bid for glamour and a touch of the exotic. The dining room was large enough to hold twelve or fifteen plain wooden tables with Formica tops and utilitarian chairs set around them. A few dusty decorations on the exposed walls had died there in a futile effort to conjure up the atmosphere of the Islands. As they hung in lifeless defeat, they were mocked by a jukebox that was thumping out an inane piece of country music with a heavily boosted bass. After he had seated himself, a waitress appeared and offered a worn menu in which all of the prices had been blocked out and new figures substituted in pen and ink.

Tallon ordered the luncheon plate, reconciling himself as he did so to taking whatever came and making the best of it. Five minutes later the girl returned with a pot of tea and a plateful of food that was three times more than he had expected. She poured out the tea for him and lingered after that for a moment or two to see if he was satisfied. "I've got some good pie today," she volunteered. "Shall I save you a piece?"

'This will be enough, thanks." The words came out more briskly than he had intended; he made amends by looking up and smiling his thanks. The girl responded immediately, smiling back. When he began to eat he found to his surprise that the food was hot, fresh, and tasty. If everything that the place had to offer was up to the same standard, he thought, then Jennifer would like it too.

When he got back to the station Francie was waiting for him. "Chief Tallon, there's a traffic ticket on your desk to be dismissed."

"I don't fix tickets." He wanted it understood from the beginning; the law had to apply equally to everyone.

Francie's hands did a little dance of despair. "Well, you see, sir, it's yours. They didn't know it was your car and it was in a two-hour zone. It isn't really fair, because it isn't marked. All you have to do is void it."

"I'll think about it," Tallon said. "Are we in the habit of giving tickets for overparking in unmarked zones?"

"Sometimes, sir."

"Then I want it stopped until the zones are properly marked. We can't expect the public to be clairvoyant about regulations. I'll take that up at the meeting this afternoon."

Young Gary Mason came out into the lobby and stiffened slightly when he saw Tallon. It seemed to him as if the man from Los Angeles could see right through him and read every inadequacy that was hidden behind his uniform.

Francie came to his rescue. "You're going to take unit two, is that right?"

"Yes. Has it been gassed?"

"It's all ready."

"Going out on patrol?" Tallon asked.

"Yes, sir—from now until four."

"Wait a moment." He turned to Francie. "Is there anything that I need to attend to right now?"

"I don't think so." The answer embarrassed her.

Tallon turned to his youngest officer. "I'll come along for a little while. I want to get to know the city better."

Mason wasted a second or two wishing that it had been someone else, then he made a conscious effort to be glad that he had been chosen. "I'll be happy to have you, sir," he said.

Within five minutes after they started out Tallon knew that Mason drove well enough to set a good example to the citizenry. The young man was being overcareful, but that was understandable. Tallon learned that Gary had been born in Whitewater and had attended the college there; consequently he had a detailed knowledge of the community that was a definite asset.

"Tell me how you joined the department," he invited.

"Well, I always wanted to be a policeman, so about six months ago, when there was an opening, I applied for it, and Chief Burroughs gave me the job."

"Did you go through a formal training program?"

"No, not exactly, but Sergeant Smallins took me out with him a good many times and taught me a lot. He's a very experienced man."

Tallon approved that touch of loyalty, but his basic concern remained unanswered. "When you come to Main Street," he said. "I want you to turn right and drive toward the city limits."

"Yes, sir." A half minute later Gary swung his patrol car around in obedience and headed south. He kept going until he was on the two-lane highway passing open fields.

"You're still in radio range," Tallon said, implying the question.

"Yes, sir—no sweat about that. Sergeant Hillman built all of our equipment himself. He's a whiz at it. We can go on twenty miles and still be in good range."

"Fine. Now I want you to hold a fifty-five-mile speed limit; stay right on it."

"Yes, sir." Mason did not understand, but he did exactly as directed. He had the feeling that he was about to be subjected to some vital test that he would not know how to handle. His hands were wet on the wheel.

"All right," Tallon said. "Now I want you to assume that you see a car coming the other way at a high rate of speed. It answers the description of a wanted vehicle."

"You want me to go in pursuit," Mason said, to be sure he understood.

"Yes, as quickly as you can without endangering your vehicle."

Gary's hands tightened on the wheel until his fingers almost felt numb. "All right; tell me when it's gone past."

Tallon waited for several seconds, then he said, "Now!"

Gary hit the brakes hard; as soon as he could he turned across the center dividing line and stopped. He backed twice before he was pointed in the other direction; then he accelerated rapidly.

Tallon checked the sweep-second hand of his watch. "Now pull over to the side and let me take it."

"Yes, sir." Gary was greatly relieved when his superior replaced him.

For the first time Tallon climbed behind the wheel of a Whitewater vehicle. He swung it around and began to drive, as Gary had done, away from the city at normal speed. "Are you familiar with a bootleg turn?" he asked.

"No, sir, I'm afraid not." In the younger man's mind there was a sudden vision of the cars he had seen on TV spinning around in free skids on dry pavement; he responded to it by tightening his seat belt. For a moment fear tc ched him, because he had never ridden through such a maneuver, then he reasoned that the chief wouldn't attempt anything he wasn't fully qualified to do.

"Let me show it to you," Tallon said. "In ten seconds we will spot the car coming the other way; you call the moment when it passes us."

A sense of excitement began to build in the young officer, which forced out the fragment of fear. "It's coming," he said.

In response Tallon hit the brake. As the car slowed he turned it to the right, toward the ditch at the side. At a thirty-degree angle he stopped it, then spun the wheel hard counterclockwise and put the shift in reverse.

"*Now*," Gary said, and hung on.

As he spoke the word Tallon released the brake; the car swung into a backward arc across the road into the other lane. Tallon shifted, gravel spurted behind the right rear wheel and in a flat three seconds the patrol car was accelerating rapidly back toward the city. It was all over so quickly, Mason required a moment or two to comprehend it. "My gosh!" he said.

Tallon spoke in a calm voice. "That turn is perfectly safe and you can do it anytime that you don't have traffic close behind you. You took thirty-four seconds to reverse direction and get up to a speed of thirty miles an hour. Using the bootleg turn I did it in eleven, and I could have cut that by three or four seconds if it had been necessary."

He pulled over to the side and got out of the driver's seat. "Try it.a time or two if you'd like until you get the hang of it; then let's get back on patrol."

Officer Mason practiced the bootleg turn twice and was delighted with his new skill. Already he had one leg up on becoming a high performance police driver. Obviously the new chief was going to make his job a lot more exciting.

Precisely at four-thirty Francie came into his office. "Everyone is ready in the courtroom," she reported. She stopped dead and then resumed on another topic. "About that ticket, sir: while you were out Sergeant Smallins took it in to the judge and he dismissed it. He said that we can't ticket cars for overparking in unmarked zones."

"Thank you," Tallon said. "Suppose you lead the way."

As he walked into the multipurpose courtroom, the nine men assembled there got quickly to their feet. That embarrassed him. "Sit down, please," he said, and then took his place behind a small portable rostrum that had been placed for his convenience.

"This is going to be brief," he announced, "because no one is out on patrol and I don't like to leave the city unguarded, not even for five minutes. Francie, if a call comes in, let us know immediately."

She fluttered loose hands at him. "Yes, sir, I have one of the girls from across the hall standing watch. She'll call us if anything happens."

"Good." He turned his attention back to the nine men who constituted the full body of his command. "Gentlemen, my name is Jack Tallon and I presume that you know where I came from and my police background, so we won't waste any time on that. Some of you may wonder how I feel about leaving a major city department to come up here; I'll answer that right now. The value of the property in this city is well over a hundred million dollars. There are about two thousand homes with an average valuation, on today's market, of about forty thousand each. That's eighty million to start with in real property. Add all of the furnishings, vehicles, business establishments and their stock in trade, and municipal improvements, and you have much more than a hundred million. That means that each of us has a ten-million-dollar share or, putting it another way, if one man is out on patrol, he's the first line of defense in the protection of that entire valuation from crime, accident, catastrophe, or whatever. There's nothing bush league about that.

"I'm perfectly aware, gentlemen, that not a great deal has happened here in the recent past that has called for police response, but that's no guarantee whatever against something major going down right here in Whitewater in the next five minutes. If we all went on a month's vacation and left no one behind to fill our shoes, how much of this city do you think would be here by the time that we got back? I can answer that one: damn little.

"So far I've only talked about property. Much more important are the lives and welfare of the people who live here. We are the professionals hired to protect them, and that is our job.

"One last point: I believe that being a police officer is a position that calls for a highly trained, exceptionally qualified man or woman, regardless of where that person is assigned. I expect every one of you to be as good as, or better than, the crack pros in New York, Los Angeles, Pasadena, Seattle, Spokane, or any other major city you want to name. That's the standard I'm setting and I intend to enforce it. Then, if a big one ever hits here, God forbid, we'll be ready. Thank you; that's all."

He did not linger to talk to anyone after that. He took his time about leaving the room, so that he could not be accused of having stalked out, then he went back to his office. The assembled men all waited until he was gone.

"What do you think?" Ned Asher asked. Tall, lean, and careful in his manner, he was the plainclothes detective.

"I think he's damn good," Gary Mason responded. Despite the fact that he was the youngest, and the newest, he was not afraid to state his opinion.

Everyone more or less waited to see what Smallins would say, but the sergeant ignored them. He put his notebook back into his pocket and left without speaking.

Chapter Five

On Thursday morning Jack attended his first meeting of the city council. Arnold Petersen introduced him to Otis Fenwell, the city attorney, then to Bill Albrecht, the treasurer, and to Marion McNeil, who looked him over in frank appraisal. He already knew Dick Collins, the full-time city manager, and it was no surprise when Harry Gilroy, the newspaper publisher, joined the group.

After coffee had been set out in paper cups, and everyone was seated, the mayor opened the meeting in very informal style. "Jack," he began, "I want to welcome you here on behalf of us all. Let me add that you will always be welcome at any of our meetings and I hope you will plan to attend most of them."

Tallon said nothing and kept his face still.

"Another thing, Jack, in a place of this size news tends to get around pretty fast. I've heard about the talk you gave your department in which you underlined the property and human values here, and the need for professionalism in our police department. We all certainly agree with you on that. Would you care to add anything to what you told your men?"

"Yes, sir," Tallon responded. "I'd like to say that I intend to keep you and the other members of this council fully informed, as far as practical, about the operations of my department. With that understood, I want to add that meetings within the police department are strictly confidential—that's part of the professionalism I talked about. When I find out who opened his mouth out of turn, he's going to hear about it from me."

He stopped in case anyone wanted to object, but no one did.

"Secondly, in my opinion some of our officers have not had adequate training for their jobs. Without reflecting on Chief Burroughs or anyone else, I intend to institute some training activities, similar to a police academy, during the next several weeks. We need to be equipped and prepared to meet any contingency that may occur."

Otis Fenwell pressed his thin lips together for a moment and a harder look came into his eyes. He was a lawyer, and therefore prepared to argue. "Give us an example of where we're deficient," he said.

Tallon was ready for that; he already knew that his predecessor had been Fenwell's man.

"If you wish, sir. I observed one of our officers making a traffic stop on Main Street. The car had an out-of-state license, so the driver was an unknown quantity. Our officer approached the car from the rear, which was proper, but he walked forward all the way to the edge of the windshield. If the driver had been armed and hostile, our man could have been in serious jeopardy; the driver could easily have gotten the drop on him. Even if the driver was only upset at being stopped, the officer's position, facing him, invited possible abuse. The officer has to control the conversation, and that position relinquished his advantage."

"What should he have done?" Marion McNeil asked.

"He should have stopped at the rear edge of the front door. In that position he can talk to the driver, keep control of the conversation, and protect himself if the driver should prove violently hostile. I believe you can visualize that. A man armed with a knife or a gun would have to reach all the way across and around his body to attack the officer. Try it with either hand and you'll see how difficult it would be."

Harry Gilroy did; being a journalist he wanted to establish the facts clearly in his mind. Otis Fenwell gave him a hard courtroom stare. "Really, do you actually expect that sort of thing up here? We don't have the ghetto areas that are prone to violence, or professional criminals."

"Sir, I can cite you offhand at least four cases of officers who lost their lives because of carelessness in supposedly routine traffic stops. None of the incidents happened in a high crime area."

Petersen spoke up, maintaining control. "I take it that the officer who made the bad traffic stop knows better now."

"Yes, sir, he does."

That ended the subject of the police department. The meeting went on for another hour while Tallon sat silently attentive to a discussion concerning a one-block addition to a sewer line. When it finally broke up he got to his feet and was about to leave when the city manager drew him aside. "Can you spare a few minutes?" he asked.

Tallon nodded and followed his new boss outside. "Have you done anything yet about a place to live?" Collins asked.

"No, I've been waiting for Jennifer; she'll be up this weekend."

"You haven't talked to any brokers yet, then."

"No."

"All right; let's take a little ride." Collins unlocked the door of his official car, got in, and turned on the radio that was tuned to the police frequency. As soon as Tallon was in and the doors were shut, he drove away.

"First of all," Collins began, "you were absolutely right about the confidentiality of police business. It was Francie who talked, and you certainly should caution her. Let me add that she was simply trying to relay her own favorable reaction."

"I understand," Tallon said.

"Now, I have a good friend at the college who's just accepted a job back East, God knows why. Before listing his home, he suggested that I show it to you to see if it would fit your requirements. He knew you were coming here, of course. My showing you the house is perfectly ethical under the circumstances, but I'd appreciate your not mentioning it to either of the brokers in town. They're friends of mine too."

"When will it be available?" Tallon asked.

"As of now. He's still here, staying with us as a matter of fact, but he's already sent his furniture and things on ahead. If you're interested, you can talk with him this evening."

"I assume he wants a fast answer."

"That's it, exactly. If you two can make a deal, then you might both save some money, but that's entirely up to you. If the matter ever comes up, Bill approached you. He's in Spokane today, which is why I'm taking you to see it."

"Of course."

The city manager turned into the southwestern sector of the city, where the newest and most desirable homes were located. When he pulled up to the curb before the house itself, spacious and inviting, with a large, beautifully maintained yard, Jack knew as soon as he saw it that it was beyond his reach. He got out of the car and followed Collins up to the door.

Within three minutes he knew that Jennifer would adore the place if there were only some way that they could afford it. There were three comfortable bedrooms, two full baths, a paneled den, and a large living room which would be ideal for entertaining. In his new job, that was an important consideration. There was also a large dry basement well equipped with shelving. The whole thing was three times the house that he might have hoped for; even the carpeting was luxurious, fresh, and unstained. "Have you any idea what he wants for it?" Jack asked.

Collins mentioned a figure that was exactly ten thousand dollars less than Jack had expected. It was still too high for him, but no longer totally out of sight.

He stopped in the middle of the huge living room and faced his companion. The city manager was close to his own age: a little heavier and perhaps a little less active, but he was obviously competent in financial matters. "You know what my salary is here," he said. "Obviously this is a beautiful place, but it's a little rich for my blood."

"First," Collins asked, "do you think that your wife would like it?"

"She'd adore it," Tallon answered promptly. "The kitchen alone would sell her."

Collins leaned against a vacant wall. "Bill is a very direct sort of guy who likes to get things over and done with. He wants to sell this place as quickly as he can, for a decent price. I suggest that you discuss it with him when he gets back tonight. For a firm commitment, from a responsible party, he might come down a little."

Tallon thought very fast, a little drunk with the idea. "Suppose I drop by about eight," he suggested.

"Fine; you do that."

During the rest of the business day the image of the splendid house remained fixed in the front of his mind. In midafternoon he spent another hour with Gary Mason, asking him questions about the residential parts of the city and the types of people that lived in each one. To Mason it was a demonstration of the thoroughness of his new chief; another example of superior police work.

When Tallon returned to his office he was still so preoccupied Francie's restless hands ceased to annoy him. He deliberately put off speaking to her about her lack of discretion and elected to read reports instead. One of his patrolmen split an infinitive in every other sentence; another wrote with the stiffness of rapidly hardening concrete. The incidents described were all minor and not really worthy of his attention.

That evening, within the space of less than an hour, he agreed to buy the house. In a three-way discussion with the university professor and the city manager, an agreement was reached. The owner came down an amount approximately equal to what the brokerage would have been; in addition, he agreed to a clause that would release Tallon if for any reason his job in Whitewater failed to last for at least one full year. When the meeting was over Tallon went back to the motel aware that he had just made the biggest financial commitment of his life. It scared him just a little, but he had been assured by the city manager that if any personal emergencies were to arise, funds would be made available to him to meet them.

He could not escape the knowledge that he had overreached himself, but he knew that Jennifer would be ecstatic. While that thought was in his mind he picked up the phone and called her. He told her to ship their household effects immediately, saying only that he had made arrangements to store them in Whitewater. Then he went to bed and slept like the dead.

On Friday he was not at his best. He could not escape from the depressing feeling that he had acted too impulsively and had overcommitted himself for the next thirty years. All of the hazards of home buying danced before him: higher taxes, increased insurance, heavier maintenance, and all of the uncertainties of a new job in a different locality.

Also it seemed to him that Sergeant Smallins was particularly distant. He did nothing that could be criticized, but the stolid, mechanical way that he went about his duties faintly suggested a political prisoner working out his sentence in some Siberian prison camp.

Tallon spoke to Francie about the confidentiality of police meetings. Her remorse was embarrassing, her hands, undisciplined. She promised fervently never to do it again, not once but three times. As soon as he could he found an excuse to send her back to her desk.

When the judge stopped in without ceremony to invite him to lunch, he was grateful for the respite. As they ate, they discussed the types of cases that came up most frequently in the local court and reached agreement on policies that were of mutual concern. It was past two-thirty when Tallon got back, but no one appeared to have noticed his absence. Some legal documents pertaining to his purchase of the house were waiting for him on his desk. He read them over carefully and found them in order, but the sum of the figures in cold typewriter ink seemed like a juggernaut.

He returned to his report reading and kept at it until he felt that he knew what type of police responses he might reasonably anticipate in the future. There had been one homicide, resulting from a bitter family quarrel, within the past decade. There had been no racial or gang-related incidents during the past five years. The most common offense for which suspects had been booked was drunkenness.

At four-thirty he shut the door of his office, pushed his work aside, and forced himself to think things out. True, he was in a new job, but he had a year's contract and it was work for which he was fully and professionally equipped. He had no need to fear failure. As for the house, which was the real cause of his concern, it was a valuable piece of property; if for any reason he could not swing it, it would be his to sell. Who would buy it, situated as it was in Whitewater, was the question. For a moment he wondered once again if he had held out if he would have been able to get it for less. Common sense told him no, the seller had been fully aware of the value of his property and the agreed-on price had been as low as Tallon had had any hope of reaching. He stayed until almost six without being able to purge the uncertainty completely from his mind.

He awoke early on Saturday, and went to his office to spend an hour or two doing some additional reading. There had been one arrest the night before: a hit-and-run driving incident that had involved only minor property damage. The suspect had posted bail and the jail remained empty. The dorm troopers at the college were making a concerted effort to locate a possible heroin pusher on the campus, but they were not hopeful of success. The one known addict had been into Seattle on a regular basis and the campus police were almost certain that she obtained her supplies there.

Sergeant Smallins was surprised to see him in and unbent enough to ask him if he would care for some coffee. When he brought in a paper cup full of a black and bitter brew, Tallon invited him to sit down and then confined the conversation to police business. There was not a lot to discuss, but the upcoming training program was adequate. Smallins continued to maintain an officially correct attitude, but he refrained from displaying any enthusiasm. "Have you heard about the beef out at the Abbott place?" he asked.

"Yes," Tallon answered. "I read the reports. So far it's entirely a civil matter and doesn't concern us."

Smallins digested that, but it seemed to bother him. "You know who owns that place, don't you?" he asked.

"Yes, but it doesn't make any difference. Unless there's an infraction, or we receive a formal complaint, it's not our problem."

"Just as you say." Since the conversation was over, Smallins gathered up the coffee cups and left.

Shortly after ten Tallon checked out with the man who was replacing Francie at the front desk. "I'm going into Spokane to pick up Mrs. Tallon," he said. "I'll take my official car and maintain radio watch."

"Fine, Chief, we'll call you if we need you." The man's tone implied that the probability was small.

As he cleared the city limits and picked up to a little more than the legal road speed, he allowed himself to relax. As the road retreated backward, the scenic splendor of the Pacific Northwest unfolded. The spectacular mountains and the great national parks were in the western part of the state, but there was a subdued beauty to the gently rolling country. He glanced at his watch and calculated that in forty-eight minutes, if the plane was on time, Jennifer would be with him and they could begin to share all this together.

At the Spokane airport he parked in one of the spaces reserved for official vehicles, cleared the security barrier by showing his badge, and waited for the sight of the incoming 727. He spotted it while it was still in the landing pattern and his sense of anticipation quickened. As it taxied into position, its two nose wheels splitting the yellow guide line, he reached the point where he could not have waited for another half hour.

She was one of the first off the plane, dressed in a new outfit he had not seen before. He gave her a chaste kiss reserved for their times in public, claimed her bag, and escorted her out to where he had parked the car. She stood and looked at it, her hands clasped in front of her, and read the legend *Whitewater Police* that was conspicuously lettered around the city emblem on the front door. She was proud, for his sake. "You ought to have something on it that says *Chief*."

He put her inside and then climbed behind the wheel. "Our entire department has four vehicles and this is one of them," he told her. "I use it when it's available, but it also has to serve a lot of other purposes."

"I see." She was a trifle disappointed.

As he drove back toward Whitewater, she supplied details concerning the shipment of their furniture. There was no significant news from Pasadena; a major 211 had gone down, but no shots had been fired and the suspects had yielded without a fight. It was another small victory in the endless war.

"Nothing at all has happened here," he told her. "Very little has for the past two years. Whitewater is a very quiet place with almost no industry. Practically all of the business is local."

She looked at him, worried. "But that's what we wanted, isn't it?"

He gave her a half smile. "It's what we've got," he answered.

At the motel he took her inside and deposited her bags. He had already informed the desk that she was coming in, which had been as unnecessary as anything he had ever done. "Do you need to freshen up?" he asked.

"Just give me a minute."

She took a little less than ten, and came out with a smile of the kind that a woman wears when she clearly expects a compliment. "Do you like my new outfit?" she asked.

"Yes," he responded. "It's very nice." He knew that she had expected more than that, but he deliberately let her dangle. "Now, would you like to see a little of the metropolis of Whitewater?"

"If you'd like."

He took her outside and installed her in the official car once more. As soon as he had the engine started, he called in on the radio and advised that he was available. The duty man acknowledged in a tone that told him nothing had occurred. "Are you hungry?" he asked.

"Later. Let's go sightseeing first."

He took her past the police station that occupied a corner of the municipal building and down the three blocks of stores that constituted the Whitewater downtown.

"Is that all of the shopping?" Jennifer asked.

"Just about. There are a couple of small groceries toward the south end of town, four restaurants, and a small library. But we do have a newspaper that comes out every week with all of the local news and features."

"Have you been in it yet?"

"Probably in the next issue."

He drove her through the middle-class residential area and up past the college. Then he was careful to come back through the section of more modest homes. For a climax he took her into the southwestern part of the city and let her admire some of the fine new homes that the college people had built. When he pulled up in front of the one he had bought, an almost savage pride surged within him. So far he had only put up a thousand dollars as a good faith deposit, but he already felt possessive about it—it was his house, his land, and his home. Or it would be.

"This one is vacant," he told her. "We can go inside and I'll show you what Whitewater has to offer."

"Jack, I'd rather not."

"I know the owner," he reassured her. "I promise you that it's all right."

With definite reluctance Jennifer got out of the car and walked with him up the sidewalk to the front door. It was unlocked; he swung it open and motioned her inside.

Once the door had been closed behind them, she could not resist exploring. She went through all of the three bedrooms and the den, and after that lingered for a few extra moments in the bright and sunny kitchen. She opened the new dishwasher and inspected the insides of the cupboards.

Still she did not suspect. He showed her the basement and then guided her back up until they were standing together in the middle of the very large living room. "What do you think of it?" he asked.

Jennifer shrugged. "It proves again that it's nice to be rich," she answered. "But I'm not complaining; I'm happy with what I've got." She was ready to leave and started toward the door.

"Well, get used to it," Tallon said, "because it's ours."

For a moment or two she froze. Then she turned to face him, incredulity and mild shock written on her features. "Jack, you don't mean . . ."

"I just bought it. Do you like it enough to live here?"

She seized a sudden deep breath. "Like it? I adore it, of course! But, Jack." She seized him and locked her hands behind his waist. "I don't believe it; it must be over a hundred thousand dollars!"

"It might cost that in Pasadena, but land is much less here, most of the building materials come from close by, and it didn't cost anything like that. It's a little more than I wanted to pay, yes, but we can make it and I closed the deal."

She said nothing at all. Then, carefully, she toured the whole house once more, opening every closet and cupboard, examining the carpeting, and looking out at the more than ample back yard. It took her quite a while before she ended up, back in the living room, once more. "We own our own home," she said, seeking confirmation.

"You wanted a new home: you're in it."

She walked over and tried the drapes that covered the big front window; they closed smoothly and easily. She faced him once more and something had cracked; her eyes were moist and she was blinking. He wanted her desperately at that moment, and his face betrayed him. "Are we safe here, together?" she asked.

He answered her by going to the front door and snapping the lock shut. Just to give her peace of mind, he checked the back door and made sure that it was locked also. An absurd little hope built within him as he lingered over the simple task; when he caught the sound of her shoes being put down his pulse quickened automatically. He looked out at the yard for a few more seconds and then went slowly back toward the living room.

She was waiting for him in the middle of the room. She held out her arms to him and he gathered her in.

"Welcome to Whitewater."

Much later, Jennifer said, "It's a nice place."

In her home, across the street and two doors down, Mrs. Lily Hope had been keeping her undivided attention on the house almost from the moment that the official car had pulled up before the door. With her binoculars, which were always on the little table beside her front window, she had witnessed fragments of Jennifer's two tours of inspection. She had also caught a glimpse of the man she knew to be the new chief of police standing in the living room and she had seen the drapes slide shut—closed in the middle of the day.

Despite her advanced age and slight physique, she hurried toward her telephone. She misdialed the first time, which made her angry: it delayed her triumph. She was already quite sure the unknown outsider that Whitewater had hired to be its police chief was a sex fiend. And she had at least thirty people to tell.

Chapter Six

On Monday morning Tallon took care of some minor routine matters and then began to draw up a training schedule. He programmed the various types of responses to be used in prowler calls, robberies in progress, attacks on citizens, bar fights, and family disturbances. Next he listed car handling and the proper manner of making various kinds of traffic stops. There were certain situations that called for maximum care, and he intended that his troops would know how to handle anything. The fact that major felonies seldom occurred in Whitewater did not influence his thinking in the least. Lightning—literally—could strike anywhere and at any time.

When he had his schedule ready, and broken down into specific teaching periods, he summoned Sergeant Smallins for a conference.

"I've just finished drawing up a training program that I want to put into effect immediately," Tallon said. "Francie is typing it up now."

"I see," Smallins responded.

"Since you are doing the department scheduling, I'd like to have you set up a suitable time when we can get everyone together."

"Normally it's very quiet between eleven in the morning and noon."

"Then let's shoot for ten-thirty so that we can have full service in time to cover the schoolchildren coming home for lunch."

"Yes, sir."

"Offhand, do you know of any house in the city that is vacant and relatively isolated?"

"Yes, sir, there is one just like that."

"Good, then if we can get the owner's permission, we'll use it for some of our exercises."

"There won't be any problem about that," Smallins said.

"One more thing: I want all of the members of the department to attend the training sessions, with exceptions kept to a minimum. Sergeant Hillman doesn't need any instruction in radio communications since he's an expert in the field, but I do want him to know what ground has been covered and where everyone stands."

As Smallins turned to go, Tallon knew that he could depend on the sergeant to follow his instructions meticulously; he valued his reputation too much to do otherwise. Satisfied that he had launched his most urgent project, he turned his attention to the daily report file and the personnel folders which he was still reviewing.

That evening he rode for an hour in the lone patrol car that was on the streets, getting to know the city better and also learning something about the policeman at the wheel.

In the morning his mind was again full of his training program. Fresh ideas had come to him and he increased his determination to make every man under his command into a top professional.

Shortly after eleven Francie appeared in the doorway and caught his attention. "Mr. Lonigan is here to see you," she said.

"Show him in," he said. He had no idea who Lonigan was.

The man who appeared in the doorway was six feet, well built, obviously in shape, and quietly dressed; Tallon spotted him as a Fed even before he nodded to Francie to close the door.

Lonigan shook hands and produced his credentials. "FBI," he said. "I'm the senior resident agent in Spokane."

Tallon waved him to a chair. "I'm glad you came by. My name is Tallon. How about some coffee?"

"I just had some, thank you. Chief Tallon, I dropped in for two reasons: the obvious one is to establish contact so that our office and yours can work together as efficiently as possible. And congratulations on your appointment."

"Thank you very much. Certainly, we'll play on the team."

"With your excellent record in Pasadena, we never doubted it for a moment. Now another matter, if I'm not rushing things."

"Not at all—go ahead."

"I understand that you're interested in a vacant house here in Whitewater. I presume that you're thinking of it as a place to live."

Tallon shook his head. "No, I've already bought a house. Not for publication: although I've only been on the job here a short while, I've already noted some serious deficiencies in the training that my men have had. I'm setting up a course to correct that and I need a house for exercise purposes."

"I see." Lonigan thought for a moment. "How many people other than yourself know of your interest in this house?"

"Enough so that it's gotten to you in a little more than twenty-four hours."

"I see your point," Lonigan said. "Since the word is out, I suggest that you go ahead as planned and use the house, but no more than you need to. Then de-emphasize it."

"Who has actual jurisdiction over the property?"

"The U.S. marshal would be the best man to answer that question. You might say that we have a fringe interest in it, which is why I'm discussing it with you."

Tallon summarized. "What you're telling me is that this house is under federal control and you want as little attention called to it as possible."

Lonigan became more cordial. "You've got it exactly. Of course, the house is in your jurisdiction and under the protection of your department in all ordinary respects."

"I understand. One thing, Mr. Lonigan: whenever you or any other agency is making use of the house for a special purpose, I want to be notified."

"I can't promise that," Lonigan said.

Tallon kept his voice conversational, but he put an edge into it. "I suggest that you reconsider that. I'm entirely capable of keeping confidences and I have to know what is going on in this community insofar as law enforcement is concerned. I don't know what Chief Burroughs's attitude was, but that's mine."

"Have you met the marshal yet?"

"No, not yet."

"When you do, I suggest that you talk it over with him."

"I'll make it a point. Do you have my private number?"

"Has it been changed?"

"Yes."

"Then I'd like to have the new one."

Tallon supplied it and shortly thereafter showed his guest out.

On Thursday morning Smallins assembled the full roster of sworn personnel in the general utility room that also served the city council. As the usual paper cups of coffee were passed around, Jack sensed that he had a job ahead of him if he wanted to instill in his men the same enthusiasm that motivated him.

With Francie assigned to cover the switchboard outside, and to relay any calls, he began his talk. "In a big city department, when a call comes in and a car responds, there is backup available. If the situation is urgent, a half dozen more cars can usually be on the scene within a very short time. In many cases the manual specifies that the first officers to arrive are to stand by until at least the first backup unit has taken position.

"This is a luxury we don't have. When you're the only officer on patrol in the whole city, your nearest backup may be thirty minutes away. Under those circumstances you've got to be good—even better than the big city man who can have all of the help he needs in minimum time whenever he calls for it.

"Today I want to take up prowler calls," he continued. For ten minutes he discussed the proper telephone techniques in answering such complaints; how to approach the scene, and why it was essential at night to check house numbers with the flashlight on the opposite side of the street from the suspect premises. He tried hard to stimulate pride in this kind of responsibility, but he sensed that he was not getting across as well as he had hoped. He countered by cutting his presentation short and asking for questions.

That helped somewhat; three or four of his officers seemed to be at least moderately interested. After the few questions dried up, he ended the session, spoke a word of thanks, and then tried to suggest that he was completely satisfied with the result.

He did not know if he had convinced any of his men, but he knew that he had not convinced himself.

He spotted Wayne Mudd, whom he barely knew, and signaled him to join him. Together they started back toward Tallon's office. Mudd was at once a little stiffly self-conscious, as though he were expecting a reprimand. "I noticed in your personnel file that you were at the LAPD academy," Tallon said.

Mudd flushed, and his manner became even more tense. "Yes, for a while—then I washed out. I fell short of the academic requirements."

"That was a tough break," Tallon commented.

"It was for me; it hit awfully hard. Chief Burroughs knew about it, of course. I don't know for sure, but I think he may have fudged the records a little so that I could be appointed up here." He paused, as though the admission had condemned him, and then added quickly, "I'm taking some courses at the college now. I really want to be a pro, small town or not."

Tallon understood, and took pity on him. It was just possible that Mudd might provide a spark that the whole training program would need. "With that kind of an attitude, you've got a very good chance of making it," he said.

Mudd's gratitude was almost embarrassing. "Thanks, Chief, thanks a lot. It means a lot to have that off my mind."

Francie met them as they walked back into headquarters and delivered a message: the furniture van had arrived and Jennifer had gone to the house to supervise the unloading.

Tallon glanced at his watch; it was not yet noon and he was not about to set a bad example by leaving early. "Call the phone company," he directed. "Ask them to get a line into the house for me, and explain why I need it as quickly as possible. Unlisted number, of course."

Francie surprised him. "Your phone is already in, sir: I took care of it as soon as you bought the house. When your wife called about the furniture, I let the phone company know to start service. You can call there now if you want to."

He went into his office in an improved mood, encouraged by that small display of efficiency.

At eight minutes after twelve he pulled his official car up in front of his new home and hurried inside. Jennifer met him, smiling and happy. "I checked us out of the motel," she said. "By the time you come home tonight, we'll be moved in. But you can take me out to dinner if you want to."

That night as he slept with Jennifer under their own roof, all the doubts of the day were washed away. There were still cartons everywhere—he had had no idea that they had so much stuff—but their refrigerator was installed and stocked with the food they had bought after dinner. The range was connected and they would be able to have breakfast together.

On Friday Jennifer worked miracles. When Tallon came home she was exhausted, but she had the living room presentable, linens had been stored in the closet, the kitchen things had all been washed and put away, and the whole house was at least one third settled.

Across the street, aided by her binoculars, Mrs. Lily Hope had kept a careful and unrelenting watch. To her regret and frustration, she had not seen anything she could either criticize or report.

On Saturday evening, after a day of heavy work for them both, they had the Petersens and the Collinses in for an after-dinner drink. It was a warm and pleasant occasion, made more so by a favorable comment or two concerning the new training program. Jennifer positively sparkled. She won over all four of her guests and made Tallon as proud of her as he had ever been in his life.

At 10:47 the phone rang and Tallon answered at once. Sergeant Hillman, cautious and careful, was on the line.

"Chief, I hate to disturb you, but you'd better get down here right away," he said. "We've got a major traffic accident with serious injuries."

"What have you done so far?" Tallon asked.

"I've sent for two ambulances; one of them is on the scene with a doctor from the hospital. The other is on the way. I've called in two backup units; they should be there in just a little while. Mudd and Wyncott have responded. I have flares out and the wrecker has been called."

"Have you notified the fire department?"

"Yes, sir, and they're standing by to hose down the spilled gasoline. Right now they're helping the ambulance people and diverting traffic."

"Sergeant, obviously you've already done all of the right things. Is there anything you feel that you can't handle?"

"No, sir, but Chief Burroughs always took personal command whenever anything like this happened."

"I see no need for that," Tallon told him. "Call me again if you need any additional backup from me, otherwise carry on. You're the watch commander."

"Right, Chief, thank you." The few words were enough to reflect Hillman's surprise that he had been trusted to use his own head. The prime principle of delegating authority to competent people was apparently something new to the Whitewater Police Department.

When he rejoined his guests, Tallon passed on the news.

"Aren't you going down?" Collins asked.

"Not unless I'm needed. Ralph Hillman has things well under control and since he's the duty sergeant, he's in command. I'm not going to step on his authority unless I have to."

"Praise God for all good things," Petersen said. "I hope that the injuries weren't too serious. If they need more medical help . . ."

"They know that you're here," Tallon told him. "I'll call in for another report in a little while."

On Monday morning there was a subtle difference in the atmosphere that pervaded the small Whitewater police facility. Sergeant Smallins was visibly less formal, Francie kept her hands under better control, and the duty men seemed to display a slightly augmented interest in their work. Tallon said good morning to everyone and then retired to his office to read reports.

The one on the traffic accident was the best that he had seen since he had assumed his new job. It was factual, concise, and reflected a man who was not afraid to put on paper what he had done under an emergency situation. One detail that Tallon had not known was included: two motorcyclists from the college had come by shortly after the accident. They had parked and been very helpful in getting the victims out of the cars and the mess cleaned up. Jack called in Francie and dictated letters to each of them, thanking them for their co-operation and response to an emergency. He had carbons sent to Mayor Petersen and another set sent to the dean of the college.

He had barely finished when Bert Ziegler, from the newspaper office, appeared at the front counter and asked to see him.

"I want to get the full story on the accident," the young reporter said when Tallon came out. "Anything extra that you can give me will help a lot."

"You're welcome to read the official report," Tallon told him. "After that, if you need any more, talk to Sergeant Hillman. He was the watch commander. Also, you can do me a favor by giving some attention to the two college students who helped with the rescue work."

"I'll be more than glad to do that; do you have their names?"

"Yes, and I've written them both letters of thanks. You might let it be known how much we appreciate citizen help."

Ziegler wrote with a blunt copy pencil on standard press paper. "We can sure use the college angle; Mr. Gilroy will like that. How about copies of the letters, can we print them?"

Obviously Ziegler, though still in the cub stage, was learning his job. "No problem," Tallon told him. "Francie will make copies for you. Anything else?"

"No, that does it. Thanks a lot, Chief Tallon."

"Any time."

The lecture on car handling under emergency conditions, which he delivered later that week, was well received. The attention level was much higher; most of his men were still quite young and high performance driving appealed to them. The only visible problem appeared to be Officer Walt Cooper, whose disinterest in his job was becoming increasingly apparent. Tallon talked with him and satisfied himself that Cooper's problem was lack of action; he was thoroughly bored by daily patrols.

At the end of his first month in Whitewater, Jennifer proudly baked him a small cake with a single candle on it. He appreciated her effort and was careful to say so, but it had been a frustrating day all around and when bedtime came, he simply did not feel like celebrating.

Mrs. Betty Weber lay on her left side, sleeping quietly, and dreaming. Ever since she had come to Whitewater, the same sequence had often gone through her mind. She was again nineteen years old and fully aware that her beauty was exceptional. Protesting, but inwardly delighted, she had allowed herself to be persuaded to enter the contest for the new Miss Houston. As her head rested motionless on her pillow, she relived once again the parade of events in which she had participated; the times that she had stood in a bathing suit, slightly turned and with her front knee bent, to smile her radiant best at the countless cameras.

They had told her that she was the new Toby Wing, a girl so fabulously pretty that she had appeared in screen musicals of the twenties just to smile at the camera as each spectacular scene drew to a close.

Then, oddly, while the contest had been still on, Betty had seen an old Dick Powell film on TV and Toby Wing had been in it; finally she understood what people had been talking about. When the next cluster of commercials had come on, she had gone to look at herself once more in the mirror. It was true—she did look like Toby Wing.

One night later, in her bathing suit once more, she had come slowly down the few steps on stage when her name had been called and had stopped to pose on the carefully marked spot before the judges. She had turned on her most enchanting smile, and thought of Toby Wing.

She had been chosen the new Miss Houston. Now, as her body rested, her mind projected for her the image of the cape being placed about her shoulders, a tiara being fitted onto her head, and flowers being put into her arms. She paraded to steadily continuing applause while hundreds of flash cubes had popped and everything in the world had been hers.

It was a wonderful antidote to the quiet and sometimes dreary life she now lived as a housewife in Whitewater. She could have gone on to the big national pageants: Miss America, Miss United States, Miss World, Miss Universe. Fabulous prizes, great acclaim, and world tours might well have been hers. But her parents had said a firm *no* and she had had to accept their decision.

That part her mind mercifully blocked out. She stirred and turned over, unconsciously listening to be sure that all was well with Wayne, her three-year-old son, who was sleeping on his cot in the far corner of the bedroom. She always brought him in with her whenever Mark was away, giving another of his seemingly endless lectures.

She did not know what awakened her—there had been no sound that she could identify. Her eyes came open and she lay motionless for several seconds, trying to orient herself. As soon as she did she sat up to look at Wayne; he might have choked or coughed in his sleep.

Then she saw the man. He was more a shadow than a reality, looming above her in the semi-darkness, his face something horrible that she could not understand. She gulped air into her lungs to scream, but a hard hand was clapped across her mouth. As she fought in sudden stark terror, she saw the blade of a long knife displayed before her eyes.

She forced herself to look up and saw only a mouth; the rest of the man's face was covered with a rubber-like mask. He looked like the Frankenstein monster.

With all of her strength she seized the hand that was covering her mouth and tried to tear it away. In response the man locked his elbow and forced her head hard down into her pillow. Then he spoke, in a voice that might have come from another planet. "Now listen," he said. He held the terrifying knife before her eyes. "Just be good and you won't get hurt. But one peep out of you, and your boy gets castrated—see?"

The hackneyed words were to her fresh and utterly horrifying; panic seized her and her body began to shake. "Now," the voice continued, "if you promise that you won't scream, I'll take my hand away. Promise?"

She felt the tip of the knife against her throat. As the hand lifted off her mouth an inch or so, she whispered, "Yes."

"All right. Now, that's the way." The man put his weight down on the edge of the bed so that the horrible mask was almost directly above her. "Now we're going to have a nice little party, just you and I." The voice became a bit more natural, but it was still forced through a deliberately closed throat.

The words were meaningless to Betty; terror seized her and images of her shattered dream flashed through her mind. She was Toby Wing and this awful thing was happening to her in a movie. In a moment someone would call "cut," and the nightmare would be over.

A small night light stood on the table beside the bed; the man reached over and turned it on.

"Nobody will see that," the man said, "but I can see you a lot better."

In the corner of the room Wayne stirred in his sleep.

The half-strangled voice came again. "Now, I'll tell you what to do and you'll do it. Be nice and you won't be hurt a bit." The mask bent closer until it was inches from her face. "Give me even a little argument and . . ." He displayed the knife once more, then he pointed it significantly toward the sleeping child. "Understand?"

Betty gathered the bedclothes around her, then she nodded. "Everything I've got—it's in the jewel box on the dresser. The money is in the second drawer, on the right-hand side. Take it!"

"That isn't what I came for, honey. It's you. Now, I can kill your kid or just cut his balls off—and you know what that'll make him—or leave him alone. You choose: tell me."

Fresh terror forced her words. "Leave him alone!"

"All right, do just as I say and I will. But . . ." He pressed the knife point once more against her throat and pricked her very slightly. "Try anything else and I'll punish you. Do you understand?"

Almost paralyzed, and blocking as much as she could of the thing that was happening to her out of her mind, she whispered, "Yes."

The man moved back to the foot of the bed. "Now you get up, nice and slowly, and stand right over there. Then, take off your nightgown. I want to look at you."

There was no hope; the only telephone was in the front hallway and she did not dare to scream. In that neighborhood the houses had been built well apart.

When she hesitated the knife pointed again toward her sleeping son. She had one hope. "I'm pregnant," she said.

The knife flickered. "Off," the voice said.

With quivering arms, Betty Weber pulled her nightgown slowly over her head. When she had finished, she dropped the flimsy garment onto the bed.

"Good," the voice said. "Good! You're a pretty one, aren't you. Now turn around."

Mechanically, Betty obeyed. A mental anesthetic had taken hold of her, making it all unreal.

She faced the wall, mercifully freed from the sight of the mask.

"Now turn back."

As she obeyed, she no longer really cared that she was on display. He had seen her now, and it didn't matter any more.

"Now sit on the edge of the bed."

Without protest she complied.

She shut her eyes. He had wanted to see her naked; all right—he had. Others had too; it wasn't that important. In fact, it didn't mean anything at all.

She heard a new sound and opened her eyes. The man had dropped his trousers. He wore no underwear and there before her, at her eye level, was his swollen penis.

Then the voice came once more, reinforced by the point of the knife that was being waved in front of her. "If you make me happy, I'll go away and you can go back to sleep. Nothing to worry about at all. Understand?"

She understood that he wanted her to say "yes," and with all of the courage she could command, she slowly nodded her head.

The man came closer. Then the unreal voice croaked again. "Do it wrong and I promise you, I'll slit that kid's belly open. *And I'll do it!* Believe me?"

Once more, as though she had been chained to the stake, Betty forced herself to nod.

The fagots were lit, the flames soared upward, and Betty opened her mouth.

Chapter Seven

When Jack Tallon became conscious that his telephone was ringing, he knew before he was fully awake that it would have to be his department calling. No one else would presume to call him at that hour or have access to his new unlisted number. By the end of the second ring he had fought off sleep enough to answer. "Tallon," he said.

Sergeant Brad Oster, who manned the graveyard shift, was on the line. That in itself was significant, because of all his men, Oster was the calmest when on duty.

"I'm sorry to disturb you at this hour, Chief, but we've got a bad one."

"Another traffic accident?" Tallon asked as he cleared the sleep from his eyes.

"No, sir—rape, and about as bad as you can imagine."

"In a private home?" The hour suggested that.

"Yes. I think you will want to be in on this one immediately."

"I'll be in in twenty minutes," Tallon said.

"Excuse me," Oster came back, "I'd like to suggest that Ned Asher pick you up; he'll be driving your car."

That told Tallon a good deal more; if the department's one detective had also been routed out in the middle of the night, Oster was pulling out all the stops without delay. An ordinary rape with a known attacker wouldn't call for a response like that. "I'll be ready for Asher," he said, and hung up.

He turned as he got up and saw Jennifer's wide eyes looking at him. He put his finger over his lips and moved his hand sideways in the air to reassure her. Then he went into the bathroom and splashed his face with cold water.

Eleven minutes later he was outside and waiting when the blue official car pulled up with Asher at the wheel. Tallon climbed in, shut the door, and asked, "How much do you know about this?"

"Very little, Chief. Brad called me and said that it was urgent. He asked me to pick you up and gave me the address. We're to meet him there."

"Who's covering the station?"

"I don't know. Probably Ed Wyncott; he lives the closest."

Tallon picked up the radio and called in. "Tallon here," he said.

"Yes, Chief." The reply was crisp and efficient.

"Have you any details yet?"

"No, sir. The victim is a local housewife, raped in her home while her husband was away. That's all Brad gave me before he went out; he was in a helluva hurry."

That violated strict radio procedure, but Tallon had heard far worse in his day. "Stay with it," he directed. "Don't give out any information to anyone except the sheriff's department, and then only if they ask for it."

"Yes, sir." The man at the station knew that the Whitewater police frequency was monitored by the sheriff's cars in the vicinity.

Asher swung the car around a final corner and drew up to the curb. He did not have to look for the number; two of the other three police units were parked in front. In accordance with the most recent training lecture, their lights were out and the sleeping residents nearby had not been disturbed. Tallon held his watch under the dash light; it was twelve minutes after three.

Sergeant Oster met him just inside the door. His uniform could have stood a pressing, but his composure was intact. "Thank you for coming," he said. "The victim is Mrs. Betty Walker, a former beauty queen, aged twenty-five to thirty. Her husband is with the college; right now he's in Boston attending some meeting. There's a three-year-old son she's been keeping in the bedroom with her while they're alone."

"In the same bed?"

"No, on a rollaway cot. Apparently the child slept through the whole thing."

"Thank God for that. Go on."

"Mrs. Weber awoke to find a masked man in her bedroom. He turned on the night light and threatened her with a knife. She hasn't said much so far, but he did force her to have intercourse with him."

"What's been done so far?"

"I got as much of the victim's story as I could, but she was hardly coherent. Then I immediately called in three more of our men and notified you. As soon as Cooper and Mudd reported, I sent them out on a search of the neighborhood. They're doing that now."

"What's the victim's physical condition; is she cut or bruised?"

"Not that I could see. She went into the bathroom and she's still there. The boy is sleeping and that's about it."

"Do you know anything about Mrs. Weber?"

At once Oster was visibly cautious. "Only very generally. As far as I know, she has a good reputation."

Walt Cooper appeared at the front door; he was in uniform, but without his tie. "We didn't find anything," he reported.

Tallon took over. "Take one of the units and check the all-night gas station for any traffic during the past forty-five minutes—local or otherwise. Check also for any male pedestrians. If you find any, stop them even if you know them and establish their reason for being out at this hour. Check both motels for any guests that have been or are still out. Get anything at all that you can."

He turned to Asher. "Ned, check the house thoroughly for signs of forced entry. Be careful that you don't destroy any footprint evidence. If you find anything conclusive, let me know immediately."

"Right. I'll be careful."

"Good." He turned back to Oster. "Brad, stay with me while I talk with the victim. I'll handle it; you take notes."

The sergeant nodded.

Tallon found the bathroom door and knocked. "Mrs. Weber," he said, holding his voice down so as not to wake the child. "This is Chief Tallon of the police department. Please come out; it's urgent that I speak with you immediately."

After a few seconds the door opened and Betty Weber appeared. A swift glance told Tallon that she was close to shock and not far from hysteria; he took her arm gently and guided her into the living room. He put her into what appeared to be the most comfortable chair and then gave her a little time in which to compose herself.

She was wearing a pink quilted robe that she had tied tightly about her. Despite the hour, and the experience she had been through, she was still strikingly attractive. Her hair was disarranged and there was no trace of makeup on her face, but her features demanded attention.

He noted that in his mind as significant. He knew very well that women who were attacked on the streets or on parking lots, were almost always chance targets, but women who were raped in their homes were almost always pre-selected for assault. This woman would definitely attract notice wherever she went.

Tallon seated himself and spoke to her very quietly. "Mrs. Weber, I know that you have just had a terrible experience. We want to catch and arrest the man who is responsible. To do that, we need your help."

Betty Weber swallowed, and then nodded with her eyes closed.

"First of all, is there anything that I can get for you?"

"No, thank you."

"Some coffee, perhaps? I'm sure we can handle that."

She shook her head sharply. "I don't want to put anything into my mouth."

He understood that with a cold chill and made an immediate decision. "Who is your physician, Mrs. Weber?"

"Dr. Petersen."

Tallon glanced at his sergeant, who went quietly to the telephone, without bothering to ask permission.

As the call was being made, Tallon began with simple, easy-to-answer questions that held minimal emotional content. "Mrs. Weber, I understand that your husband is in Boston."

The young woman used a handkerchief and then took a little better grip on herself. "Yes, he is. I don't know what will happen when he comes home and finds out . . ."

Tallon made a quick shift of subject. "Are you employed, Mrs. Weber?"

"No, I just take care of the house—and Wayne."

"Were you out at all today?"

"Just to the market, otherwise I've been in the house all day."

"Did you have any visitors?"

"Nancy Jorgenson stopped in for a little while this afternoon. Not for long."

"After dinner you put your son to bed?"

"Yes, about nine-thirty. I let him stay up a little to see a TV program. Then I put him down."

"And he's still asleep."

"Yes." She stopped and listened, but there was no sound from the bedroom.

"What time did you retire?"

"About twelve. I watched the eleven o'clock news and then made myself a cup of tea. After I drank it, I went to bed."

"Did you receive any phone calls during the evening?"

She shook her head. "No, nothing."

"Now, without straining yourself, please tell me what happened."

Betty Weber twisted the handkerchief in her hands until she had made a rope of it. It was a large square one that probably belonged to her husband. "I went to sleep right away; I was tired and Mark wasn't here to talk to. It must have been . . ." She paused and rubbed her forehead hard with the heels of both her hands.

"I woke up. I can't say that I heard something, but I must have. I sat up to see if it was Wayne, then I saw that there was a man in the room."

Ned Asher was hovering in the background; when Tallon signaled him to talk, he reported, "The back door was forced; there's no doubt about it. The wood is splintered where a tool was used to push the latch open. As soon as it's light, I'll get some pictures and check for footprints."

"How was the door when you found it?"

"Standing slightly ajar; I'm about to check it for prints."

It was confirmation, but Tallon had already accepted the fact that a rape had taken place. He turned back to Betty Weber. "This is very important," he said. "Please describe him."

Betty shook her head. "I can't very well. You see, he was wearing a mask; an awful thing like the kids have at Halloween. He looked like Frankenstein."

"The mask, then, covered his whole face?"

The partial question made her draw back within herself. "No, the bottom had been cut off—just below the nose. I could see his lips. And his . . . mouth."

"What sort of clothes did he have on?"

"I *can* tell you that. He wore a blue shirt, the kind men wear when they're doing manual labor, and blue jeans. He had a leather belt about an inch and a half wide; I noticed it when . . . he took his pants down."

"How big was he?"

Betty paused. "A little bigger than medium-sized, I'd say. He looked bigger, because I was lying down when I first saw him."

"Could you guess his age?"

"Between twenty and forty; that's all I can say."

She stopped, pulling a deep breath into her lungs and strengthening her resolve. When she continued, her voice was coolly factual, as though she were talking about something that had happened at some other time and place to a person who was a stranger to her. "This may help: he can't be too old, because he had two orgasms, once the regular way, and once in my mouth."

"Excuse me a minute," Tallon said. He got up and then turned. "Was he a white man?" he asked.

"Yes."

He dialed the station number. "I have a description of the suspect," he said, and supplied the few details that he could. "Alert the sheriffs. If they stop anyone, have them try to locate a Halloween mask of the Frankenstein monster. It's cut off at the bottom, below the nose."

When he had finished, he sat down once more. "May I call you Betty?" he asked.

"Yes, of course."

"All right, Betty, I want to say something to you. I *do* understand what you've just been through and if it will help, let me add that I believe you in every particular. I have no doubt at all."

"It does help," Betty said. "I know that the police are sometimes very suspicious . . ."

"Only when we have reason to be," he interrupted her, "and that isn't the case now; you don't have to convince me of anything. Now, please tell me what happened after you found him in your bedroom. Particularly anything that the man said. And the way in which he threatened you."

Betty Weber sat still. She didn't want to continue, but she knew she would have to. As calmly as she could, she told her story and, terrible as it was, somehow the sympathetic man sitting and listening to her made it easier.

She recited the facts, repeating almost word for word what her rapist had said to her. When she came to the point where he had pressed the knife into her throat, she lifted her chin and felt the spot. A fleck of red showed on her finger, and she wondered if it was that bit of physical evidence that had convinced Tallon to believe her.

She was interrupted close to the end of her story by the opening of the front door. Another policeman came in with Dr. Petersen behind him. Tallon greeted the physician quietly, then, to spare the victim as much as he could, he briefed him in her presence. His recital of the facts was concise. "I felt you should be called," he concluded. "First because she had been raped. In addition, she was compelled to perform fellatio on him. She endured this because he had threatened to kill her child if she refused."

There was a dangerous flush of blood in Arnold Petersen's face. He helped Betty to her feet and said, "Let's go into the spare bedroom."

It was a good twenty minutes before he came out again. He shut the door behind him and then conferred with Tallon in a quiet voice. "There are several things you will want to know," he said. "She definitely has had sexual intercourse within the past two hours or so and I don't doubt her rape story for a moment. I've known Mark and Betty ever since they came here and she is positively not promiscuous. She's a former beauty contest winner. Someone picked her out, found out where she lived, and learned that her husband is out of town."

"No argument," Tallon said.

"She's two months pregnant, so we don't have to worry about a possible conception, but venereal is another matter. I'm going to take her to the hospital for certain safeguarding procedures. While we're there I'll also run some tests in case the results are needed later as evidence in court."

"Good," Tallon agreed. "How about the boy?"

"I was just coming to that. The Jorgensons are very close friends of the Webers and Nancy knows what to do in an emergency. I'll take Wayne over there if you will have someone take Betty to the hospital. I'll meet you there."

"Does Betty know what your plans are?"

"Yes, I just told her. So if you want to talk to her any more, you can now, but for God's sake, take it easy."

"Depend on that," Tallon said.

A minute later Petersen came out of the bedroom with the still sleeping child in his arms. A policeman held the front door open for him and he was gone.

Betty Weber came back into the room and sat down slowly where she had been. "Do you want me to finish?" she asked. Her voice was flat and tired.

"If you feel up to it. The more you can tell me, the better our chances will be to make an arrest."

"I understand," Betty said. She continued her account like an automaton, forming the words dispassionately. She told of the hot breath of her attacker on her hair as he had worked himself up to a second orgasm and then, how he had penetrated her so deeply she had feared that she would lose her child. Throughout the recital, her face remained a mask.

When she had told it all, Tallon thanked her as quietly as she had spoken. He did not waste words assuring her that the utmost effort would be made to find her attacker. "If you're ready now," he said, "I'll drive you to the hospital myself. That is, if you don't mind a police car."

For the first time she smiled, a very little. "I'm glad it's that," she answered. "I'll feel safer."

He was en route when a call came in over the radio; he was wanted at headquarters. Fired with hope that his men had found something definite, he delivered his passenger at the hospital, where Petersen was waiting for her. As soon as he was free he drove to his office in code two condition, without the siren, but with the warning light burning on top of his car.

Oster was waiting for him there with Mudd and a civilian they had in custody. Tallon evaluated the man quickly: he was twenty-five to thirty, husky in build, and obviously defensive. He was being detained in the day room, where he sat in a hard chair that offered little comfort, either physical or moral. When Tallon came in, he stood up. "Will you please tell me what this is about?" he said.

Tallon ignored him for a moment while Oster reported. "His name is William Rose. He was observed on foot going down an alley and cutting between buildings as if he wanted to avoid being seen. He then got into his car and drove three blocks before he turned on his lights. He has no explanation for his actions."

With a tightened jaw Tallon nodded his approval of his men's work, then he indicated that he wanted to be alone with the suspect. A few seconds later he was facing the man, whose visible discomfort was mounting steadily. "Sit down," Tallon directed.

The man sat.

"I want your address," Tallon said.

The suspect protested. "Look, I don't know what this is all about . . ."

"You can have your choice," Tallon interrupted him. "You can answer my questions now, or I'll have you put in a cell under suspicion of a major felony."

"My God," Rose responded. "I haven't done anything like that!"

"Where do you live?"

"In Spokane."

"Your address?"

Rose supplied it, this time without hesitation.

"What is your occupation?"

"Civil engineer. Please, will you give me some idea what's happening?"

"Presently. Why were you on foot in Whitewater in the middle of the night and why did you drive your car without the lights on?"

Rose moved in his chair and then held out his hands. "Look," he protested again, "this isn't a federal case. I don't understand . . ."

"Answer my questions," Tallon snapped.

"Maybe I should call my lawyer. If you're arresting me, don't you have to read me my rights, or something like that?"

Tallon did not soften. "Mr. Rose, at the moment you aren't under arrest: you're being detained for questioning. A crime has taken place and you're a definite suspect. Does that make things a little clearer?"

Rose swallowed hard. "May I ask what crime?"

"Criminal rape."

"Oh, my God." For a few seconds Rose seemed to slump in his chair, then he obviously made a decision. "If that's the case, I'd better give it all to you, because there's no way in God's green earth that I'd ever do a thing like that. Will you keep this confidential, please?"

"I'll consider that after I hear what you have to say."

"All right, I'll accept that because I have to. I live in Spokane, as I told you; I'm married and have a family. I also . . . have a girl friend who lives here. I come to see her occasionally. When she's free she calls me; then I tell my wife that there has been a malfunction and that I have to go in. She's never questioned that."

"You work for the city, then?"

"Yes—I do."

"She called me tonight; her husband is in San Francisco. I came here and we spent some time together."

"Were you intimate?"

"Yes. I left her home a little less than an hour ago. To protect her I tried not to be seen; there are nosy people everywhere. I thought that I'd gotten away all right until the police car stopped me."

Tallon kept his own emotions under control. "I'll have to have the name of your friend," he said. "Your story will be checked out thoroughly, for your own protection. If it doesn't hold up, you will be in very serious trouble; do you understand that?"

Rose nodded. "Completely. It will stand up. But please, you can ruin my life and hers if this gets out."

Although he did not change his manner, Tallon sensed that it was a no go. The story was too easy to check, even if Rose had a girl friend who was willing to lie for him. "Mr. Rose," he said, "I've got to investigate this thoroughly, and I will. If any part of what you have just told me isn't accurate, correct it now. I don't need to emphasize how important this is."

"It's the God's truth, so help me."

"Then I will release you if you can supply full identification and all information concerning your companion. But I want you to call in to my office at four tomorrow afternoon; failure to do that will result in a warrant being issued."

"I'll call; you can absolutely depend on it. I'm not a criminal. Will we . . . have to face charges?"

"If the lady confirms your story to our satisfaction, then I'll consider it a matter of normal conduct between consenting adults and the report will go into our confidential file."

Rose came to life and the defensiveness left him. "I don't know your name."

"Tallon. I'm the police chief here."

"I think it would be best if I called my friend right now and told her what the situation is. You can listen in on the call."

"I think it would be best if you don't call her," Tallon answered. "Even though we have an automatic system, at this hour the call might be monitored; many of them are. I suggest that you give Sergeant Oster all the information that we discussed, including your ID. Then call me at four tomorrow. Insofar as we can, Mr. Rose, we'll be discreet."

Rose stood up and held out his hand. "I very much appreciate that, sir. And I hope to hell that you catch the real criminal."

After a slight hesitation Tallon took the offered hand for a bare moment. "Don't worry about that," he said. "We will."

When Tallon got back home, the eastern sky had an elliptical arc of pale washed blue that was growing brighter, second by second. He opened the door as quietly as he could and found Jennifer waiting for him in the kitchen, reading the Spokane paper from the day before. She looked up with inquiring eyes.

He kissed her. "I could use some breakfast," he said. "Then I've got to get right back to the office."

He went into the bathroom to shave.

At a little after eight he met with five men of his force, the maximum number that he could muster under the circumstances. Although most of them were fully informed as to what had happened, he spelled out the known facts and then gave them a quick outline of his plan of attack. "I want every resident within three blocks of the Weber residence interviewed," he said. "If people aren't at home, call back until you do see them. Find out in particular if anyone saw any kind of a vehicle, even a bike or a motorcycle, parked where it doesn't usually belong. Check also if they heard anything or saw any pedestrians. Emphasize that it makes no difference if they saw someone whom they knew or not. Try to talk to every member of each household, kids included. I want every house covered without exception." He designated three officers to handle that assignment, Walt Cooper among them. He noted with some satisfaction that Cooper seemed to have found a fresh determination to do his job properly. Part of the reason could lie in the fact that he had a young and exceptionally pretty wife.

Tallon turned to Sergeant Smallins. "Frank, I want you to take charge; I'm going into Spokane to see the sheriff. I'll be back as soon as I can. Answer any reasonable questions by the news media; we won't be able to sit on this one and there's no use pretending. In a town of this size I don't think we'll be able to protect the victim's identity."

"How about her husband?" Smallins asked.

"Dr. Petersen called him and he's on his way back here. Arnold broke the news, so he's prepared." He addressed himself to his detective. "Ned, go back to the scene and make as thorough an examination as you can. If you need help, call in. Relieve Jerry Quigley, who's out there now, and tell him to get some sleep, because I'm going to need him later today."

"Who's going on patrol?" Smallins asked.

"That's your decision, Frank; handle it the best way that you can."

"All right," the sergeant answered. The words had a shade more life in them than they had had the last time he had used them.

Tallon took a minute to phone the sheriff in Spokane, then he jumped into his official car and headed rapidly toward the highway.

The city council meeting on Thursday morning was grim. The only item of business discussed was the rape; there were many questions and Jack did his utmost to answer them all.

He minced no words. "I'm going to give it to you completely straight," he said, "but please don't repeat anything that I tell you outside this room."

"We won't," Dick Collins assured him.

"First, then, I want you to know exactly what we're up against. We have almost no description at all of the rapist; he was masked and he wore the most common type of clothing. There was nothing distinctive about his voice, and he disguised that. We have no hair color and have no data on possible visible scars. We can't fix his age any closer than somewhere between twenty and forty, that's the best that the victim can give us."

"Have you been able to do anything at all?" Marion McNeil asked.

"Yes, we've literally searched the city for the suspect. We have one man under investigation at the moment. We have interviewed and questioned the occupants of every home within a three-block radius of the Weber home; unfortunately no one saw anything at all that we can use. We checked with the sheriff in Spokane and put out a statewide request for information on any other known rapes with the same MO."

Harry Gilroy maintained a prudent calm. "What can I put in the paper?" he asked.

"You can state that the police department is conducting an investigation with full co-operation from other law enforcement agencies. That we have checked the records of every registered sex offender within a two-hundred-mile radius and that many of these men are now being questioned. Meanwhile, until this man is caught, I have increased the night patrol of the city."

Gilroy made notes on a folded piece of copy paper.

"Can you add anything to that, confidentially?" Otis Fenwell inquired. He was tight-lipped as he spoke.

"Nothing substantial," Tallon admitted. "The suspect we are investigating doesn't look too promising. He claimed that he was in the city to visit his girl friend and so far she is backing up his story. The only concrete things we have are negative: the victim is quite sure that she didn't know her attacker and had never met him anywhere."

"How about race?" Harry Gilroy asked.

"Caucasian. Incidently, one thing we haven't determined is the man's mode of transportation. None of the nearby residents spotted any unaccustomed vehicles: no bicycles, no motorcycles, not even a pedestrian. It's pretty damn hard for anyone to come and go without someone seeing him, but unless someone is lying, this man did."

Bill Albrecht, the city treasurer, was thinking hard. "Suppose the rapist lives in the immediate area. That would explain it."

Tallon nodded. "That's right. But my men checked on the alibis of every male of the proper age that lives within the area we covered. There was no one unaccounted for; the late hour helped us there. Also, you remember that the victim told us she was sure she had never seen or met the man who attacked her.

"Our examination of the scene gave us very little help. The rear door was forced open; it's a simple lock and there's no burglar alarm system. There were no strange fingerprints in the house. The Webers have a paved patio that showed no footprints—not even the ghost of one."

"What you're telling us," Otis Fenwell interjected, "is that you don't have any clues at all."

"That's correct, Otis. I told you I would give it to you straight and I'm doing it now; we've pretty much exhausted every avenue of investigation. I've alerted every police department in the state and in the five nearby states. As of now, there is not a damn thing more we can do."

"Then what chance is there that he can be caught?" Marion McNeil was sharp, which was not like her.

"Well, we may get a break; that very often happens. Someone may phone in an anonymous tip. One elderly woman, who refused to give her name, did, and talked to Sergeant Smallins. She was sure she knew who the rapist was, and named him."

Marion sat up straighter in her chair. "And who did she name?" she demanded.

"She named me," Tallon told her. "She claimed knowledge that I was a sex fiend—those are her words."

"I know who that was," Collins volunteered. "Her name is Lily Hope. She lives quite near you, on the other side of the street. She's the worst gossip in town, a pathological case."

"Thank you for the warning," Tallon said.

Marion tapped a pencil on the table top. "If you don't get a break, as you say, what then? You realize how many frightened women there are in this city right now."

Tallon could have ducked it, but he didn't; he was never built to do things that way and he gave it to her straight out. "We expect to learn more, and probably will, if and when he strikes again."

Chapter Eight

During the next two weeks Jack and Jennifer Tallon went to three parties and gave one of their own. Despite the good will and the mood of relaxation, the specter of the unsolved case refused to be exorcised. Jennifer was delightful, but not even her charm could dispel the awareness that there was substantial concern in the city. The whole community knew that the new police chief, the experienced expert who had been imported from Southern California, had not yet solved the most notorious crime committed in Whitewater during the past several years.

It was generally understood that there was a dearth of workable clues, but that did little to help. During the third week a minor burglary was committed and solved; it would have helped more if the culprit had not turned out to be a twelve-year-old boy. There was not too much credit attached to capturing a child.

Tallon continued his training program; he took his men out and schooled them in the proper way to respond to a complaint of a prowler, a peeping Tom, a suspected thief, a rapist on the premises, or the possibility of murder. He also appeared before the city council to ask for an appropriation to buy walkie-talkie radios for his small force.

There was considerable debate before the funds were allocated. Otis Fenwell and Bill Albrecht were opposed and voted against the measure. The city attorney was pointed in asking if the proposed new equipment, had it been available, would have helped to capture Betty Weber's attacker. Tallon had no satisfactory answer to that. He was still well received, but it was abundantly clear that the police department was not in good repute at the moment and the new chief had lost a little of his aura.

He made another trip into Spokane and again checked the records of all known sex offenders in the eastern part of the state. Once more he came up empty-handed. As he drove back to Whitewater he was in a fine rage, lashing out in his mind against the circumstances that had given him almost nothing with which to work.

Francie read the signs as soon as he returned to his office and passed the word that the new chief was in a rotten mood. That evening Tallon took a car himself and went out on patrol in the city, thereby effectively doubling the force that was in the field. Harry Gilroy, who had spent a lifetime observing things, saw him and understood. There were conscientious doctors who had patients they could not save, and lawyers who had had innocent clients convicted on circumstantial or perjured evidence. He hoped, for Jack's sake, that something would break soon.

Mrs. Lily Hope reported to her intimates that the new police chief was driving around nights looking for more women to rape.

On Wednesday morning, at 9:41, a call came through on the land line: an Oregon car, license number unknown, was reported headed northward toward the Canadian border at a high rate of speed. The vehicle was believed stolen; the two men supposedly in it were prime suspects in a liquor store holdup that had gone down just before nine. Shots had been fired and a clerk who had been alone in the store had been wounded. The location of the fleeing vehicle had not been established and there was no exact description.

As soon as he was notified, Tallon took immediate action: he had the car on patrol advised and sent Wayne Mudd out in another unit to guard the highway that passed through the main street of Whitewater. If the wanted car came into the city, it would be up to his force to stop it. Then for the next few minutes he sat in his office and carefully debated his next step. Both of the officers he had out were young and inexperienced; if by any chance they were to run into two hard-core professionals who were known to be armed, the results could be disastrous.

The proper procedure, of course, would be to stay where he was and let his troops in the field handle the matter. That would be fine in Pasadena and he wanted it to be fine in Whitewater, but he couldn't make it add up. Gary Mason, willing and eager, was twenty-three years old with a few months of experience behind him—experience that had never included a situation of the kind he might face within the hour. Wayne Mudd, taller, quieter, was twenty-six and an admitted washout from the LAPD academy. A nice guy for whom the previous chief had made an exception and had given him his job.

That narrowed it down to Smallins and himself. Sending his sergeant would be the proper organizational thing to do. Smallins might be qualified, but he didn't know the man well enough yet to be sure.

He got up and went to the front desk. "Francie," he said. "Call Wayne back in; I want to ride with him."

He fastened his badge to the outside of his coat and then picked a shotgun out of the small arsenal in the day room. As soon as Mudd pulled up outside, he went to join him.

"Do you want to drive, Chief?" his patrolman asked.

"Yes, I'll take it," Tallon said. He slid behind the wheel and handed the shotgun to Mudd. "There may be two men in the car, both armed," he added. "They've crossed a state line after a shooting two eleven, and in a stolen vehicle. That means the slammer for sure, so they aren't going to be easy to take."

"I'm glad that you're along, Chief." There was no shame in the words, and no cowardice; Mudd meant exactly what he had said.

"Thank you. The chances of their coming through here are slight, but we've got to be ready, just the same."

"Yes, sir!" A tingle of anticipation ran down the young policeman's spine; at the same time his abdomen tightened with a quick spasm of fear. He knew that big city men went up against such situations all the time, but they were highly trained academy graduates. For the first time he questioned whether he was actually qualified to wear the uniform he had on.

Tallon drove to Main Street, turned left, and headed north toward the outskirts of the city. At one of the quiet side streets he turned off and parked the car facing the highway where it was semi-hidden, but where he could see a block and a half in either direction.

He picked up the radio. "Whitewater One," he reported. "We're stationed at the corner of Main and Balsam."

Francie's voice came back. "O.K., Whitewater One, nothing new has come in."

"Mason, do you hear me?"

The fresh young voice came back quickly. "Yes, sir."

"Stay on the south end of town. If you see a suspect car, put it on the air and then follow, but keep well behind if it's being driven legally. If the driver runs a light or does more than forty-five in town, pursue at a distance, but let us intercept here. Is that clear?"

"Yes; I'm not to take it."

"That's right. There's two of them, so let's have three of us."

"Yes, sir!"

Gary Mason put his mike back into its bracket with a sense of gratitude. There was a chance of some real action, but he had not been asked to stop a car and take two armed and dangerous suspects into custody unaided. He would have been willing to try, but the chief would

his unit. Gary Mason reacted almost instantly; he threw his car into gear and before Tallon could make it back to Mudd's vehicle, he pulled up beside him. "Get in!" he yelled.

Tallon hesitated a split second, thinking of the shotgun in Mudd's car, then he yanked the right-hand door open and threw himself onto the seat. As he slammed the door shut Gary hit his lights and siren, gaining speed as fast as his engine could gulp gasoline. The Chevrolet had been modified for very high performance; the speed of its takeoff had established that. The police car was a standard vehicle with no special racing equipment, but Gary knew it thoroughly and had it well over seventy in a matter of seconds. Behind him, in the mirror, he could see Wayne Mudd less than a hundred and fifty yards back and gaining slightly. Mudd could drive, there was no argument about that.

Tallon pulled the mike from its clip. "Whitewater One," he said.

"Go ahead, Chief," Francie answered.

"We're in pursuit of a blue Chevy, Oregon license . . ."

"Wait a minute," Francie cut in, and there was an interval of four or five seconds. "I'm sorry, I dropped my pen."

Tallon gave her the number. "Call the sheriff and tell him."

"Shall I get some help?"

"No, we'll handle it, but advise that we're northbound from Whitewater in hot pursuit at high speed." If any of the sheriff's units were monitoring him, they would know what to do.

At the wheel Gary Mason was bent forward, his fingers locked around it until the knuckles were white. The speedometer read eighty-five plus, but the vehicle held the road and the shocks were good.

A curve loomed ahead. The Chevrolet slowed to approximately seventy to take it; Mason kept his gas pedal close to the floor and led into the turn like a true professional; the car tried for an instant to rise onto its two right wheels and then settled down again; the center of gravity had been low enough to keep it right side up.

By that dangerous maneuver they gained more than a hundred feet. Three seconds later a tiny star burst into the upper center of the windshield and the sound of a shot could be heard. Tallon reached again for the mike. "Whitewater One, still in pursuit and we're being fired on. Call the sheriff and ask for a rolling roadblock ahead."

He took out his handgun, leaned out into the lashing slipstream, and leveled it with both hands toward the car they were pursuing. The scream of the wind tore at his ears and the rocking of the car gave him an almost hopelessly unstable platform. Holding himself as rigidly as he could, he squeezed off two shots aimed at the blue Chevrolet's gas tank. Then, although he knew that his chances of success were close to zero, he tried for the left rear tire.

That was enough of that. He took out his keys and with one of them he unlocked the shotgun that was stowed at the base of the front seat. Praise be to God it was there; the other three units didn't carry one. With the weapon in his hands he turned toward Mason and saw that the young officer was as intense as before, but he showed no signs of fear. "Give it all she's got," he said.

"Doing that now," Gary answered.

Almost as he spoke, the car ahead began to ease off its mad pace. It came without warning, forcing Mason to let up on his own gas pedal to avoid overrunning his target; if the other car was about to attempt some abrupt maneuver, he was ready.

"Left lane!" Tallon barked, and thrust the muzzle of the shotgun out the window on his side.

The blue car continued to slow gradually; as it did so Gary maintained a position on its flank where Tallon would have the best angle of coverage with the shotgun. As the suspect car began to pull onto the shoulder, Tallon saw for the first time that its left rear tire was losing air and was already half flat.

Apparently he had been as lucky as hell; any one of the three shots he had fired might have done the trick. Then he knew better; if he had hit the tire, it would have gone down at once and would be totally flat. Something else, obviously, had caused it to fail.

Gary Mason pulled up, jumped out, and, taking shelter behind the engine hood, pointed his own weapon. Even at that moment it gave Tallon a savage burst of satisfaction to see how his training program was paying off in the field. He held his own position as Wayne Mudd pulled up behind him.

"Throw out your guns!" he ordered. "Then come out with your hands up."

For a tight few seconds he thought that the men in the Chevy were going to make a fight of it. Then the left rear door of the blue car opened slowly. The passenger in the rear seat began to emerge, but he had not discarded any weapon. The driver remained frozen and still.

Wayne Mudd, a shotgun in his hands, ran up and took cover beside Mason. Even in the face of that firepower, the suspect's hand jerked up, an automatic still in it. Mason fired; the man fell out onto the pavement, the gun bouncing from his fingers.

Tallon jumped out and held the shotgun on him while Mudd covered the driver. The man behind the wheel raised his hands. "All right, God damn it!" he shouted. He opened the door beside him and got out without resistance.

The man lying on the pavement was holding onto his leg. "You didn't need to shoot me, you son of a bitch," he yelled. "I was throwing it out; you saw me."

As instructed Gary said nothing; he came out from behind the hood of his car and looked a question at his chief.

"Cuff your prisoner," Tallon instructed. "Then see if he needs any first aid."

As though he had done it many times before Mason rolled his man over and fastened his hands behind his back. Then he turned him face up and checked the area of bright red on his trouser leg. "I think it's just a flesh wound, no need for an ambulance."

Mudd took care of the driver. He put the man in position, facing the car and leaning on it, and patted him down. Then he cuffed him briskly with only a little awkwardness; he had never done that to a genuine suspect before.

Tallon checked the interior of the Chevy. He found a second gun in the glove compartment and removed it by the trigger guard. The rest of the vehicle seemed to be clean. By the time he had finished, the two prisoners had been put into the patrol cars. The back seats were fitted as cages; a heavy grill protected the driver and the rear door could not be opened from the inside. The handles that controlled the windows had been removed.

He picked up the microphone in Mason's car. "Whitewater One," he said.

Francie came back with a little distortion and at reduced volume. "Go ahead, Whitewater One."

"Cancel the roadblock, we have the suspects in custody. Shots were fired and one of them is wounded in the leg. We'll take him directly to the hospital; have Sergeant Smallins meet the unit there."

"Yes, sir. Is everyone all right?"

"Yes, we're O.K. Have the wrecker come out and pick up a blue Chevy north of town, you have the number. I'm coming in with Mason and the second suspect."

He put the mike back into its clip. "Mudd, I want you to take the wounded suspect to the hospital. He's Mason's prisoner, but I'd rather you handled him. Mason, I'll ride with you back to the station."

Gary was very serious. "Yes, sir, whenever you're ready."

When the patrol unit with Tallon, Mason, and the suspect who had driven the blue Chevrolet pulled up in front of the headquarters entrance, there was a reception committee. Sergeant Hillman, who was not technically on duty, met the car, Francie momentarily deserted the desk to come out front, and Bert Ziegler was on hand from the paper. It was Francie who first saw the bullet hole in the windshield and who called attention to it while her hands wove mad patterns in the air. "You could have been killed!"

Tallon ignored that. He stood by while the prisoner was unloaded by Mudd and the sergeant and taken inside, then went back into his office closely followed by Bert. "Let's have the story, Chief—all the details," the reporter demanded, and sat down without an invitation.

"Talk to Mason and Mudd," Tallon told him. "They did the driving and captured the suspects."

"Chief, there's a hot rumor out that one of them is the rapist. Is that true?"

"I'd say not a chance in a million."

Ziegler was disappointed, but he had the grace to leave without pushing any further. As soon as the young man was out of the office Tallon put in a call to Jennifer. News traveled fast in Whitewater and he didn't want her to worry.

Before the lunch hour was over, it was throughout the city. Tallon went down to the garage and inspected the Chevrolet more thoroughly. The left rear tire had simply torn apart under the strain; it had not been hit. There was a genuine bullet hole that had barely caught the extreme right end of the gas tank. The other two shots had missed.

By the time he got back to headquarters, positive ID's had come in on the two suspects; they were definitely the wanted men. Tallon had been certain of that fact, but he still welcomed the official confirmation.

Francie carefully listened in while Gary Mason gave his account to Ziegler. Although the young officer maintained a proper professional attitude, he made the most of his chief's fearlessness when a bullet had barely missed his head and then described Tallon's awesome skill with a gun when he had leaned out the window of a car careening at more than eighty miles an hour and had not only hit the gas tank, but also had shot out the left rear tire of the suspect car.

After the interview, which was supported and supplemented by Wayne Mudd as soon as he got back from the hospital, Ziegler was resourceful enough to call the garage where the fugitive car had been taken. From the manager he learned that the left rear tire was indeed flat and there was an unquestioned bullet hole in the gas tank. That was a story and Ziegler knew it; he hurried back to the newspaper office and gave it all to Harry Gilroy.

In contrast, it was remarkably quiet at the Whitewater Police Department the next day, particularly after a sheriff's van had taken the prisoners away. Almost no calls at all came in. When the paper arrived in midafternoon, Francie had to be restrained from posting the feature article on the bulletin board in the lobby. Sergeant Smallins told her not to, fully aware that everyone would see it anyway. His instructions

were given with a crispness that Francie had not heard from him before.

By Saturday evening Tallon's stock had risen spectacularly. His success even reached Mrs. Lily Hope, who, for the moment, did not dare
to phone any more whispered conjectures about him, sensing that they
would not fall into receptive ears.

There was a party at the Albrechts' at which Jack and Jennifer were
the unwilling center of attention. The city treasurer made a valiant
effort to redeem himself for his opposition to the requested police radios; whatever thin walls had been erected crumbled away.

By the following week, Tallon was both accepted and respected as
the chief of police. Furthermore, he had the satisfaction of knowing
that he was doing a superior job.

It all ended abruptly on Thursday night, when the rapist found another victim.

Chapter Nine

The call came in at one forty-seven in the morning. Sergeant Oster answered the phone with a brisk, "Whitewater Police, may I help you?" and held a pen poised.

A female voice responded. "Could I speak with a policewoman, please."

"I'm sorry, ma'am, we don't have any female officers. What can I do for you?"

There was a hesitation before the next words. "I'd like to see any officer then, as soon as possible."

"Are you at home, ma'am?" There was something indistinct in the voice, but Oster couldn't define it.

"Yes, 227 College Lane."

"One moment, please." He pushed the hold button and used the radio microphone. "White One, see the woman at 227 College Lane. Unknown trouble."

From the single cruising patrol car Officer Jerry Quigley responded and gave an ETA of ten minutes; he happened to be some distance away.

Oster came back on the telephone line. "Hello?"

"Yes, I'm here."

"Officer Quigley will be with you shortly. In the meantime, is there anything I can do?"

There was a much longer pause, then Oster realized that she was crying. "I . . . guess not."

"Excuse me, but are you ill?" He was suddenly aware that she had first asked to speak to a policewoman.

There was no answer although the line was still open. He tried to make his voice considerate and sympathetic. "Ma'am, if you've had an accident, or have been assaulted in any way, please tell me now."

Again there was silence, then something like a suppressed sob came over the line. "I've just been raped," the voice said.

Oster was already flipping the file beside the telephone to the chief's unlisted home number. "We'll be right there to help you," he said, and broke the connection.

By chance Tallon was still awake. He was sitting in his pajamas in his favorite chair, reading the current issue of *Police Chief* magazine.

The first ring of the telephone snapped him out of his contented mood and a sudden fear enveloped him. He picked up the instrument. "Tallon," he said.

"Chief, this is Brad Oster. We just got a call from what sounded like a young woman. She said that she'd just been raped. Quigley's on his way."

An almost violent emotion filled Tallon; then he controlled himself and answered in something like his normal tone of voice. "I'll go right there. What's the address?"

In less than five minutes he was unlocking his official car that stood outside. His hand shook as he fitted the key and he lost several seconds. As soon as he had the door open he hit the seat and fired up. As he rolled away from the curb, he picked up the microphone. "This is Tallon; I'm on my way. Anything new?"

"Not yet, Chief. I've called in Ned and three of the other guys. As soon as they report in, we'll start a search."

"Good. Where's College Lane? I only know the general area."

Oster gave him precise directions. "Do you want me out there?" he asked.

"Yes, after you've been relieved. You're the watch commander."

"Right."

When Tallon pulled up at the address he had been given, he noted that the front door light was on and that the door itself was ajar. It was a much more modest home this time, but still a respectable property in a good neighborhood. He parked and walked rapidly up to the doorway. He tapped and almost immediately Quigley admitted him.

"I've only got a little so far. The same MO as last time; the victim was alone in the house." He seemed much more mature than his twenty-seven years as he led the way inside.

The girl was seated on a sofa that was backed up against the front windows of the room. She was about eighteen, Jack thought: a dark, fairly attractive brunette who would probably have looked a lot better under any other circumstances. Now she was sitting defensively, her hands wrapped around her abdomen, her face locked in an agony of shock. Her moderately long hair hung in confusion; her slim shoulders were hunched forward as though she was trying to shield herself against the world. She had on a light blue robe that was tied at the waist with a frayed cord. It had once been quilted, but many washings had robbed it of all shape and it gapped open at the top so that from where he stood Tallon could see much of one small neat breast. She held a hand towel that she had been using to wipe her eyes.

"Miss Edelmann," Quigley said carefully, "this is Chief Tallon."

The girl swallowed; it was a major effort for her to clear her throat and speak. "Thank you," she said, as though no other words would come to her.

Tallon sat down, after moving a chair so that he would not be squarely in front of her like an inquisitor. "What is your first name, Miss Edelmann?" he asked, very calmly and quietly.

The girl used the towel on her eyes for a moment, then she sat a little straighter. "Janet," she said.

"Were you alone in the house, Janet?"

"Yes."

"This is your home?"

"I room here. I'm a student, at the college."

"Who owns this house?"

"Jim and Frieda Morrison."

"Jim Morrison, the attorney?"

"Yes. They went . . ." She stopped dead for a few seconds, then she released her hands from across her body and rested them at her sides. She swallowed again and her shoulders visibly relaxed. "Jim and Frieda went to Las Vegas on a travel package of some sort that's good during the middle of the week. They asked me if I would be all right alone and I told them, 'sure.'"

Tallon kept perfectly still and was grateful that Quigley had sense enough to stay in the background.

"I went to bed early, I was tired. Just before I did, I checked all of the doors and windows, and everything was fine. Then I went to sleep right away. When I woke up, there was a man in the room. He was bending over me, and he was holding something sharp against my throat."

"Was there enough light for you to see him?"

"Yes, because I leave a night light on. I could see him; I wish I hadn't."

"I know what a terrible shock that was, Janet, but do you remember at all what he looked like?"

Very calmly she nodded. "He was fairly big and dressed in work clothes—blue jeans and a work shirt. But he had a mask on, a rubber thing that made him look like Frankenstein."

"So you couldn't see any of his face at all."

"Yes, I could. The bottom of the mask was gone; I could see his mouth. And I can tell you something about his hands, because the first thing that he did was to put his hand across my mouth. It was rough and the skin was hard and tough."

"Janet, that's very important. Thank you. That's new information, and we need every bit we can get."

He hoped his words would help to calm her, but she appeared to ignore them. She continued almost automatically. "Right then and there I knew what I was in for, because I knew all about the last time that it happened. I sleep with my bedroom window open, so I suppose he got in that way."

Tallon turned his head enough to speak to Quigley. "Have Ned check on that the moment that he gets here. And call Oster and set up the same procedure we used last time."

He turned back to the girl. "Excuse me; please go on."

The brief interval seemed to have helped her. She showed a little more self-possession as she folded her robe closed. "I'm still pretty shaky," she admitted. "But I'll tell you anything that I can so that you can catch that . . ."

"You're doing fine," Tallon encouraged her. "Just don't skip anything."

She kept her voice even as she resumed. "I always sleep nude because I can't stand any nightclothes twisting around me. So when he pulled back the covers, there I was. He really looked me over, even though there isn't that much to see. He waved the knife again and then put it back against my throat."

"What kind of a knife, Janet?"

"It wasn't an ordinary kind: the handle was a sort of plain wood and it had been sharpened a lot so that it looked pretty awful."

"I believe that. Go ahead."

"Then he spoke to me in a kind of funny voice, it wasn't natural. He said something like, 'Listen, little girl, be good and you won't be hurt a bit. But if you let out one yelp, I'll cut your tits off.' Then he made a gesture with the knife, as if he was actually doing it. I was terribly frightened, then."

"You had a right to be," Jack told her.

"Then he felt me and played with me a little. After that he stood up and took his pants off. He didn't have any underwear on. He had an erection and it looked terribly big to me. He pushed it right in front of my face."

Tallon let her stop for a moment. She was showing a lot of courage and he didn't want her to lose it, but there was something he had to know. "Janet, this is a tough question, but I have to ask it. Had you ever faced anything like that before?"

She shook her head. "I'm a little bit of a freak, I guess; it's just a thing I have. I don't mind skinny dipping or anything like that, but I'm not a swinger."

"Let me make this easy," Tallon said, "as easy as I can. Did he force you to take his penis into your mouth?"

"Yes."

"And he threatened you with mutilation if you didn't comply?"

"That's right."

He stopped, the anger flaming inside him to the point where he had to fight for his composure. Janet sat quietly looking at him, apparently waiting for him to continue. When he didn't for several seconds, she spoke again. "I know you don't want to ask it, and I understand." She looked at him without faltering. "He did make me go all the way, and when I tried to resist, he put the knife on me and the point actually went in. I don't mind showing you." She opened her robe at the top and showed a small, still bleeding wound on her left breast. "After that I was too terrified to do anything else."

"Janet, how old are you?"

"Eighteen."

"I'm going to catch this man if it's the last thing I ever do. When he's on trial, will you be willing to testify against him?"

Janet nodded. "Of course I will."

"Good girl, you can add me to your list of admirers."

"I'm afraid I'm not much to admire right now."

Tallon ignored that. "Janet, when you called us, you said that you had been raped. Did you mean that literally?"

"Yes, I did."

"So this man, with his knife, forced you to have sexual intercourse with him."

"Yes."

"I'm almost through, Janet, and forgive me for asking, but did he ejaculate again in your body?"

The girl looked at him steadily, but a touch of uncertainty tinged her features.

"I think so," she answered, "but I can't be sure. I mean, I couldn't swear to it on a witness stand. He made me bleed quite a lot and it hasn't really stopped. You see, I was a virgin."

In the chilled silence that followed the ringing of the telephone was like a sharp dagger thrust of noise. Tallon picked it up. "Yes?" he asked.

"Oster here, Chief. Ned's on his way with his equipment. I got hold of Walt Cooper and Ralph Hillman; they're making a neighborhood check right now. Ed Wyncott is coming in too; he'll check the downtown."

"Good. This is a very bad one: tell them to check everything possible —they're not to take anything at all for granted."

He went back to his chair and sat down once more. "Janet, who is your doctor here?" he asked.

"I don't have one; I haven't been sick."

"Now, I'm going to drive you down to the hospital and I'll have Dr. Arnold Petersen meet us there. He's a physician and a gynecologist and the right man, I think, to take care of you. He's also the mayor and a man completely to be trusted."

"Do I really need to go?"

"I think so. Not to prove your story, but to see that you receive any needed treatment. After you've been seen by Dr. Petersen, they'll probably want to keep you for the rest of the night. I don't see how you could sleep here after what's happened."

Janet looked with sudden gratitude at him. "Thanks," she said. "Thanks a lot." She sensed that she no longer had to fight; others had taken over for her.

Tallon went to the telephone.

Throughout the rest of the night the Whitewater Police Department gave of its best. For five blocks in every direction from the address on College Lane, the streets and yards were scoured for evidence. A number of sleeping residents were startled and had to be assured that they were in no danger. Two officers on foot covered every inch of the downtown area for any possible stragglers. The all-night gas station attendant was questioned, but he had nothing to contribute. Both motels reported that no guests had been seen either leaving or returning after midnight. There was an absence of activity that was in itself quite remarkable.

At the house where the second rape had taken place Ned Asher examined the whole exterior and dusted the bedroom exhaustively for fingerprints. With a flash camera he photographed the ground directly underneath the window that had been open. There he found definite evidence of entry and probable exit, but the person responsible had been cautious enough to scuff out his marks before leaving the scene. Ned made a careful note to check for dirt on the side of the suspect's shoes—if and when a suspect was taken into custody.

Tallon got very little sleep. He tossed and turned in his bed during the short time that he was in it, then he got up, shaved, showered, dressed, and tormented himself by trying to reason out evidence that wasn't there. Jennifer prepared his breakfast without saying a word, understanding his mood and his absolute need to be left alone. When he quickly finished his coffee and left for his office, her heart went with him.

He had hoped fervently for at least a few shreds of evidence, but the total of the whole night's intense work was a taunting void. His men had done their best, he was satisfied of that, and he also knew that he could have done no better himself.

There was one avenue open. He went through the things on his desk that required attention and then left immediately for the hospital.

Janet was still in bed when he got there, under observation. Praise be to God they had put her in a cheerful room where the morning sun was burning bright patterns across the floor. She was sitting up waiting for him and he knew that Francie had phoned ahead for him, something he had forgotten to ask her to do.

"How are you feeling?" he asked.

"A lot better, thanks. And I like Dr. Petersen, thank you for getting him for me."

He drew a chair and sat down. "Do you feel like talking a little?"

"It's all right: go ahead."

He spoke informally, as though he were discussing a new book. "Janet, we've learned quite a lot about rapists and their methods of operation. Certain things trigger them, and cause them to choose one victim over another. I want to talk with you not so much about what happened, you've already told me that, but about your life since you came to Whitewater. By comparing what you can give me with the information we gathered last time, we may find some parallels. Once we do that, we may be a long step ahead in capturing this . . . man."

"I understand," Janet said. "I'm only worried that if Dad hears about this, he'll take me out of school here, and I don't want that. Somehow I don't think that that man will ever come back again."

"Neither do I," Tallon agreed. "Rapists seldom repeat with the same victim unless it isn't really rape at all, and in your case it definitely was. We're going to catch him, you can depend on that, and you can help to make it a lot sooner by answering some questions."

For almost two hours Jack interviewed her, and not once during that time did she falter. She had chosen the college at Whitewater largely because a close friend of hers went there and had encouraged her to enroll. Her family lived in Seattle, where her father was employed by the Boeing Company. Her mother was a legal secretary. A careful questioning about her mother's possible role in any cases involving rape drew a total blank. She was employed by a legal firm that dealt almost entirely in estate management and related fields; it did not handle criminal cases.

Janet herself had been born in Cleveland and had lived there with her family until her father had joined Boeing seven years before. She had gone to high school in Seattle. She had been moderately popular, but despite her good looks and obvious intelligence, she had never really been part of the "in" crowd. She attributed this, in part, to her old-fashioned outlook toward sex—which was the phrase she used.. "I had illusions about waiting for the right man and it simply doesn't work like that any more."

"Is there anyone, perhaps in the background, who might have been frustrated by your refusal and tried a little too hard?"

"Some guys did get upset when I said 'no,' but no one was violent about it. There were plenty of other girls, and nobody seemed to want me in particular."

"Janet, did you ever enter a beauty contest, even a very local affair?"

She shook her head emphatically. "No, Dad would have killed me if I had done anything like that. He's a wonderful father, but he's a fundamentalist who believes that the Bible forbids blood transfusions and things like that. Frankly, he turned off some pretty nice guys that were interested in me. That's really why I came to college here; so that I'd be out of that influence."

He traced every one of her interests, every hobby that she had ever had, even for a short while, and nowhere could he find a match-up with Betty Weber, the first rape victim. The only thing he could find in common was that they both lived in Whitewater, but Betty was a permanent resident, while Janet only attended college there.

Both were attractive, but where Betty Weber was spectacular, Janet Edelmann was not. She was a nice-looking girl, but she was nowhere in Betty Weber's class.

No match. Jack went back to his office in a dangerous mood.

Ned Asher was waiting for him there, unshaven and tired, and ignoring it. "I only found one set of fingerprints in the bedroom," he reported. "They were all over the place, so they have to be the victim's. I couldn't find anything else in the house that would give me a lead. Apparently he was in the bedroom and that was all."

"I want a complete description of the house," Tallon said. "I want to know how it's landscaped, what kind of flowers grow in the yard, and if there's a patio in back. What I'm after, Ned, is any point of similarity, no matter how small, between this house and the Webers' place. If they both have green shingles, that might be it."

Asher listened with dead seriousness. "I'll go after it," he promised. "I know that strange things trigger these birds."

"Good. Make the inspection, then go home and get some rest. But call me right away if you spot anything at all."

It was after twelve and Tallon went to lunch with the damning knowledge that he did not have a single solid clue—not even the fragment of one. When he got back, Dick Collins was waiting for him.

The city manager came right to the point. He carefully shut the door and then said, "I want to give this to you straight, so you'll know what's going on. It's all over town that there's been another rape. There are a lot of wild rumors, but the general understanding is that a college girl was attacked where she rooms."

"That's right," Tallon confirmed.

"Jack, you and your men did an outstanding job in nabbing those two wanted men: it made us all look good. But that wasn't a Whitewater affair, and this is—a damned serious one. I know you're doing your best, but I should warn you that if you don't nail this bastard that's got every woman in this town frightened of her own shadow, the flak is going to be unbelievable."

"If you want my resignation, Dick, you can have it right now."

"I don't and you know it, Jack. All I'm trying to do is to tell you what the score is so that you can protect yourself. Personally, I know how fortunate we were in getting you to come here."

The city manager got to his feet. "I'll back you all the way, you know that, but if anything does break, for God's sake let me know. Then I'll be able to tell the council that something is going on and that they'll have a full report in due course."

Tallon saw his visitor out and returned to his desk to hear his phone ringing. It was his private line, so he picked it up promptly, and answered.

"This is Harry Gilroy, Jack. I've heard about the new rape; I guess everyone has. Is there anything I can do to help you out?"

Tallon was grateful. "At the moment, Harry, no—but thank you."

"One thing: Bert wants to come up and get the story, but it occurred to me that this might not be the best time. With a weekly we don't normally have to rush."

"Not now—please!"

"Got it. Rest easy, you've got at least three days before we need a thing." The newspaper owner hung up.

There was one more thing to try. Jack laid out two blank sheets of ruled yellow paper on his desk and put down on them, respectively, every fact that he could remember about each of the two rape victims. Somewhere there had to be a parallel, something that they had in common that would provide a clue.

He had been at it hard and heavy for more than an hour when Ned

Asher appeared in his doorway. As soon as Tallon waved him in, he delivered his news without wasting a moment on preliminaries. "I've got something," he declared. "It isn't much, but it might help. I've got a witness at the Northside Motel who definitely saw an old pickup truck, that she thinks was a Ford, driving out of town about one-thirty last night. She is certain that there was only one occupant and that it was a man. He went right through the red light at the corner without even slowing up, as if he were running away from something."

"Is she sure of the time?"

"Yes. She'd been up late because she had had trouble getting to sleep. She went outside and sat on one of the patio chairs, hoping that the night air would make her feel better. She had looked at the clock just before she left her room and she had been seated for only about five minutes when the incident occurred."

Jack shuddered with relief—at least there was something!

"Ned, that's great. I'll talk to the witness right away."

"By all means if you want to, Chief, but I think I got all that she has."

Tallon caught the tone and responded to it immediately. "Then there's no need for me to see her at all. I know you don't have the license or you would have said so. I thought you went home."

"I'm all right, and I feel a helluva lot better than I did. She says that the truck is white, dirty, and had nothing lettered on it, like a firm name."

Tallon leaned forward. "Check immediately with the all-night gas station attendant to see if he saw the truck. He might remember it if he did, since he's on the south side . . ."

Asher's broad smile stopped him. "I already did that, Chief. Joe Meyers was at the station from twelve o'clock on. He not only didn't see the truck in question, he's certain that no such vehicle went through here any time during the second half of the night."

Chapter Ten

Tallon's first act was to notify Dick Collins that he had a new lead and that Ned Asher, his detective, had dug it up. After promising to keep the city manager posted on any further developments, he called the few men who were on duty into his office.

After he had shut the door, he gave them the new information. "From now on, every white pickup truck that you see on the streets of Whitewater is suspect," he told them. "Particularly at night, but don't discount the daytime, because this man is picking his victims; he's choosing them somewhere. Keep this absolutely within the shop, but I want every white pickup checked in one way or another. If you see any kind of traffic infraction, stop the truck, check the driver's ID, and inspect it on the inside if you get the chance. Fortunately, there isn't any locked trunk on a pickup. If the infraction is minor, take the license number and let the driver go with a warning. And it makes no difference whatever if you happen to know the driver or not."

He dismissed them all but Sergeant Smallins. As he waited for the room to clear, he noticed that Smallins seemed to have lost a little weight. "You seem a little slimmer," he said.

The sergeant nodded. "I was getting a little too heavy; too much desk work. I'm down six pounds so far."

"Keep it up."

"I intend to."

"You remember the suspect we picked up after the first rape. I'd like you, personally, to find out exactly where he was when Janet Edelmann was attacked. And check up on his girl friend here; find out if he was visiting her."

After Smallins left, he called Asher back in. "I want you to go home and get some sleep, and that's an order," Tallon said. "When you come in tomorrow, I want you to call on Mrs. Weber and get from her a list of every place that she's been seen in public during the past three months. Find out where she's been shopping, where she goes to church, whether or not she uses the library, where she buys gas—the whole works. She's very co-operative and if you're patient with her, the list should be pretty solid."

"I understand, Chief. After I do that, you want me to see Janet Edelmann and put her over the same set of hurdles."

"Right! And the moment that you hit on any common ground, I want to be notified immediately. But don't stop if you get one match-up; this isn't a big city and there could be a good many similarities. Stay with it all the way through."

When he was again free he called the sheriff in Spokane, filled in the watch commander with the information on the white pickup, and asked for maximum co-operation. The lieutenant he talked with promised that the vehicle files would be checked at once for any likely leads.

For the first time, Tallon felt that he had something to go on. He turned back to the yellow sheets on which he had been making his listings. Sergeant Smallins interrupted him some forty minutes later. "Report," he said. "The young lady in Whitewater: her husband was back on the night of the rape and the family was in all evening. No chance for a visit from the boy friend."

"Good. And what about him?"

"He was out and can't prove his whereabouts. He says that he went to a movie; he had a fight with his wife and left alone. No one saw him that he can produce. In short, no alibi."

"Get the ID on his car."

"It's a Ford Mustang; I've got the plate number. We'll watch for it."

Francie appeared to tell him that he had a visitor. "The Fed from Spokane. Mr. Lonigan."

That was all that Tallon needed to complete his day, but he recognized the need to co-operate with the FBI. He had Lonigan shown in.

For the first few minutes they discussed the rape cases. "I know that this isn't your beat," Tallon said, "but if you run into anything at all that might help us here, please call us immediately."

Lonigan promised that he would extend maximum co-operation in any way possible. "We often run into things in the course of our own work, so there is a chance that we may be able to help. My best guess would have been that it's someone in your own community, but the truck incident changes all that. Smaller cities have been used before by hard-core offenders who are looking for relatively easy pickings. No reflection on your department, but in a major city backup is usually there when you need it; here you might have a problem."

"We know that," Tallon said.

"Now, to come to the point: if you don't have any objection, a man will be here in the morning to install a special telephone on your desk."

"A direct line to where?" Tallon asked. "The safe house?"

"That's it. Do you remember the big bank heist in Seattle about four months ago?"

"I wasn't in the area then, but I remember hearing about it."

"We have three suspects in custody, that's open information. What isn't known is that we have a key witness, a cashier who disappeared after the robbery and who hasn't officially been seen since."

"And you have him," Tallon supplied.

"Her. Actually, she appealed to us for protection, and she had reason to. Five men hit the bank; we've got three, which leaves two at large. We think they may know we have the witness, and we feel that they would go the limit to knock her out of the picture, because she can make a positive ID of the three we have. Without her, our case would be materially weakened."

"When will she be moving into the safe house?"

"Tomorrow. A van will arrive with some furniture in the ordinary way. The family will consist of a man and his wife, plus her brother who lives with them."

"One witness, two bodyguards."

Lonigan leaned back and relaxed a little. "Call me Roger," he said.

"Jack."

"Good, Jack. This is the word: you'll be kept informed of all that's going on, but we're asking you not to tell anyone else. Not the mayor, not the members of your staff—no one."

"What about an emergency?"

"In that case, use your own judgment. But right now secrecy is essential, because this is a big one. We're up against a team of the toughest pros in the country. Frankly, we debated letting you in on it, but we decided that we didn't have any choice."

"No, you didn't," Tallon agreed.

"The direct line will stay open and you're welcome to call and check at any time. They won't call you unless you're needed. If it ever rings, you'll know."

"What if I'm not here?"

"Tell your watch commanders that it's a special phone and to answer it if it rings. They'll be given directions. If no one talks, have them call you immediately."

"Roger, I think you're making a mistake in not letting me tell my sergeants; they can definitely be trusted."

"All right, we'll consider that. In the meantime, you know the drill."

When the FBI man had gone, Tallon evaluated this new responsibility. He didn't object to it, but the timing was bad. Until the rapist was caught, he would have little time for anything else.

His private line rang and he answered it. It was the college police chief with a piece of information: a heroin user had been turned up on the campus. The dorm troopers were investigating. After he had hung up, Tallon reflected that he would let them handle that one. Then he wondered how in hell things were going in Pasadena.

As had happened before, Marion McNeil and Bill Albrecht were holding an impromptu meeting in the office of Harry Gilroy, the newspaper publisher. They were close friends and spoke freely in each other's presence.

"It's an absolute outrage," Marion blazed. "The sort of thing that could only come from a disordered mind!"

"I agree," Albrecht said, somewhat more calmly. "No intelligent person is going to believe it for a moment, but the fact remains that it's all over town and some people are pretty sure to think that it could be so."

Harry Gilroy put a pointed question. "Have you any idea where the rumor started?"

"Where do you think?" Marion snapped. "That insane old woman who peeked in my shopping bag last week to see what kind of brassiere I had bought—Lily Hope."

"Can you prove that?" Gilroy asked. Like any publisher, he could smell libel a mile away.

"I don't have to; she lives right across the street from the Tallons and you can bet that she watches them constantly."

Albrecht remained calm. "To get back to the realm of facts, it is being widely circulated that our new chief of police is the rapist who's got the city terrified. I wish to heaven that everyone was sensible enough to realize that it's impossible, but suspicion will feed on the fact that these crimes did begin shortly after he came here. And it's also true that he's all over town, day and night."

"Because that's his job," Gilroy noted. "I happen to know that he's been taking extra patrol shifts himself at night, to increase the coverage in the city. And I don't think that he's putting in for overtime."

"He isn't," Albrecht said.

Marion asked, "Is there anything we can do, legally or otherwise, to shut that old woman up?"

"I wish that there was," Albrecht answered. "A while ago she spread the wholly unfounded rumor that some municipal funds were missing. She got that from a remark I made to my wife in the supermarket: I said that the council had wanted to do something, I don't even recall now what it was, but that I hadn't been able to find the money. That's all there was to it, but I almost had to request an extraordinary audit to clear that one up."

"Does Jack know?" Marion asked.

"I honestly can't answer that," Albrecht told her, "but if not, he should be tipped off."

"I can tell him," Harry Gilroy said. "I live in the next block beyond him. I should just catch him coming home."

At the college, the rumor that the new Whitewater police chief was the rapist spread rapidly. It was neither believed nor disbelieved, but there were enough students on the campus to whom all cops were pigs to encourage the idea and give it the appearance of substance.

The dorm troopers had an unusually bad night and they had no idea what had brought it about.

As soon as he received the news, Jack Tallon's first reaction was one of outraged fury. After Harry Gilroy had left, he came down off the walls and made a massive effort to get control of himself. While she was preparing the last things for dinner Jennifer almost wept. It was her fault, all hers: she had persuaded him to take the thankless job up in this Godforsaken place, thinking that they would be so much happier together. When they sat down to eat, she didn't waste a moment.

"We've got to get out of here," she said. "I don't care if you take a job mixing Orange Julius, you're not going to be subjected to this one day longer. I haven't told you, but I miss Pasadena terribly, and all our friends there."

Tallon reached out and put his hand on top of hers. "Now listen, I'm way ahead of you, and I know just how you feel. But realize something, Jenny: if I were to pull out now, how do you think it would look?"

"As if you're too big a man to put up with such an outrage. And you are!"

He shook his head. "That isn't the way it would be read. It would look like a confession; the suspect who flees the scene. Think about it. Right now the one thing I can't do is leave. I'm going to catch that son of a bitch, and when I do, the cheap gossips around here are going to have egg running all over their sniveling faces."

"I don't see how you can be so calm," Jennifer said.

"I'm not, I'm raging, but I also know that in a fight the first man that loses his cool gets licked. I blew it for a few minutes, but now I'm all right. And if you think that I'll allow one senile old woman to drive me out of the place where I choose to live, you've got another guess coming."

As Jennifer bent over her food she offered a silent prayer of thanks.

Across the street and slightly up the hill, Mrs. Lily Hope had carefully watched both the arrival and the departure of the newspaper publisher. Since she was sure that it was the first time that Gilroy had been to the Tallon home, it was to her a vivid proof that he was bringing a pre-emptive message from the city council. Otherwise, why would he call just before the dinner hour?

Once more she was whispering into her telephone.

Chapter Eleven

Jack Tallon had a wretched night. Sleep would not come and the burning anger refused to leave his body. Jennifer tried her best to soothe him, but he was almost hostile in his rejection of her. She understood and sympathized deeply, knowing that at that moment it was beyond her scope to offer him anything that would ease or divert his mind. He got up, took a Valium, and returned to bed to pitch and toss for the rest of the night. .

When he arrived at his office the following morning, Ned Asher was waiting to see him. The young detective was obviously concerned and the lines in his face suggested that he had added a year or two to his age within the past twenty-four hours. His movements had a touch of awkwardness in them that was not natural.

"Chief, there is a damn ugly rumor running around town—are you aware of it?" he began.

"Yes," Tallon answered.

"Then I just want to tell you that the rest of us in the department are as mad about it as you must be. It's an outrage."

The intention, if nothing else, helped Tallon to feel better. "Thank you, Ned," he said. "I very much appreciate it."

Asher drew breath as if to say something more, then he thought better of it and quietly left the office. Tallon sat down behind his desk just in time to answer his private phone; Harry Gilroy was on the line.

"Jack," the publisher said, "I'm sending Bert over to see you. He's got some questions to ask that I gave to him. Answer them in your own words, and then trust me."

"I'm not sure that I want to say anything for publication right now, Harry," Tallon answered.

"I said, trust me. I know what I'm doing."

"I do trust you, but you'd better fill me in before Bert gets here."

"All right: it's still true that people believe what they see in print.

For the sake of the dim-witted members of our community, I'm doing a recap story on the search for the rapist. In the course of the copy I'm going to mention the fact that you were notified at your home immediately after the crime was reported, in both instances."

Tallon tried to think, but his emotions clouded his usually logical mind. "Harry, I'm not sure that's a good idea."

"You talk with Bert; he's on his way."

"All right."

Within ten minutes the young reporter was shown in. He sat down, opened a notebook, and surveyed a list of questions he had carefully written down. "In cases of rape, Chief Tallon, I know there must be certain standard methods of investigation. Can you tell me a little about them?"

Before Tallon could respond, Judge Howell walked in without an invitation. "Bert, please be kind enough to excuse us," he said.

Without a word, the reporter shut his notebook and left the office.

As soon as he was gone, the judge shut the office door and then sat down. "Jack," he began, "I've asked Francie to hold your calls for a few minutes unless there's something urgent. Now, listen carefully: You're new here and I've lived in this town for a long time; I know it better than you do. No intelligent person is going to believe for a moment that you're responsible for these rapes, but people like to repeat a juicy story, especially when they don't have anything better to do. I want a commitment from you that you won't take any action whatever to counter this wild rumor except to continue your efforts to catch the man who is the actual criminal."

Tallon shook his head. "If you're asking me to take it lying down, I can't. I've been awake all night over this and as of this moment, I've had a Goddamned bellyful of Whitewater. I'd resign this morning except that I obviously can't—you know why."

"Jack, listen to me." The judge's voice revealed a toughness that Tallon had not known was there. "I want you to forget this matter and leave it to me. You stay here and run the police department. And don't blame Whitewater, we're not all a bunch of imbeciles up here. I'll give Harry Gilroy a call and turn him off. Now, remember, you're under injunction to keep hands off, and I mean it."

"If you say so, Judge."

"I do say so. You already have some friends in town."

Twenty minutes later the judge was comfortably seated in Otis Fenwell's office. The city attorney had had to cancel an appointment, but the fact that the judge had come to see him gave the call priority.

"Otis," Howell opened, "I'm fully aware that you haven't too much enthusiasm for our new police chief, but I'd never accuse you of not being willing to give him a fair chance."

Fenwell was cautious and deliberate. "I'd have to say that you are probably right on both counts," he acknowledged.

"Are you aware that there's a helluva rumor going around town?"

"Yes, I've heard of it. It's preposterous."

"I'm glad that we agree on that." The judge hitched his chair an inch forward. "From now on this is confidential."

"So understood."

"To begin with, all of this nonsense was started by Lily Hope. I presume you know of her."

"I certainly do."

"I have now contacted certain responsible women that I know: the kind whose testimony would be believed in any court. Four of them have agreed to sign a deposition attesting to the fact that Mrs. Hope phoned them unsolicited and told them flat out, with no reservations, that Chief Tallon is himself the rapist who attacked Betty Weber and one of the college girls."

Fenwell rested his chin in his long, bony fingers and thought; it took him several seconds to reach a conclusion. When he did speak, his voice was completely dry and unemotional. "There's a complication, Sam, that pretty much spoils your case. Tallon is a public official; to a considerable degree that denies him the usual protections against slander or libel. The courts have been holding, as you know, that you can say almost anything about a public official without being in jeopardy. If Tallon were just a private citizen, then, based on the depositions you mentioned and live testimony in court, he might have the basis for an action against Mrs. Hope. But as the chief of police, he's virtually powerless."

"Agreed, and if he did file an action, he'd be almost compelled to win it or he'd get caught in the backwash."

"True," Fenwell agreed.

"Now, Otis, to my great regret, there isn't any clear-cut statute or ordinance under which Mrs. Hope can be charged."

"However," Fenwell observed, "she may not know that."

The judge took a cigar out of his pocket. "Now you're beginning to get the picture. You know, of course, that she once spread a rumor that you had taken a bribe."

Fenwell nodded gravely. "Yes, I know that."

The judge paused and changed his tone. "Otis, if she ever got hold of even one tenth of what I know about this town, or you either, for that matter, there'd be nobody left to pay the taxes."

Fenwell mellowed slightly. "That's for sure." He tapped a folder on his desk. "Here's a good example."

The judge looked over and read the identifying tab. "Hell, yes," he concurred. "That would probably send her into permanent orbit."

"Then maybe we ought to tell her," Fenwell said. "But I don't think that I will. What are you going to do now?"

The judge rose. "I'm going to get some hard evidence, just for the record," he answered.

From the outer office the judge made a phone call to the newspaper office and then dialed once more. When he was through he thanked the secretary and went outside to his car. A few minutes later Betty Weber opened the door for him.

"Come in, Judge," she said. "I put the coffeepot on as soon as you called; it's hot and ready."

"Thank you." Howell walked in and seated himself comfortably in the living room. Moments later Betty came in from the kitchen with a small tray. She set out two cups, cream and sugar, spoons, and a small plate of bakery cookies. As soon as she had served him and was ready to listen, the judge opened the conversation.

"Betty, I don't want to be hard on you, but I've got two or three questions to ask you—not specifically about what happened to you, that's already fully on the record."

"I don't mind," she said. "I'm pretty well over it now. I hope they catch the guy, of course, but as it worked out, it might even have been a good thing for me." Her tone had more acid in it than the judge had ever heard her use.

"Why?" he asked.

"Because of Mark and me. I never told you, I never told anybody, but our marriage was pretty much of a joke."

She paused to sip her coffee; the judge did not interrupt her.

"He married me because I was a showpiece. He brought up that beauty contest thing time and again, as though it was all that he could find to be proud of in me. I felt just like a fish having its picture taken, hanging by the gills while some guy stands beside it to show how proud he is of his kill."

For a moment her jaw tightened and harsh lines formed around her mouth, forecasting what she might look like in another ten to fifteen years. Her beauty momentarily vanished from her face and the judge looked away, knowing that she wouldn't grow old gracefully—not unless she put her mind at ease first. "Wayne helped, of course, but gradually the novelty of having a son wore away and he became more of a kid who was a nuisance than anything else. To Mark, that is. So we decided to split up."

"News to me," the judge commented.

"We didn't want anyone to know. Then I found that I was pregnant; I must have gotten careless." She reached across a small table and picked up a pack of cigarettes.

When she had lit one, she continued. "Frankly, we didn't know what the hell to do. I'm Catholic. Then . . . it happened. Mark came flying back from his girl friend—I knew there was one—and we've been a lot closer ever since."

"I've heard it said that there's some good in everything," the judge remarked.

"Not for that college girl, Janet Edelmann. We met and talked. It was a complete horror for her, and I don't know if she'll ever get over it."

The judge decided that it had gone far enough; he signaled that by rattling his coffee cup in its saucer and then took over. "Betty, I'm going to ask you some questions I don't think you've answered before. Take your time, but please give me the most accurate answers you possibly can."

"All right." The lines around her mouth had eased and she looked young and lovely once more.

"After it was all over, how did the man leave your house?"

"He dressed, quickly, and then ran from my bedroom, not very fast. He said to me, 'Now, stay away from that Goddamned telephone or I'll be back.' Then I heard him running through the house toward the back door."

"Fine, Betty, I've got that. Now, what was the next thing that you did? I don't care how trivial it was."

"I went into the bathroom and spat as much as I could. Then I used a mouthwash—full strength. I did that three times."

"How long did it take—two minutes?"

Betty thought. "Less than that, Judge. Say a minute at the most."

"Then what did you do next? Don't skip anything whatever."

"I went right to the telephone and called the police."

"Did you look up the number?"

"No; I asked the operator and she connected me immediately."

"Good. How long was it before the police answered?"

"Right after the first ring; the man must have been sitting right beside the phone."

"So from the time that the rapist ran out of your bedroom until you were actually talking with the man at the police station was less than five minutes?"

Betty leaned forward and snuffed out her cigarette; she had hardly touched it. "Not that long," she answered. "Three minutes at the outside. Why?"

"Let that go for the time being. Do you remember who you talked to at the police station?"

"Yes, a Sergeant Easter, or something like that. He was very helpful."

The judge got to his feet. "If anyone asks if I was here, don't deny it —it might be misunderstood. But otherwise, keep this entirely to yourself. I mean *entirely*. Now, may I use your phone?"

Janet Edelmann was in the commons when she was told that she was wanted by the dean of women. She gathered up her books and went to the office, vague fears in her mind. The dean, however, was considerate; she showed Janet into a private office, introduced Judge Howell, and then left them alone.

"Is this about the rape?" Janet asked.

"Yes, it is, but not what you may think. Sit down."

Janet sat, hesitantly, and on the front edge of the chair.

"I want to check one or two very small points with you, but they're extremely important. So will you help me as much as you can, please?"

"Yes, your honor."

"After you were attacked, the man put his clothes back on, I assume."

"Yes, he did."

"Then what did he do?"

"He went out the window."

"Did he say anything to you?"

"Yes, he said that if I went near the telephone he would know and he would come back."

"Then what?"

"He disappeared."

"Now, Janet, from the moment that the man disappeared from your sight, tell me exactly what you did. Every tiny detail."

For a moment an aftershock ran through the girl and she found it difficult to speak; the reopened raw memory was too vivid. Then she began to recite, "I lay still in bed for maybe half a minute, no more than that. Then I recovered and I almost jumped to my feet. Even though it hurt, I wanted to get out of that bed as fast as I could. It had my blood on it."

The judge was listening intently, but he did not let it show. "Go on," he prompted.

"As soon as I was on my feet, I ran for the telephone."

"You weren't afraid of the man's threat, then."

"I never thought about it; I just dialed the operator and asked for the police. She put me through right away."

"After you dialed the operator, how long was it before she answered?"

"Just a few seconds. Almost at once, I'd say."

"She put you right through to the police?"

"That's right; I said that."

"I know you did. How long was it before the police answered?"

"Oh, that was right away too. I remember because I was . . . well, every second seemed like an eternity."

"I understand. Then you told the police what happened."

Janet hesitated, not allowing words to be put into her mouth. "No, not exactly—I asked to speak to a policewoman. The man who answered told me they didn't have any. Then I said that I wanted to see any policeman. He told me to wait."

"And you waited—for how long?"

"Ten or fifteen seconds."

"Then what?"

"He came back on the line and told me that Officer Quigley would come and see me. He asked what was wrong and I told him."

"Janet, you've been a great help. Now, one more question, and this is very important: How long do you think it was from the time that your attacker disappeared until you told the police exactly what had happened?"

"You mean, over the telephone?"

"Yes."

Janet rubbed her forehead with her fingertips, then she looked up. "Less than two minutes. Maybe only one. Say two."

"Thank you very much. What did you do after that?"

"I went into the bathroom and vomited."

The judge nodded, then he got up and put a hand on her shoulder. He warned her carefully not to say anything about the interview to anyone and then told her to wait five minutes after he had left before she went out of the building. He had no idea who might be watching.

Jack Tallon ate his dinner almost in silence. There were too many things pressing on his mind for him to want to talk, and he sensed that Jennifer understood. When he had finished he tried to read for a little while, but his mind refused to focus on the words. He turned on the television, but the supposed drama was so obviously aimed at a nine-year-old intelligence, he could not relate to it. When a commercial urged him to become the first in his block to own a microwave oven, his disgust overflowed and he snapped the set off. He didn't care at that moment if he ever turned it on again.

"I'm going down to the office," he said. "I have some things to do. Then I may take out a car for a while. Don't wait up for me."

Normally Jennifer would have protested, but she had been a policeman's wife long enough to understand the pressure he was under and the absolute need in him to be doing something to fight against the thing that was drowning him. She kissed him good-by, putting a promise in it as she did so. For a moment he held her very close and she thought he was going to change his mind and stay; then, gently, he pushed her away. Moments later she was alone.

Tallon spent only a few minutes in his office, hoping for some shred of news, but nothing had come in since he had left at five-thirty. He had a cup of coffee with the two men who were on duty, then he took the keys of his own patrol car off the board. "I'm going into the field for a while," he told Ralph Hillman, who was the watch commander. "If the rapist sticks to his pattern, he could be due to try again anytime."

"Fine, Chief," Hillman said. "It's good to have you out there."

Tallon went out to where his car was parked against the curb, started it up, and checked the gas. It had been filled at the city pump some time during the afternoon; the simple fact that that had been done properly heartened him a little. He started out to drive through the parts of the city he knew least; he wanted to memorize the name and location of every street and each of their individual characteristics. As he passed by the safe house he noted that there was a light on inside. Apart from the fact that it was somewhat isolated, it looked like any other residence.

When he had covered the whole area, he turned toward Main Street and cruised slowly past the motel where the white pickup had been spotted. He continued on downtown. Two blocks ahead of him he spotted the taillights of a car that was weaving more than it should. He fed a little more gas and gradually closed the gap.

When the vehicle ahead of him reached the empty intersection of Main and Fawcett, it went straight through the red light as though the signal had not been there. Tallon pressed down on the gas and reached for the mike. "Whitewater One," he reported. "I'm making a traffic stop on Main south of Fawcett. Stand by for the vehicle ID."

As soon as he was less than half a block behind the car he was after, he flipped on the Twin-Sonic lights overhead and then touched the electronic siren for just a moment. In response, the car ahead of him obediently pulled over. Tallon parked behind it with a three-foot overlap, read the license number into the microphone, picked up his pinch book, and got out.

There were four males in the car he had stopped, all of them in the seventeen to eighteen age bracket. He approached the driver and stopped at the rear edge of the front door. Before he could speak, the young man asked, "Now what the hell is it?" His tone was angry and hostile.

Tallon did not react. "You went through a red light about two blocks back," he answered. "May I see your driver's license, please."

"Who are you? I don't know you, and you're not in uniform. If you're a cop, show me your badge." He made it a pre-emptive order.

Because a citizen had a right to demand that, Tallon displayed his shield briefly and then put it away. He took the driver's license and returned to his vehicle.

"Whitewater One," he radioed. "Do we know a Ronnie Keyhoe, age seventeen, and is there anything on the car?"

Hillman came back promptly. "Ed Wyncott will back you up, ETA two minutes. Nothing on the car, but we know Ronnie well. Unless I'm mistaken, Judge Howell has him on probation right now. Mostly traffic offenses. What did he do this time?"

"He ran the red light at Main and Fawcett." Tallon put the mike back on its clip and returned to the vehicle he had stopped. He unfolded his pinch book and began to write up the citation.

"Hey, fuzz," Ronnie declared from the front seat. "You're wasting your time. That ticket'll be fixed tomorrow."

"I don't think so," Tallon answered. He didn't bother to look up.

"Shit, man, tickets get fixed all the time around here. Don't you know that?"

Tallon remembered the parking citation he had received himself the first day he had been on the job. "Not without a good reason," he said, keeping the conversation brief and restrained. He completed the write-up and handed the book to the driver. "Sign right there, please," he said. "That's not an admission of guilt, only a promise to appear."

"And what if I won't?"

"Then I'll have to take you to jail." He put a measure of hardness into those words; he was in no mood to be pushed around by a juvenile.

Ronnie drew breath, but before he could speak the other patrol car on duty appeared at the intersection, its overhead lights on in silent warning. Ronnie saw it, grabbed the offered pen from Tallon's hand, and made an illegible scrawl on the ticket.

"That won't do you a damn bit of good," he told Tallon. "My dad will call the chief and take care of it before you're out of bed in the morning."

"Why don't you see the chief yourself," Tallon invited.

"I may just do that, pig. You know why they call cops pigs, don't you?"

Tallon nodded. "It's an abbreviation for Patience, Integrity, and Guts. Go ahead and see the chief in the morning if you want to." He handed the citation over. "Maybe he'll believe you."

"I will, shithead. There's four of us and one of you. Where are your witnesses, hey?"

"That's enough," Tallon barked. "I've taken all I intend to from you. Now, go home."

"So long, sucker," Ronnie shouted. As if to defy the slip of paper he had been given, he started the car moving with a racing engine and burned rubber on the dry pavement as it accelerated.

Ed Wyncott pulled up alongside. "Everything all right?" he asked.

Tallon nodded. "Cool and under control. He's a very powerful young man; he's going to see the chief in the morning and get the ticket dismissed."

Ed grinned in amusement and drove away. Tallon closed his citation book, got back into his car, and radioed that he was back in service.

Hillman had a message for him. "Chief, a man just phoned in and said that he wanted to see you personally as soon as possible. He wouldn't give me his name, but he said that he had met you the day you spoke at the Kiwanis Club."

"Why wouldn't he give his name?"

"I can't say. I told him that you were out on patrol. He asked if you would stop by the Hawaiian Gardens, he's there now with his wife."

"How am I supposed to know him?"

"I presume he'll introduce himself. Ed, do you read me?"

"Loud and clear," Wyncott answered.

"Since this guy refused to give his name, I suggest that you back the chief up—just in case."

"Right. No problem."

"I'll see what it is," Tallon said, and started his engine.

Because it had a liquor license, the Hawaiian Gardens stayed open at night, normally until about eleven. Tallon drove back up Main and swung into the parking lot. His mind was open on this one, largely because the man who wanted to see him had his wife with him. That all but eliminated any likelihood of physical action. He pushed open the door and went inside.

The place was virtually deserted. The low-powered colored spotlights that picked up the decorations added a small illusion of warmth in the absence of the main overhead lights. Tallon walked slowly up the row

of five booths as though he were on a break and couldn't decide where
to sit.

"Chief Tallon."

A man had risen in booth four, his hand lifted in greeting. Tallon
could not remember ever seeing him before.

"Phil Jones; we met at the Kiwanis Club. This is my wife, Diane.
Won't you join us?"

It appeared very casual; Tallon seated himself and said the proper
things to Jones's wife. When the lone waitress on duty appeared, he
was careful to appear relaxed and friendly. "I'd like one of those big
fruit punches you make," he declared.

The waitress had seen him several times before and still thought that
he was damn good-looking. "Is that all?" she asked. "A little rum in it,
maybe?"

Tallon shook his head. "Not while I'm driving a patrol car."

The waitress smiled. She didn't believe the things that they were saying about the new police chief, but if she woke up some night and
found him in her bedroom, that wouldn't be too hard to take. She made
up an extra special punch and wrote a check at the lunch rate, not the
night bar price.

After she had served it and gone, Jones dropped his voice and spoke
very quietly. "Thank you for coming," he said.

"It's part of my job," Tallon answered. He looked up as Ed Wyncott
came walking through to be sure that all was well. He spoke briefly to
his patrolman as though they had met accidentally and then turned his
attention back to Jones and his wife.

"We had made up our minds never to tell anyone," Jones continued,
"and we've stuck to that decision. But now we can't anymore, for several reasons, so we have decided to confide in you. If we tell you something, will you agree to keep it absolutely to yourself?"

"If you're going to confess to a crime, I can't," Tallon answered. "I'm
a sworn peace officer, as you know. However, if you have any other
kind of information, I'll hold it in the strictest confidence."

Jones looked at his wife, who nodded openly.

"All right, Chief Tallon. We know, of course, about the two terrible
rapes that have happened here recently. We've followed what's been
published very closely. While I was at a three-day sales meeting in
Spokane; Diane was raped in our bedroom. By a man wearing a Frankenstein mask who threatened her with a knife."

"My God!" Tallon said softly.

"We decided to tell you, because we might be able to give you some
clue you wouldn't otherwise have. But we want it kept secret, because
Diane's family was very opposed to our coming out here. They're plan-

ning to visit us shortly and if they were to learn what happened, there would be almighty hell to pay."

Tallon quietly took some of his drink and then set the glass down. "Thank you very much for confiding in me," he said. "Unquestionably you did the right thing. If I may, I'd like to talk with Diane about it in detail. I know it won't be pleasant for her."

Diane herself responded to that. "It's quite all right, I understand. But there are two things you should know right now. First: it happened almost two months ago, before you came here. I was probably the first."

"But we don't dare to come forward and scotch the rumors that are going around," Jones added.

Tallon made a hand gesture. "That's not a consideration, so don't let it bother you. What's the other thing?"

Diane lowered her head for just a moment, then she looked at him quite calmly. "I can tell you one thing about your rapist that you may not know. He's diseased. I know, because he gave me a case of gonorrhea. We found it out when I infected my husband."

Chapter Twelve

It was not easy for Tallon to keep himself under control. He managed to hold his voice somewhere near its normal level, but only by making a conscious effort.

"I assume that you're having medical attention," he said.

"Yes, we're going to Petersen, partly because we knew he had taken care of the other two victims. It was in the paper." Jones was not having too easy a time himself.

"Did you see Dr. Petersen at the time of the attack on Diane?"

"No. We thought about it, but she didn't seem to have any physical ill effects, thank God no pregnancy resulted, so we kept it to ourselves— for the reasons I already gave you. I didn't want Diane stared at every time she went into the supermarket."

"But now it's a different situation."

"Exactly."

"When did you find out?"

"This afternoon for sure. We talked it over at dinner and decided that we had better tell you."

"So Dr. Petersen knows."

"Yes; we told him when Diane had been attacked, so he knows also that the rumor going around isn't true. Not that I'm suggesting he needed any reassurance."

"Thank you." Tallon folded his fingers together and thought for a few moments. "It would be a great help to my department," he said, "if you will allow me to tell my key people that another attack did occur. We need every bit of data we can get, and alibi checking could be very important when we get that far."

Jones looked carefully at his wife before he answered. "It's awfully damn hard to keep a secret in a town like this, once the basic fact is known. Someone might guess."

Tallon shook his head. "I don't think so," he disagreed. "There are more than two thousand women in Whitewater who might be considered possible victims, and more than twice that many if you include the girls at the college. Unless you yourselves tip someone off, I don't see how it can possibly come out. Arnold Petersen won't talk under any circumstances, and I can absolutely guarantee that I won't."

"I think it would be all right," Diane said. "The reason we decided to tell you was to help, if we could, in catching the man."

Tallon gave her his full attention. "How soon can we talk together?" he asked. "Every hour now could be important."

"We could go up to our house now," Diane answered. "But I'd rather not have the police car parked right outside."

"Suppose that I come in half an hour in my own car? It's inconspicuous, especially at night."

Jones agreed with that. "I think it would be best to get it over with as soon as possible. We'll be ready when you come."

Tallon finished his punch and left a dollar on the table. Jones tried to hand it back, but Tallon shook his head. He drove immediately back to the department, turned in his patrol car, and wrote a number on a card. He dropped it into an envelope and sealed the flap, then he gave it to Brad Hillman. "I'm going to have a drink with some friends," he said. "If an emergency arises, and you have to reach me, the number is in here."

Sergeant Hillman nodded. "I understand, Chief. Let's hope that it's a quiet night."

As he drove off Tallon was not looking forward to the interrogation he would have to inflict on Diane Jones. Fortunately she was intelligent and the passage of more than two months should have given her enough perspective to avoid any fresh emotional shocks.

At ten the following morning the Whitewater City Council met in executive session. Tallon was present by invitation, and so was Judge Howell. Arnold Petersen presided in his role as mayor, but it was the judge's show since he had asked for the meeting.

"A few days ago," he began, "I became aware of a very ugly rumor that was circulating through the city. I didn't believe it for a moment, but my opinions aren't evidence. Therefore I decided to make a personal investigation in order to get some concrete and provable facts."

"You're referring to the rumor that Jack Tallon is the rapist," Marion McNeil said. "To put it on the record."

"That's right. I have now talked with a number of people who heard the rumor and I have depositions from four of them, all women of unimpeachable reputation, and all confirming the same source. So that is definitely pinned down. Next, I interviewed both of the rape victims and got some detailed information to which they both will swear. I now want to report to this council a fact that we all knew: it is an absolute impossibility for that vicious rumor to be true."

The judge sat back and relaxed.

Arnold Petersen spoke quietly, but with authority. "Thank you, Judge Howell. I'm sorry that this issue ever arose, but you've certainly resolved it. Have you anything more to tell us?"

"Yes, I think the time has come when we will have to do something about Lily Hope. I've constantly excused her on the grounds that she's a lonesome old lady, but this time she's come perilously close to causing some very serious trouble. I arranged to have her quietly warned some time ago, but it had no effect whatever."

"What do you have in mind?" Marion asked.

"I haven't made a final decision yet, I'm still thinking about it." He turned to Tallon. "Jack, if I do decide to take some action, I'm going to ask you not to interfere in any way."

"I can't disobey the court," Tallon said.

"Damn right you can't," the judge agreed. "Now let's get on with other business."

In response to a summons, Sergeant Smallins and Ned Asher came into the chief's office. "Is Ralph Hillman in yet?" Tallon asked.

"He and Oster are both here; it's payday," Asher answered. "Do you want them too?"

"Yes," Jack answered.

When his three sergeants and his detective were assembled, he shut the door and then sat down again. First, he explained about the new telephone on his desk and what procedures were to be followed if it rang. When he had done so, Ralph Hillman spoke up. "Chief, I think you should know that we're all familiar with the fact that there's a safe house in the city. We've been onto that for some time. Is that where the line is from?"

Tallon thought quickly. "Suppose I leave it that you can draw your own conclusions on that point."

Smallins nodded. "The marshal made you promise not to talk; we understand."

It would have been senseless to deny that, and Tallon didn't want to. He took a quick pride in the fact that his men were not as naïve as Lonigan had assumed. And he was also glad that Sergeant Smallins seemed to have moved over to his side of the fence. He was a sound man and Tallon genuinely liked him; understandably, he wanted Smallins's good opinion in return.

"Since that's out in the open," he said, "keep an eye on it. Not conspicuously so, just precautionary."

"The patrol men have been doing that since the new occupants came in," Oster told him.

Tallon realized that Smallins had known it was a safe house when he had nominated it as a likely place for a police exercise. He still had things to learn about his city, and his staff.

"Here's something you may not already know," he continued. "There is a third rape victim. Same MO, undoubtedly the same man."

That did create a stir, in fact a considerable one. Smallins swore out loud, after that it was quiet.

"What I have told you is not to go out of this room," Tallon cautioned. "I have some more details you should know. I've talked to the victim and her husband at length and they've supplied some fresh information; the Lord knows we need every bit we can get. I've promised the victim that her identity will be protected; she came forward to help us and that commitment must be kept. I don't even want it known that there has been a third attack, is that completely clear?"

No one spoke.

"For the time being, the rest of the men are not to be told. I'm not implying that I don't trust them—I do—but there is a very delicate situation here."

Ralph Hillman, quiet and thoughtful as usual, spoke for the group. "Chief, if any of us do happen onto anything that might reveal her identity, you can be sure that we won't let it out."

"I am sure," Tallon told him. "Now, here's what I have: the victim was attacked approximately two months ago in her husband's absence. She was raped after she had gone to bed by a man wearing a Frankenstein mask. It was a complete mask and covered all of his face, so no oral sex was involved. However, he did infect her with gonorrhea."

Brad Oster, who had only been a sergeant for five months, spoke up. "I hate to say it, but that doesn't help us too much. He's probably been cured by this time, and no doctor is going to give out any information. Sometime, somewhere, he had a girl who gave him the dose, but how in hell are we going to trace that?"

Tallon nodded. "You're absolutely right, but we can warn the other victims, and that's already been done. Later, we can try for a court order allowing us to examine medical records if we zero in on a suspect. Meanwhile, I've got a little more, mostly negative. I've interviewed the victim at length, checked out her home, and looked into every other angle that I can think of. Nothing matches up. There isn't any neighborhood pattern. The types of houses are entirely different. There's no relationship in the work that the husbands do, and one of the victims is unmarried. In fact, you know she was a virgin. There's no similarity of appearance or occupation between the victims, except for the fact that two of them are housewives. They come from different parts of the country, one from Houston, one from Seattle, and the third victim from —somewhere else. Betty Weber is a beauty contest winner; the other two women are attractive, but not in that league at all."

Sergeant Smallins shook his head. "I've got to admit it," he said. "I don't know anything we can do that we haven't already done."

Tallon drew a deep breath. "I agree, but nevertheless we've got to do more. First of all, I'm putting myself on a regular schedule for night patrol; until this bastard is caught I want two cars out all of the time between midnight and four A.M.; that's the period during which he strikes. Also, I want to set up a fast reaction program so that if he tries it again, we can have as many of our people on the scene as possible in the minimum time. Between the hours that I gave, I want every officer we have who's up and dressed to be in uniform—just in case. We're going to get him: we've got to get him, and I don't want to let him hit a half dozen more victims before we do."

He stopped for a moment, but there was no comment.

"Now I want to ask something," he continued. "Is there any other young woman here in Whitewater who might be considered to be in Betty Weber's class as far as looks are concerned? Have we any other conspicuous beauties?"

Ralph Hillman and Brad Oster were both prepared to answer that; Oster spoke first. "Mary Clancy down at the hospital." He looked around and received confirming nods. "I don't think you've met her yet, Chief, but she is something. She's a nurse and, believe it or not, single. A very intelligent girl and about as good-looking as it's possible to be. In fact . . ."

Tallon interrupted him. "Would you say that she was a likely target for the rapist?"

"That's just what I was going to say, Chief. I thought about her right after Betty Weber was hit."

Sergeant Smallins had been thinking. "Is it your idea to set her up as a decoy?" he asked.

Tallon nodded. "Yes, if she's got the nerve to go along with us."

Three hours later Mary Clancy was ushered into Tallon's office by Ned Asher, who knew her well. The moment she walked in Tallon saw that the reports had not been exaggerated. She was a striking beauty: auburn-haired with wide apart green eyes that commanded immediate attention. When she smiled, she became irresistible.

He rose and welcomed her. When she had been seated, and the door had been closed, he thanked her for coming and then spoke directly to the point. "Miss Clancy," he began, "you know, of course, about the two very vicious rapes we've had here recently."

She nodded. "I know, sir. Both of the victims were at the hospital."

"I don't want this circulated about," Tallon continued, "but as of this moment, we have almost no clues to work on. Furthermore, most rapists follow a definite pattern, but this man apparently does not. We've investigated every angle possible, and we've come up with nothing."

The nurse nodded, but she did not speak.

"Now, Miss Clancy, I have two choices: I can wait for the man to strike again and hope for some additional evidence, or I can try to entice him out and trap him—before he can attack another victim."

"How can I help?" Mary asked.

"First, let me give you a piece of very confidential information. I mentioned a moment ago that most rapists follow some sort of pattern. They can be excited by some very odd and unusual things. Several have been caught because they attacked victims who had hung their undergarments out on a washline to dry, others have been motivated by illogical strange fetishes. For example, one case was solved when it was discovered that the victims always lived in houses with white stone roofs. You don't have them up here, but they're quite common in Southern California."

"Possibly he had been rejected by a girl who lives in such a house," Mary suggested. "Or he might have had a mother fixation."

Tallon nodded. "You understand. Now, I have been very careful to conceal this fact, but in each of the rapes, the victim wore a yellow dress the day before she was attacked. That isn't a great deal, but it is something."

"Yellow dresses are quite common," Mary told him. "Since only two women were involved, it could very easily be a coincidence."

That was true, of course, but Tallon could not tell her that the "coincidence" covered three cases, not just two. When he looked up again, he saw that the strikingly lovely girl sitting before him was apparently thinking very carefully. From that he made a swift deduction. "Miss Clancy, do you often work professionally with Dr. Petersen?"

"Yes, very frequently."

"Would you say that you were familiar with the majority of his patients that he might treat at the hospital?"

"Yes, I would say so." She spoke with an undercurrent of caution that gave him hope.

"Let me put a very general question to you, Miss Clancy. Without entering into the field of medical ethics, do you have any reason to believe that the rapist we are discussing might have infected one of his victims with a venereal disease?"

Mary Clancy took several seconds before she responded to that question. Then she was very cautious. "It's a medical possibility, Chief Tallon, of course that's obvious. I wouldn't care to go beyond that. Dr. Petersen would be the man to approach for an opinion."

"I understand. I believe, Miss Clancy, that we are both observing our respective professional ethics. I will go so far as to say that I am withholding some information that I was given in confidence."

"Would that information in any way have caused you to ask me that question about infection? Please don't answer that if you feel that you should not."

Tallon was fairly certain of his ground then. "Asking you to consider my answer as a medical confidence, as well as a police one, yes."

"Was your confidant a man or a woman?"

"Both."

Mary Clancy carefully crossed her legs and rested her hands in her lap. "A recently discovered infection?"

"Yes, so I understand."

"Chief Tallon, I still cannot break a medical confidence, although I'm convinced that we're speaking of the same thing. I believe that you are suggesting that the yellow dress coincidence may be a little more significant than appears on the surface."

Jack Tallon felt a sudden surge of hope. He liked the girl before him and in her he recognized a kindred spirit: someone with professional standards and the integrity to maintain them. He knew that she could be trusted, and that was what he needed most. "I won't argue that conclusion," he told her. "Now let me come to the point. I understand from Ned Asher that you share an apartment with another nurse, who often works a different shift than you do."

"Yes, that's right."

"You live on the ground floor."

"Yes."

"How far ahead of me are you now?"

"Far enough, I think. You've already told me that you want to try to entice the rapist into a trap. I'm to be the bait. You chose me not because of my medical skills, but because someone suggested to you that I might be the type of person who could attract him. If I agree, then you propose to have me show myself conspicuously around town in a yellow dress in the hope that I may be chosen as the man's next victim. Meanwhile you will have a watch maintained over my apartment for a period of time. After that, I will be on my own."

"Let me add just a little to that," Jack said. "Since all of the rapist's known activities have taken place in Whitewater, a local man is likely to be responsible. I do have one piece of rather thin evidence to the contrary, plus the known fact that criminals of this type often deliberately go to smaller communities where the police cannot saturate a given area within a short time. We don't have the manpower, and they know it."

Mary nodded, retaining her composure. "Chief Tallon, asking me deliberately to provoke a rapist is quite a tall order. If he is local, he might well discover that you are giving me protection—and when that protection is withdrawn. I admit that the prospect isn't too inviting."

"Will you consider it? I thought of using a policewoman from Spokane, but this is still a very small city and it would be known that she was from outside."

"I'll consider it," Mary said. "But please don't press me for an immediate decision—I have to think about it."

"Of course. Meanwhile this conversation is totally confidential."

"Absolutely. I want very much to see this man caught."

"He will be. Thank you, Miss Clancy."

"Mary, please."

He thanked her again and showed her out. She was a striking girl, but he was still unsure that the rapist would prefer her for a victim; he still had no real idea what set the man off.

Two hours later Mary Clancy phoned from the hospital to say that she would co-operate. In a suitably guarded manner, she asked for further instructions.

As soon as she was off the line, Tallon called Arnold Petersen and asked for an immediate meeting with him and Dick Collins, the city manager. Fifteen minutes later the three men were gathered in Petersen's professional office. Quickly and precisely Tallon outlined his plan. "We're asking a great deal of Miss Clancy," he concluded, "but I think she can handle it."

"Definitely," the mayor agreed. "She's a topflight nurse and highly dependable. And if her appearance doesn't entice the man, then he must be a strange bird indeed."

"He's that anyway, I suspect," Collins added. "One thought, Jack: so that she can have the benefits which she's entitled to in the event that anything unfortunate happens to her, would you have any objections if she were to be sworn in as a policewoman? I realize that that normally entails a great deal of professional training, but I agree that if we bring in someone that's fully qualified, everyone would know very shortly that she wasn't a local girl."

"I would favor that," Petersen said. "Strictly from the legal protection angle, and the other benefits that would accrue."

"Then it's settled," Tallon said, "because that's what I came to ask."

From Petersen's office he called the Spokane office of the telephone company and talked with one of the investigators, who promised him full co-operation.

The following day an installer arrived to put a new telephone into Mary's apartment. While he was there, he spent some time in her bedroom and other parts of the small suite. When he left, a number of invisible alarm buttons were in place; a touch on any one of them would flash an immediate warning on the police switchboard. Two of the units were placed so that even if she were in bed, they could be activated without it being noticed. Later in the day a test run showed that the system was working perfectly.

At four-thirty that afternoon Mary Clancy was formally sworn as a member of the Whitewater Police Department. She wore a yellow dress for the occasion. Then she spent most of the next day, in the same dress, being seen in all of the public places that she could logically arrange to visit.

After that, it became a waiting game.

For three days and three long, painfully alert nights, nothing happened. A few traffic stops were made. One out-of-state motorist abused Ed Wyncott as a "hick cop," but the tall, bespectacled young officer kept his cool and wrote out a ticket without visible emotion. Ronnie Keyhoe appeared in court and, because of his past record, paid a considerable fine. He was cautioned from the bench that the next time he appeared, if it was within the span of one year, he would be sentenced to jail. Judge Howell concluded by suspending his license for a period of sixty days.

There was nothing whatever from the safe house. The watch for the white pickup truck continued, but no suspicious vehicles were sighted. There was no boredom in the small headquarters building or riding with the men out on patrol; soon something would break, and everyone both knew and felt it.

Shortly after nine on the fourth day, a Captain Long of the Spokane Sheriff's Department called and asked to speak directly with Tallon.

"We had a rape incident last night that may interest you," he reported. "The attack was made by a man who wore a Halloween-type mask and who threatened the victim with a knife."

Despite himself, a quickening of his heartbeat took hold of Tallon; he could almost feel his face flush.

"The mask," he asked, "was it a Frankenstein type, cut off at the bottom?"

"I can't answer that offhand," the captain answered, "but we did get a break. The victim screamed; a neighbor heard her and called us."

Tallon could hardly contain himself. "Yes?" he demanded.

"We got there in time," Long continued. "We were too late to prevent the rape—that had already taken place—but we do have the suspect in custody."

Chapter Thirteen

As Jack Tallon took his official car into Spokane he was in a mood to drive a great deal faster than the legal limit. He understood fuel conservation and all that, but there were times when a man needed to feel the power of a machine under him, and exercise that power with the skill and control that he knew he could command. When he reached the city he slowed to a respectable speed, drove to the big building that housed the complex sheriff's department, and parked in one of the slots reserved for law enforcement personnel.

Captain Long was waiting for him in his office. Tallon had not met him before, but the business of getting acquainted took only seconds. "The suspect is under interrogation right now," Long said. "I can give you a look at him if you like."

"I'd also like to ask him a few questions," Tallon added.

"Not for a little while, if you don't mind. We've got him just about where we want him, and I don't want to break the pattern."

Tallon understood that and the need to accept the necessary delay. He followed his host down some corridors and then into a room where a one-way mirror allowed him to see the suspect while a hidden microphone supplied the sound. For a few seconds he heard nothing; his attention was riveted too intently on the suspect, who was seated, in the other room, only a few feet away.

He was a lank youth with a pimply face and shoulders that were almost embarrassingly weak. His whole body was abnormally thin, so that his legs suggested narrow poles that had been thrust into his trousers. He was sitting on a hard chair; on the small plain table before him there was a grotesque rubberlike mask and a wicked-looking knife. It was as though he had been stripped naked and there was nothing about him that had not already been laid bare.

Long turned up the sound and Tallon listened to a little of the dialogue. Within half a minute he knew that the suspect had already admitted his guilt, that he had no particular remorse, and that he was defending himself on the grounds that the woman he had attacked had been enticing him for weeks. It was a cop-out; the suspect was a specimen that would pass through the judicial process toward a sure conviction at the finish.

The women who had been attacked in Whitewater had described their assailant as big, but in the fright-filled atmosphere of a darkened bedroom, almost any man could appear that way. Even more so with a knife in his hand.

One of the two detectives conducting the interview picked up the mask and had the suspect put it on. The result was grotesque: a spiritless body abruptly topped by a green-hued face that resembled no actual living thing. Then the suspect was directed to pick up the knife and hold it in his hand.

He complied mechanically, acting like an unwilling performer in a child's play. He held the required attitude, but he made it empty and meaningless.

"He doesn't look like much, does he?" Long said.

"He could be a user," Tallon commented. He was still trying to paint pictures in his mind that would not take form: the man in the room before him forcing his will on Betty Weber and Janet Edelmann.

"He's admitted to using weed," Long told him. "The stuff gets him excited and then he has to have an outlet."

"Have you asked him about the two rapes we've reported?" Tallon tried to keep his voice casual, but it was difficult.

"Yes. He's denied both of them and claims that he has an alibi for the time of one of them. That interested us, because we didn't supply him with any dates—we only put the question generally."

Tallon thought carefully before he spoke. "I don't think it would do a great deal of good to bring our two victims here to view this man; they only saw their attacker at night and with his mask on. But there's another way: do you think you could let me have that knife for a few hours? Both of them spoke of its being distinctive and they might recognize it."

"How about a photograph of it?"

"I'd rather have the real thing, if possible," Tallon answered. "I know that it's important evidence and I'll be properly responsible for it."

Long turned from the window. "Could you get it back to us some time this evening?"

"For certain. I'll have a man bring it in and deliver it to the front desk."

"Fine. If one of our cars happens to be out your way, I'll have our people pick it up and save you the extra trip."

A half hour later Tallon was driving back to Whitewater with his mind whirling. He would have preferred to have had the man captured by the members of his own department, but if manna had fallen from heaven, he was not going to complain about the flavor.

His motions as he guided the car were mechanical, his mind only giving them precisely the amount of attention that the road before him demanded. He pulled to the left and passed a white pickup truck without being consciously aware of the kind and type of vehicle that it was. The gossip against him had been decisively shot down in the council chamber; now if only the right rapist was in custody, his life would take on a wholly new and much more welcome hue.

He drove straight to the college, where Janet Edelmann awaited him in the dean's office in response to his radioed request. In the presence of the dean of women Tallon cautioned her to be careful and certain in any identification she might make; then he showed her the knife.

At first she was afraid to touch it; then she examined it gingerly, put it down, and shook her head. "It isn't the same one," she said.

Tallon pushed his own emotional response to that into the back of his mind. "Are you quite certain, Janet?" he asked.

"Yes," the girl answered. "I'm positive."

"All right," he said carefully. "Now, is it anything like the weapon that was used to threaten you?"

"Well, it's a knife, but the one . . . I saw . . . had a wooden handle —I remember it. It looked homemade."

Tallon thanked her for her co-operation and put through a call on the dean's phone to Mrs. Betty Weber. Twenty minutes later he was back in his office, staring at the knife that lay on the desk before him: a piece of evidence that had been denied to be the rapist's weapon by his two leading witnesses. He knew that he could show it to Diane Jones, but even if she thought it to be the same knife, it would still be no good. He accepted the fact that one of two things was true: either the rapist in custody in Spokane had changed knives, or he wasn't the man wanted in Whitewater.

He called Long and gave him the news. At the same time he asked if the suspect's quarters could be searched for another knife—this one with a homemade handle.

"We'll be glad to look for you," the captain said, "but it isn't going to wash. On the date of your first rape in Whitewater, the suspect was in jail doing five days on a minor rap; he couldn't pay the fine. He said that he had an alibi, and that's about as good a one as you can get."

Jack Tallon hung up the telephone and called on the emotional reserves that he had built up over his many years' experience as a policeman. One bright glimmer relieved his feelings: the way was still open for the rapist to be caught by his own department and locked in his own jail. He wanted that to happen almost as desperately as he had ever wanted anything in his life. Hanging on to that thought, he called in Sergeant Smallins, gave him the news, and asked to have the knife returned to the sheriff's department in Spokane.

When the day was at last over and he went home, he found Marion McNeil sitting in his living room. It was a touch of disappointment: he had wanted Jennifer so that he could tell her his troubles and receive the comfort that she always had waiting.

"Welcome home," the councilwoman said. "How about a substitute wife for a little while?"

If he had been in a less depressed mood he might have taken that as an invitation and kissed her; instead he simply asked, "Where's Jennifer?"

"We've been shopping all day in Spokane. She invited me to stay for dinner and I accepted. After I did, she ran out to get a few things. Now, how can I make you happy until she gets back?"

"Step right into the bedroom," Tallon said.

"Certainly, but will we have time enough before your wife comes home?"

That bit of mock dialogue picked him up in a way that he needed; the fact that Marion had indicated her prompt willingness, even in jest, restored a little of his faith in himself. He mixed two drinks and gave Marion hers with a small flourish. "Liquor is quicker," he reminded her.

"Maybe I don't need it," she teased him. He realized then that she had read his mood as soon as he had come in and had instinctively known that he had needed an ego build-up. He had met more beautiful and attractive women, but Marion had a certain solid foundation that gave her an appeal that was individually her own.

Tallon dropped into a chair and, since she was a member of the city council, he told her what was on his mind. She listened sympathetically, then came and sat beside him. "Jack," she declared, "however this works out, you know that we're all behind you. You'll nail the bastard eventually."

At that moment the front door opened and he rose to help Jennifer with her small load of groceries.

He enjoyed his dinner and felt much more like himself after it was over. Marion stayed for a little while and then drove away after giving him a good night peck on the cheek. Normally Jennifer would have gone into the kitchen after that to clear away the dinner things, but instead she mixed two drinks and silently handed him one of them. That was a signal they both understood: she wanted to talk.

The way that she sat down beside him told him that there was no anger in her, no bruised hurt that she had been holding inside and now wanted to unload. It had to be something else.

He sat quietly, giving her time, until she broke the silence. "I'm sorry," she said. "I'm terribly, terribly sorry."

"About what?"

She pushed her body closer to his, seeking to reinforce the tie between them. "You were doing so well in Pasadena. You would have made lieutenant before long and everyone respected you. I made you come up here to this Godforsaken little place where . . ." Her voice began to break, ". . . they say terrible things about you . . ."

She turned herself around so that she could look directly into his face. "Marion told me how Judge Howell had to conduct a personal investigation to prove your innocence. Next time there might not be any Judge Howell. I can't stand the whispers—the utter, unbelievable small-mindedness of it all! And the rapist—one Goddamned vicious criminal and if you don't catch him, there goes your job and after that, where are you?"

He started to speak, but she wouldn't let him. "You know that I came from a small town and that was the way to live—I thought. Peace and quiet, without any street gangs, hypes, and the crazy things that go down every day. But it isn't that way at all now! It's as though you were in a shooting gallery and anyone who wants to can take ten shots at you for a quarter."

"I came with my eyes open," he began.

"You came because I almost made you," she cut in. "I pestered you and bugged you because I wanted it my way. I kept telling myself that it was for your good, that you'd be safer up here, that our lives together would be happier, that . . ." She made no attempt to finish.

Tallon put his arm around her and offered his comfort. "Let me tell you a little about gossip," he said in his calmest, quietest tone. "The people who invent and spread it are only trying to attract attention, and to look as if they know more than others do. They don't understand that everyone despises them for it."

Jennifer shook her head, rejecting his explanation. "We've just bought this beautiful home—a better one than I ever thought I'd have —but now I know that we're being spied on from across the street every minute of the day. It's ruined everything for me!"

She took hold of herself. "I might as well tell you the rest of it; I called Pasadena today and talked to Captain Youngblood. I told him that you didn't know anything about my call; that it was my own idea.

I asked him if you wanted it, if you could have your old job back. They've just had a budget increase and he said that you'd be welcome anytime."

He pressed his fingers lightly into her upper arm, to steady her a little. "Jennifer, in case you've forgotten, I signed a year's contract with the people up here."

"But they'd let you out of it!"

"I don't want them to. If I quit now, it would be a massive failure on my record. There's no other way, I've got to stick it out. Now relax: we'll get the rapist, and Judge Howell has a plan to shut the gossip up. Better days ahead, kid."

He stopped there because there was nothing more that he could say. He loved Jennifer with all his heart and he was confident that he would find a way to work things out.

At just after two in the morning one of the campus patrol cars pulled quickly into the emergency entrance bay at the hospital and one of the three dorm troopers got out. Opening the front door on the right-hand side, the campus patrolman lifted out a young woman. It required a considerable effort, but he was a well-built man and he managed it without undue difficulty. As he walked toward the entranceway, the girl he was carrying lay completely limp, her hair hanging down from her head.

A nurse saw him coming and held the door open. She was an ample person, middle-aged, who radiated an efficiency that even the depressing hour of the night could not extinguish. "In here," she directed at once, and held open the door of the emergency room. As soon as the patient had been carried inside, she picked up a microphone on a small stand and paged Dr. Lindholm.

Within two minutes a very young physician pushed his way through the door, prepared to face whatever crisis he had been summoned to meet. The patrolman gave it to him without preamble. "She's Liza Heilberg, a sophomore student. Her roommate called us when she passed out. She's been unconscious since I picked her up, I don't know why. Her roommate didn't know either."

Dr. Lindholm stretched out the patient on the examining table and carefully rolled up one of her eyelids. After inspecting the pupil, he made a gesture. "Please wait outside, if you don't mind," he said. "I'll let you know as soon as I have any news." As the officer left, the matronly nurse came hustling in, pushing a piece of equipment on wheels. The door shut behind her.

Almost half an hour later Lindholm came out and gave his report. "At present it looks as if she'll be all right, but I want to keep her awhile and run some tests. My finding at present is that she overdosed on heroin, but there may also be some complications. I don't think she's a confirmed addict, but if she'd taken much more, that would have been it. You'd better notify her parents, her doctor if she has one here, the dean, and the police department."

The campus patrolman knew all that, but he understood and didn't take offense; the doctor was simply being thorough and that was the way he wanted doctors to be. He drove back to the campus knowing that he had a job of investigation ahead of him.

A few minutes later Sergeant Oster put down the manual he had been reading on weight control and answered the phone. He took down the pertinent information and typed a brief note for the chief. Since it was the second heroin incident involving the college students within recent weeks, he knew that Tallon would want to be advised.

As soon as he had read the memo in the morning, Jack phoned the hospital. He was told that he could not interview the patient; the doctor had left orders. Also, as soon as her parents had been notified, they had engaged legal counsel to represent her. The attorney, in turn, had left strict instructions that his client was to talk to no one other than her doctor and not to answer any questions whatever unless they were medically necessary.

The dorm troopers made little progress with their investigation on campus. The patient's roommate claimed that she knew nothing whatever about Liza's use of heroin and that she was sure there had been a mistake somewhere. Throughout the rest of the campus community no one had anything to contribute.

Toward noon Jack Tallon had a brief conference with the president of the college. They mutually agreed that the heroin traffic on the campus would have to be cut off at the earliest possible moment, but neither man had a significant plan to offer. The dorm troopers remained the first line of defense; if they were not able to resolve the problem, then the Whitewater police would have to be called upon for help.

After that somewhat frustrating interview, Tallon had a surprisingly agreeable lunch with Otis Fenwell. He told the city attorney about the drug problem and discovered that he had a sympathetic listener; for the first time he felt that he had established a rapport with the older man. The subject of the rapist did not come up, which was another small blessing.

Tallon spent a good part of the afternoon mapping out the training session he had called for the next day. He was satisfied that he was getting good results with the program: the men under his command were showing some added interest in the various techniques he was teaching them. One thing was definite: he had broken the pattern of ennui that had characterized his department before he had arrived. Despite the small size of Whitewater, and its naturally quiet, semi-rural atmosphere, it was now understood that major crime could invade it at any time, and that violence could explode in its peaceful streets without warning.

It very nearly did when the city council met at its regular.time the next morning. The moment that Marion McNeil came into the room, electricity crackled in the air. She was furious and barely contained herself until Arnold Petersen had formally called for order. Then she took the floor without invitation.

"I want to confess that I came as close to committing murder last night as I think that I can," she said, biting off her words. "You all remember our last discussion with Judge Howell. Now Lily Hope is spreading the rumor that I'm having an affair with Jack! When I heard about it I called her directly and told her to keep her foul mouth shut. And do you know what she told me? She said that if I behaved like a public woman, I could expect to be talked about!!"

"What triggered her this time?" Dick Collins asked.

"I spent a day with Jennifer; we went into Spokane. When we came back, she asked me to stay for dinner. After she had gone out to get a few things, Jack came home and we were alone together for ten minutes or so. She must have seen us." The recollection brought her dangerously close to the boiling point; her breathing was not normal and she was unable to keep her hands still.

Petersen looked at the judge, who was present by invitation. "Sam?" he asked.

Howell appeared calm, but it was deceptive. "That's her rumor for today. Earlier this week she was hinting broadly that Mary Clancy was going into the call girl business, the way that she was showing herself around town. And there isn't a more decent girl in this city than Mary, I happen to know."

"Can we do anything about it?" Petersen asked.

"We're going to do something about it; I'm at the end of my patience with her." He looked toward Tallon. "Jack, tomorrow morning, about ten or so, I want you to send a car out to her house and have her picked up. Have your man treat her gently, she's frail, but it must be made clear to her that she's in trouble. There happens to be a statute making it illegal to interfere with a public official in the performance of his duty. On that basis bring her in. Marion, I want you to sign a formal complaint."

"Gladly!"

"I'll grant her an immediate hearing, in court, and have an attorney there to represent her. Otis, you can present the evidence. I'll listen to her attorney, of course, but if in my considered judgment she deserves it, I'm going to place her under injunction not to use her telephone for any purpose other than emergencies and ordinary business. The first time that she gossips over the line, she will be in contempt of court."

He paused and softened his tone. "That may be a little hard on her, but if something isn't done, something drastic could happen. She has gotten some people mighty damn mad at her."

"Including me, right now," Marion said.

That afternoon Arnold Petersen took a call at his office from the traditional irate housewife. She demanded that as mayor he dismiss the new police chief at once and ask the sheriff to investigate. She had it on "good authority" that the new chief was, himself, the criminal rapist who had every decent woman in the city terrified. She stressed the word "decent" as much as she could. And wasn't it true that the rapes had begun shortly after he had come to the city?

After he had received his confidential instructions, Sergeant Smallins ventured a comment. "At one time I tried to get Chief Burroughs to do something about Mrs. Hope, but he felt that it wasn't a police matter and let it ride. Ralph Hillman and I both felt that since she lives alone, someone might get mad enough to go after her. Considering the sort of stuff she spreads, I think that she's been lucky."

In his office Judge Howell phoned a young attorney who was building a reputation and alerted him to a possible call from the court to defend a client who would probably have no legal counsel of her own. Otis Fenwell submitted a formal complaint that was signed by Marion McNeil as a councilwoman of the city. Through the designated proper channel the police department was then instructed to pick up Mrs. Hope and bring her in to answer the charge. The letter of the law was strictly observed and the paperwork was all in proper order.

Upon being notified of his duty, Jack instructed Sergeant Smallins to pick up Mrs. Hope himself. "Go easy on her," he advised. "But let her know that officially she's in trouble."

Frank Smallins smiled. "I'll do my best," he promised. Conscious of the role he was playing, and secretly a little happy in it, he got into one of the official cars that was plainly marked as a police vehicle and patrolled for a little while until it was time to drive to Lily Hope's address. En route he rehearsed his manner and put himself in exactly the right mood.

He pulled up at the curb and got out with proper dignity, knowing that he was already under observation. He walked up to the door and pressed the bell with full official dignity. Then he waited.

When there was no response he rang once more. There was no doubt whatever that she was there, but perhaps she had guessed his mission and was trying to hide. When a third ring brought no results, he went around to the back. He knocked there, but once again there was no result.

He hesitated for a few seconds and then tried the door. It was unlocked. He knocked once more and when there was still no response, he cautiously peeked inside.

The small kitchen was in order with one or two dishes left on the drainboard. "Mrs. Hope," he called, and waited.

Hearing nothing, he concluded that he had ample justification to investigate. It was reasonable to believe that something might be amiss. He walked down a short hallway into the living room and there, lying on the floor, he found the body of the woman he had come to arrest. He bent over at once to see if he could help, but the flesh had long since turned cold and a stiffness that he understood held her body almost rigid.

Beside her lay a short stepladder, off which she had obviously fallen. On the carpet, between the body and the fallen ladder, there was a pair of binoculars. The sergeant carefully noted where the ladder had stood before it had tipped over. There was only one possible place; a space had been cleared for it by moving a table away from the front window. The shade was drawn, but at the upper right-hand corner a slot had been cut out of the opaque fabric to provide a small and inconspicuous window.

Frank Smallins carefully noted the exact position of the stepladder, then he picked it up and fitted it onto the slight indentations that still remained in the carpet. He climbed up one step and looked through the hidden slot in the curtain; it provided a direct line of view at an angle across the street and into the living room of Jack Tallon's home. In order to made doubly sure of his deduction, he picked up the binoculars and with their aid looked once more toward the chief's house. He discovered that he could see inside with remarkable clarity, despite the sheer curtain that Jennifer had hung. He saw her distinctly as she was running a vacuum cleaner across her living room carpet.

He got down immediately, grateful that what he had unwittingly seen had been so innocent. Mrs. Hope, being small, had been standing on top of the short ladder. Either she had leaned over too far, or else she had turned too quickly in the darkness. Or perhaps she had only missed her footing. Her lights would have been out so that she could look from darkness into light. He glanced at the light switch; it was in the down and off position.

Carefully and meticulously he replaced the binoculars just where they had been and put the stepladder once more on its side exactly as he had found it. Then he went to the telephone.

Chapter Fourteen

The first reaction that Jack Tallon had after he heard the news was mild surprise; then, despite himself, he felt a vast wave of relief. He regretted that someone had died, but the emancipation that had been granted him was too powerful, and he could not help himself.

The replay ran through his mind: first the exhilaration of buying a finer home than he had ever expected to own, then the discovery that almost directly across the street were the relentlessly prying eyes of Lily Hope.

He and Jennifer had had to accept the fact that they were doomed to be under constant surveillance, their privacy almost utterly destroyed. He remembered almost bitterly the day he had come home at noon, full of love for Jennifer and a desire to hold her in his arms. She had reluctantly pushed him away, saying, "We can't—she'll know." With a stab of resentment he had known that she was right.

Now that relentlessly wagging tongue had been stilled; the constant spying had abruptly ended. He almost wanted to thank God for it, except that it would be the completely wrong thing to do.

He called in Ned Asher. "Mrs. Lily Hope has just been found dead in her home by Sergeant Smallins," he said. "Apparently the result of a fall."

"Good God," Asher said. He, obviously, had mixed emotions too.

"I want you to go out there and conduct an investigation," Tallon continued. "According to Frank she fell off a ladder and that was that. However, Mrs. Hope was known to have some enemies. Therefore I think it would be a good idea if you made a thorough check and filed a report. And notify the coroner. If anything at all doesn't look right to you, let me know."

"I'm on my way," Asher said.

As soon as his detective was out of the office, Tallon phoned Jennifer and told her what had happened. By the way that she reacted he knew that she could not help but view it as he did—a sad event, but one that would bring immediate benefit to their lives. It was hard not to celebrate.

He notified the judge, who was slightly startled, then obviously much relieved. "You'd better have Francie pass the word to the council members. And notify Harry Gilroy that Bert Ziegler won't be needed."

Sergeant Smallins returned. "I notified the pastor of her church," he reported. "They'll take over all of the arrangements. She attended regularly, so there is someone to look after her."

There was a tap on the open door and Bert Ziegler, his press camera in his hand, looked in. "Excuse me," he said, "but Francie's tied up on the phone. I saw Frank Smallins come in alone; how about the prisoner?"

Tallon waved him inside. "I'm sorry, Bert, you should have been called sooner. When Sergeant Smallins went to her home, he found her dead on the living room floor. Detective Asher is out there investigating right now."

"Lily Hope—dead?"

"I'm afraid so."

"Any evidence of foul play?" His reporter's instincts were almost quivering.

"So far none; she fell off a ladder."

"I'll tell you something, Chief—not too many tears are going to be shed."

"I understand, Bert, but it's all over now. Let her rest in peace."

"After what she did to you, I've got to hand it to you for taking that attitude. Thanks for letting me know."

A little after noon Asher came back. Tallon was still in his office, so the detective gave a verbal report. "I checked thoroughly, as you directed, and there's no evidence of any kind of interference. The coroner came while I was there and he made an inspection of the body. He told me that he's going to take another look at the funeral home, but his preliminary examination indicated that she had fallen exactly as we found her and that the shock had been more than enough to kill her. The arm that was underneath her was fractured, proving that she had fallen on that side. She tumbled in the dark, which made things that much worse for her."

"I want a full report, in writing."

"Yes, sir." Asher hesitated, then he spoke again. "I think you might want to know that she was spying on you at the time. She had cut a little window in her front shade so that she could see what was going on, and there was a pair of binoculars lying on the floor. A surprisingly good pair. I checked the focus and the line of vision."

"Thank you for telling me," Jack said. "Include that in your report."

As soon as Asher had left, he reached into his desk and pulled out three long sheets of yellow ruled paper that he had covered with carefully written, detailed notes. The problem of Mrs. Hope had been settled; now he could concentrate on the rapist.

He had organized everything carefully on the layout sheets. Each one represented one of the rapist's victims with corresponding facts on the same line so that back and forth comparisons could be made with minimum effort. He had made such comparisons at least twenty times, but now he was ready to try once more. On a new day, with a fresh mind, it was possible that he might see something that he had so many times missed. When he had had only two victims it had been almost impossibly difficult; there had been very limited data with which to work. The third victim had added a great deal to his available information. Two things being the same would not mean a great deal; three things, on the other hand, would very much increase the importance of a positive finding.

He worked with intense concentration, letting nothing distract him. He considered each set of parallel facts in turn. Two of the women were married, one was single. One family owned their home, the second family rented, Janet Edelmann roomed. Their ages were twenty-six, eighteen, and thirty-one. One came from Houston, Texas, one from Cleveland via Seattle, one from Denver. One was a high school graduate, one was a college student, one had earned her degree. One home was moderately pretentious, the other two were upper middle class. One victim was blond, the second quite dark, the third had brown hair and eyes. Their heights varied by seven inches: Betty Weber was five feet four, Janet Edelmann was quite tall, Diane Jones was petite. They went to different churches, had varying tastes in food, and chose different forms of recreation and entertainment. Betty Weber was spectacularly pretty, Janet Edelmann was normally attractive for her age, Diane Jones, while only slightly older, had a definite married look about her.

Out of forty other sets of parallel facts, nothing significant would match up. When he was convinced at last that no concealed item had escaped his careful scrutiny, Tallon began to search for areas not covered—for possible questions he had not asked. He had one thin thread, the fact that all three victims remembered wearing a yellow dress shortly before they were attacked, but they did not agree on the time interval.

He ended up as he had feared that he would: there was simply not enough to go on. A yellow dress, and a white pickup truck that had been seen running a light, as so many hundreds of motorists did when they thought that no one was looking—especially so late at night. There was only one way: increase patrols, maintain a fast response mechanism, and wait for a break.

Francie came in without knocking. "Chief, Jerry Quigley just called in: a suspicious car with four men in it is headed toward the eastern part of town. He said to tell you right away."

Tallon didn't waste a moment wondering if she knew about the safe house or not, he swept up the special telephone and waited only six seconds for a response. "Yes, what is it?" came over the line.

"Tallon here. One of my men has just spotted four men in a car headed your way. He didn't like the looks of it."

"Thank you. We'll be ready."

"So will we." As Tallon hung up, he saw Smallins in the doorway. "Perimeter the safe house," he ordered. "Suspicion only, so far."

"Gotcha!"

Counting himself, Tallon had five men on duty. As he reached the corridor, he almost collided with Ned Asher, who had seized a shotgun from the weapons rack.

"Let's go," Tallon barked, and ran for the front door. He unlocked his official car and jumped in; as he did so Asher hit the passenger seat. Within seconds he was away from the curb and rolling. Ned turned on the radio.

Moments later Quigley reported once more. "Turning north onto Brewster. I'm keeping well behind, but they've probably spotted me."

Francie acknowledged. "The chief and the others are coming," she advised.

Quigley came back, completely cool and restrained. "Tell them that the car I'm following has made two turns that don't fit with any destination. They're doubling back."

As he picked up his mike, Tallon visualized his man: tall, slender, wearing glasses, but perhaps the most improved member of the department. "Good, Jerry, we read you. Smallins and Mudd will be in unit three."

"We copy," Smallins said over the air.

"All right," Tallon said into his mike. "Perimeter the house, just as we practiced. Don't break the pattern unless something goes down."

"Right," Quigley acknowledged.

"Will do," Smallins answered.

Within four minutes Tallon had his men on the scene and deploying. As he had instructed, the police cars were kept away from the area directly in front of the house. Ned Asher, who was in plain clothes, remembered to display his ID on the outside of his breast pocket; the training was paying off. With a stab of pride Jack saw his men take their positions according to the book, and without any one of them showing the least evidence of concern or fear. They were beginning to look and act like professionals.

Tallon held one of the two portable radios that had so far been delivered. "Quigley," he said.

"Yes, sir."

"We're positioning at the house—do you know which one?"

"Affirmative."

"Keep me posted, but don't take any chances. Under no circumstances try to go it alone. Ignore any traffic violations."

"Will do. Chief, they're just turning your way now."

"Keep it cool."

"Right."

"Smallins, did you copy?"

"Yes, sir, we did. We're ready."

"You know that there are four of them."

"We do."

"Don't provoke anything, no matter what you do. But if they start anything, we'll finish it."

"Right you are."

Again, no doubt, no signs of fear.

"ETA half a minute," Quigley warned from his car.

"We're set. Remember that there are two men in the house. Don't get in their way."

Tallon spotted the car coming a good block away. His sharpened instincts told him at once that it was not an ordinary vehicle; Quigley had done a good job in spotting it. Ned Asher had his shotgun held with the muzzle down, but he was ready to position it within a second if he needed to.

The car began to slow down; Tallon estimated its speed at twenty-five miles an hour. At that pace it went past the safe house and continued on down the road. There were four men in it, and all four had been looking out intently. They had seen the police cars and, just perhaps, someone had made an instantaneous decision to abort what might have been their mission.

Jerry Quigley rolled past in his patrol car, keeping well behind as he had been instructed.

Tallon used his handset. "Sit tight," he instructed. "They may well come back."

"Don't worry," Smallins retorted.

"Francie," Tallon said.

"Yes, Chief?"

"Call the sheriff on the direct line. Tell him we have a suspicious car that is still in the area. If they ask for the address here, give it to them."

"Right away."

"We're tailing the car and will advise when it leaves here, if it does. Four men aboard. They used an evasive driving pattern with many turns."

Within a minute Francie was back on the air. "Chief, they will pick up the car after it leaves here. They're setting up a roadblock."

After that it remained quiet for a long ten minutes. The men held their posts until Quigley called in once more. "Subject car is leaving Whitewater, headed south. It's already past the limits and picking up speed."

"O.K.," Tallon said. "Well done, guys."

The front door of the safe house opened and a man came out. Jack spotted him as a Fed before he had walked ten feet, then watched as the man came up to him. "Chief Tallon?" he asked.

"That's right."

"Thanks a lot. We saw your perimeter and let me say that it was damn well done."

"Kind of you," Tallon answered. "Now perhaps I can tell my men what's going on here."

The federal man refused to react. "I'm sure they all already know. Anyhow, thanks again."

"Did you recognize anyone in the car?"

"Not for certain. The sheriff's men can take over. They always like to make new friends."

Tallon shook hands briefly. Ten minutes later he called the men who had taken part in the operation into his office.

"Fortunately, nothing went down," he said. "But if it had, you were all properly positioned and ready. We would have handled it, even against four tough-minded hit men if it had come down to that. As far as I'm concerned, it was a professional operation all the way and the Fed I talked to thought so too. Well done."

As if to cap the day's activities, Gary Mason went on patrol on the second shift and within his first hour of duty he handled a hit-and-run with major injuries. The bootleg turn that he executed in the downtown area on Main Street attracted some notice, but no criticism. He apprehended the suspect car, took a prisoner into custody, and came into the station a half inch taller than he had gone out. The suspect was processed, allowed a phone call, and then put into a cell.

The man had looked in the yellow pages of the thin Whitewater phone book and had called an attorney at random from among the five who were listed. He chose Jim Morrison, who came down to headquarters to meet his client. Before he went into the small cell area,

Morrison asked one question. "Is this guy in any way a suspect in the rapes?"

Ralph Hillman, who had taken over the watch, remembered that Morrison and his wife were the hosts for Janet Edelmann—one of the victims. "As far as I know, no connection at all," he answered.

Morrison went back and conferred with the hit-and-run driver. The suspect had genuine need of an attorney: he was already on probation for another major traffic offense and the fact that he had fled the scene after causing serious injuries was deadly.

Jack Tallon went home with the feeling that a good day's work had been done. He did not know whether or not the marshal would move the critical witness from the safe house, and he did not much care. Quigley had done an exceptionally good job in spotting the suspect car. That reminded him; he went to the telephone and called Harry Gilroy at his home. When he had the publisher on the line, he did not waste words.

"Harry, we had a little incident this afternoon that caused everyone on duty to respond."

"I've heard about it."

"I thought you would. Mum's the word."

"Jack, it's a good story, it's legitimate news, and your department deserves some real credit."

"Thank you, but forget it. Nothing happened. Write about the hit-and-run capture. You might mention Quigley's name as having averted a possible serious incident earlier in the day, but don't go any farther. Some important people wouldn't like it."

"If you say so, Jack."

"I'm afraid that I do. Explanations later."

"I understand. Thanks for the call." Gilroy hung up.

That evening Bill Albrecht and Marion McNeil came over for drinks and some relaxed conversation. The little party went exceptionally well, possibly because all four of those present knew that they were no longer under scrutiny. It was past one before the moment of break-up came. Bill carefully kissed Jennifer and thanked her for a wonderful evening. He was still speaking to her when the phone rang.

The effect was electric. There was a sudden abrupt quiet and a sharp chill seemed to fill the air. As the bell began its second ring, Jack picked up the instrument, an unspoken, fervent prayer racing through his mind. "Tallon," he said.

The other three stood stock still while he listened on the line.

"I'll go right over," he said into the phone. "Did the patrol man get anything at all?"

As soon as he had been given the answer he hung up the phone and stood, his hand still resting on the instrument. Then he turned, and Jennifer was startled to see a controlled fury on his face. When he spoke, his voice sounded as if he wanted to cry. "The rapist. This time it was . . . a sixteen-year-old baby-sitter."

"Is she all right?" Marion asked quickly.

"She's at the hospital," Tallon answered. "The people who had hired her came home and found her almost unconscious on the floor. She's very badly shaken and can't talk coherently."

"I want to come," Albrecht said.

Marion plucked his arm. "I think we should leave this to Jack. Let's go home and thank God that this is one they can't blame on him."

As Tallon drove to the hospital, he knew that it was already far too late to make a thorough search of the neighborhood where the rape had occurred; the man would be long gone. A traffic check in the downtown would be almost equally hopeless.

He picked up the radio mike, grateful that Sergeant Hillman had installed a set in his private car. "Tallon," he said. "I'm en route to the hospital. Anything new?"

Brad Oster answered him. "Nothing since I called you. Ned is on his way to the house with Mudd."

"All right. Raise me at the hospital if you get anything at all."

"Yes, sir."

When Tallon walked through the swing doors into the emergency section of the hospital, the same substantial nurse met him with a brisk, "Yes, sir?"

"I'm Chief Tallon of the police department."

"Oh yes, sir—I've been expecting to meet you before now. It's about the rape, isn't it?"

"Yes. What is the girl's condition?"

"She's been given emergency treatment by Dr. Lindholm, and admitted. Right now she's sleeping under sedation. You won't be able to talk to her until tomorrow morning at the earliest."

Tallon knew that the nurse was thoroughly experienced, practical, and capable; she spoke that way. "Perhaps you will answer a couple of questions for me," he said.

The nurse halted him. "I can call Dr. Lindholm; I think that would be better."

"All right."

Within five minutes the resident joined them. "Since this is an official police matter," he said, "I'm not going to quibble about ethics, because I know that you can get a court order from Judge Howell with one phone call. The girl was definitely raped. There was a good deal of bleeding, because she was menstruating, she was virginal, and there is some tissue damage. Fortunately, not too severe. Psychologically the impact was very bad; she was incoherent when she was brought in and in a state of partial shock. I've treated her, sedated her, and taken some specimens for examination. You know that semen can be typed now."

Tallon was grim. "Thank you, Doctor. Now, is there anything else you can give me—anything about her condition, or anything she may have said, that might help us? You know how desperately we want that man."

The doctor nodded. "I certainly do know; my wife has been very wary . . . being alone at home nights. There isn't too much that I can give you beyond what I've already said. I don't know if this is of any significance or not, but the patient has a definite pricking, deep enough to draw some blood, on her left breast just above the nipple. I frankly can't explain it."

"I can," Tallon said. "That happened to the last victim; the rapist pricked her with the point of a knife. Did you check to determine if your patient had been forced to perform oral sex?"

A shadow crossed Lindholm's face. "No, dammit, I didn't think of that! It isn't too late; I'll take care of it immediately."

"Just a moment, Doctor, before you go. As of two months ago, the rapist was diseased. Gonorrhea."

"I've already taken a precaution against that, but thank you—every little bit helps. May I go now?"

Tallon touched his arm. "One more question before you do: did the patient say anything—anything at all, that might be of help? Think hard!"

The doctor paused, obviously anxious to get away. "Nothing, really," he answered. "She was incoherent, I told you that. She did say something about the book she had been reading."

"What was that?" Tallon pressed.

"*Frankenstein*," Lindholm answered.

Chapter Fifteen

During the remainder of the night, Jack Tallon did not get one wink of sleep. He lay in bed, on his back, his mind too highly charged to allow him any rest.

Fury burned within him until it seemed almost as though it would boil the blood in his veins. A dozen assorted woes phalanxed to plague him, like a cloud of vultures swooping to tear at his flesh. Unrelenting was the knowledge that he didn't belong in Whitewater; he had been trying to fit himself into an environment where he knew that he could not cope.

In this small community he would always be talked about as long as he remained the chief of police. He had allowed himself to be panicked into buying far too expensive a house; he added thirty years to his age and saw how old he would be before the mortgage would be finally satisfied. Then he asked himself if he could reasonably still expect to be the chief of the Whitewater police at that time. If he did, would he be able to stand it?

He was an outsider, the big city policeman who was expected to solve all of the police problems with the dazzling virtuosity of a Sherlock Holmes and the up-to-the-minute resources of the Federal Bureau of Investigation.

To become chief of police in any respectable community you had to go up through the ranks and hold many different assignments, in both the uniformed and plainclothes divisions. He hadn't even made lieutenant, let alone captain: he was still Sergeant Tallon and the people who had hired him knew that.

He hated any kind of fraud, and to play at being chief in a small town was a kind of self-delusion that he abominated. It was the same as posing as a five-star general in some tiny banana republic where the rank was ridiculous.

In a few days he would be going to Seattle to attend a regional intelligence conference—an exchange of information between law enforcement agencies in the Pacific Northwest. He would go as "Chief Tallon," but considering the size of his department, in that company he would be lucky to be rated Agent. He had always detested puffing and blowing; now, unavoidably, he was doing it himself.

If he were in actuality a fully qualified chief of police, he would spread an effective dragnet and snare the rapist that had the whole city terrified. How many more times would his ineptitude be tolerated; how many more women would be degraded because he hadn't performed his duty?

He made a decision: at the end of his year he would sell the house for whatever he could get, swallow his loss, and go back to the kind of living he understood. Jennifer would know why; they had been together long enough. Perhaps this year stuck up in the eastern part of the state of Washington would cure her of the belief that small town living was the one way.

He pounded his pillow with his fist and tried again for the comfort he could not find. He looked toward the window and saw a lightening that meant an unwelcome new day.

When he reached his office in the morning, Lonigan was waiting for him. "Come in," Tallon invited, and sat down behind his desk, still in a wretched mood.

"Do you have a place here that serves good coffee and maybe some breakfast?" Lonigan asked.

"Sure—a block and a half away."

"Can you spare a few minutes?"

Tallon got up again. "Why not," he answered.

In the back of the small cafe they sat down together, well by themselves. The single waitress working at that hour took Tallon's order for coffee and the FBI man's more substantial one for the number three breakfast.

When she had left the table, Lonigan began. "Did you know Chief Burroughs?" he asked.

"No, we never met."

The federal man toyed with a fork. "He was a very decent sort, but he lived by the general rule that it's best not to rock the boat. He ran his department that way. As he saw it, Whitewater was a rural bedroom community and the police department more or less of a formality. So the men who worked for him went about their jobs without a great deal of enthusiasm."

"I discovered that when I came up here," Tallon said. "I'm not criticizing Burroughs, but the department was way below standard."

"Agreed, and that opinion will remain between us. So you can see why, when you came up here, none of us expected too much. Co-operation and all that, but the Whitewater force wasn't taken too seriously."

"You made that quite clear," Tallon responded.

"Jack, please try to understand our position. We're into the heavy stuff all of the time: bank holdups, organized crime, kidnapping, and internal security. The people we're up against run all the way from some relatively innocent radicals to the KGB."

"I do understand, Roger, and now let me tell you what we're up against. At the college there is a heroin problem that could explode into major proportions—and horse isn't minor league drug trafficking."

"Agreed," Lonigan said.

"And while we have that on our minds, we also have a rapist who so far has hit at least three women here. And rape, you will recall, used to be a capital offense. Just yesterday a sixteen-year-old girl was attacked; at the moment she's in the hospital and all but out of her mind."

The conversation stopped when the waitress arrived with the orders. She set down Tallon's coffee and put a sizable plate of food in front of the FBI man.

After he had tried his eggs and had had a swallow or two of coffee, Lonigan was ready to talk again. "Jack, we deal all of the time with small departments, some of which are close to zero in real professionalism. I'll give you this and gladly: you've performed a small miracle since you came up here, you proved it at the safe house incident. Your men showed a class we never expected to see. So suppose we bury the hatchet. I started it, so let me stop it."

"Fair enough," Tallon answered. "I think what got my fur up was your refusal to let me tell my men what they were supposed to be protecting when they're out on patrol. If they didn't know, they might get caught in the middle of something damn dangerous and not be prepared to deal with it."

"Point taken."

"Another thing: there's a rule of intelligence that the fewer people who know something, the better. Excuse me, but that's bullshit. By not telling people who should know, risks can be greatly increased, not decreased. I know of an incident where an undercover man was shot because no one told a police commander that there was another officer operating within a group under surveillance. They didn't think that the commander was to be trusted; an innocent man paid the price of that stupidity."

The Spokane man nodded. "I assume that you did tell your men."

Tallon flared. "No, I did not! I told you that I wouldn't and I kept my word. They already knew—they told me."

"I see. Jack, have you ever thought about federal law enforcement?"

Tallon understood how that was meant. He drank his coffee. When he had finished he said, "The next time that you have a problem anywhere in our area, let us know. We'll be more than glad to co-operate."

"You can believe me when I say that we will," Lonigan said.

When he got back to his office, Tallon was in a better mood. The air had been cleared with the local FBI office and a good rapport established. The marked improvement in his department had been noted. The trial was coming up and soon the safe house would again be empty.

That gave him an idea and he called the sheriff's department. Three minutes later he hung up with something new to think about, and he understood why Lonigan had come down to Whitewater. The car that had been reported as a result of the safe house incident had been stopped at a roadblock. It had not been an easy job and one man had been slightly hurt. Of the four suspects in the car, all had been armed and two were wanted in New York for extortion and murder. That suggested strongly that they were in some way connected with one of the major crime families. They had been turned over to the FBI.

In a sudden somber mood, he called in Sergeant Smallins and gave him the news.

"I'm sorry, Chief," Smallins said. "I assumed that you'd already heard. They were hard types all right."

"It's quite possible that they were connected," Tallon offered.

"That doesn't make them bulletproof," Smallins responded, "and we were there with the firepower."

Francie came in, hands fluttering, though not as badly as before. "There's a Mr. Clay to see you," she reported. "I don't know what about."

"Ask him to come in."

The man who entered within a few seconds was fortyish and stockily built. His hands clenched and unclenched as if they were demanding the right to be made into fists and to strike out in anger. "Chief Tallon?" he asked.

Tallon stood up and held out his hand. "Yes. Sit down, please."

His hand was ignored and the man did not sit down.

"Last night," he almost spat out the words, "my sixteen-year-old daughter was raped and driven out of her mind by a man who won't have ten seconds to live if I catch him. *I want to know what you're doing about it!*"

Tallon sat down himself and kept his cool. "When I was notified, I went immediately to the hospital. At the same time I sent our detective to the house where the crime occurred to get every bit of evidence that was available. At the hospital I was told that your daughter was under sedation and that it would be impossible for me to interview her. I left word that I was to be called as soon as she would be able to talk to me—regardless of the hour."

"God damn it, man, you don't need to talk to her to know what happened! The same thing that happened to two other young women in this town after you took over. I'm telling you that you'd better get your ass out of this office and find that rapist or there's going to be almighty hell to pay. And you aren't going to talk to my daughter; she's been through all she can stand—and maybe more. As soon as she can be moved, my wife is taking her back to San Francisco, where we won't have to depend on a police department like this one for protection. You couldn't protect a damn Jersey cow from being raped!!"

"Now listen," Tallon snapped back, "anything you can tell me about the rape I want to hear, but I'm not going to stand for abuse even though I know you're upset."

"Then what are you going to do?" Clay challenged.

"What we have been doing—run every lead, no matter how thin, right into the ground. Watch police files from every other part of the Northwest. Keep maximum watch over the city as far as our resources permit. Listen to every piece of information we can get, and hope to God that we get a break."

Clay seemed to digest that. "Can you imagine what it's like to have your sixteen-year-old kid ruined for life?" he demanded.

"No, because I haven't got one of my own and I won't pretend. But I have got a wife that's young and attractive, and right now she's alone nights most of the time because I'm out driving a patrol car to beef up our effort to catch this man. And we will get him, you can bet every damn dollar that you've got on that. Mr. Clay," he said, as calmly as he could manage, "please sit down."

He won a small victory when Clay did sink onto the edge of a chair.

"Now, I want to catch that man so much that I can't possibly put it into words for you. I need help, specifically information. He isn't perfect, he's got to leave a clue somewhere and that's how we're going to get him. The more you can tell me, the better our chances will be. Now, will you answer some questions so that we can bring this rapist to justice?"

An hour later, after Clay had gone, Tallon looked over his notes once more with meticulous care. He was going to give them intense study, but he already knew that they contained nothing that was in any way new or helpful. And in exchange for the interview, he had had to give his promise not to talk to the latest victim or shadow her in any way.

He had had no real choice in that; she was a minor and her parents had the right of refusal.

He got out another sheet of long yellow paper and began to organize his fresh facts in the same format he had been using. Even after that had been done, there was nothing that held any promise; there was no starting point whatever for a further investigation.

Wayne Mudd was driving the one patrol car that was on duty in the city. For almost four hours he had gone up one street and down another, following an irregular pattern both because it was good procedure and also because it helped somewhat to relieve the boredom. During the whole time that he had been out, nothing whatever had come over the radio to give him anything specific to do.

Fortunately, he was used to such patrols and had come to accept them as part of his job. Other people worked much harder to earn their paychecks and he enjoyed the status of being a police officer. He would have been a little happier if he had seen any prospect at all of eventual promotion, but in a ten-man department that always hired its chiefs from somewhere outside, the most that he could hope for was eventual sergeant's stripes.

Because of his failure at the Los Angeles police academy he questioned in his own mind whether or not he would be able to hack it on any big city police force. He knew very little about ghetto problems, narcotics, the work of morals squads, homicide investigation, and gang control. Since his wife was four months pregnant, he knew that he had very little choice but to remain where he was at least until the baby was born, all of the bills had been paid, and a reasonable amount of savings had been built up. His days as a high school star athlete seemed far behind him, as well as his initial excitement at going into police work. Chief Burroughs had hired him because he was locally popular, physically well equipped for the job, and he had been one member of his generation who hadn't gone in for long hair.

He turned another corner and looked down another quiet street that did not seem as though it had ever needed a policeman since it had first been surveyed. When he again reached Main Street he glanced at his watch and decided that it was time for a short break. He crossed the highway, U-turned on the other side, and drew his car up to the curb. Then he shut off the engine, released his seat belt, and took the sandwich he had made for himself out of the glove compartment. He also had a Thermos of cold milk with which to wash it down.

He sat quietly, watching the limited traffic that went up and down the highway as he ate. The latest training session had been on high performance driving. He knew that there were many tricks with cars;

Tallon had shown them all a few. He had learned how to hold the wheel during pursuit, how to turn a corner at the highest safe speed, how to make a skidding reverse in case of a real emergency. As he sat and reviewed the practical lesson, he wondered how a man of Tallon's background and record had ever been persuaded to leave that exciting arena to move to Whitewater. Someday, perhaps, he would know the chief well enough to ask him that question. With Burroughs he would have hesitated, but Tallon was closer to his men and when something did go down, the chief took an active part. But he didn't simply stand around to be seen and seize credit for being on the spot; he was a working troop. Considering his dazzling display of marksmanship during the high speed car chase, he was a damn good man to have to help out.

The rapist was the only thing that had prevented him from being a sensational success, but no one could accuse him of not trying. It was the breaks, that was all, and the man had simply been too clever. It was Wayne's guess that the criminal did not live in Whitewater; he was someone from the outside, Spokane perhaps, who picked a place where he was not known as a sort of private poaching ground. He could find out who was out of town, leaving an unprotected wife or daughter, by reading the paper, which was on sale in Spokane and wherein all of the comings and goings were meticulously published.

That gave him an idea that he thought was good enough to suggest to the chief: the victims were always attacked when the man of the house was away. If they all used the same travel office or the same airline. . . .

Almost without being aware of it he saw the truck go through the red light. For a second he did not react; the light had been about to change and the infraction was only a matter of a second or so. But it had been a violation and he was reaching to start the engine when it hit him—it had been a white pickup.

He took a second or two to snap his seat belt into place, then he turned down Main Street after the vehicle. He switched on his overhead lights and used the microphone. "White One," he reported. "Stopping a red light runner on Main. Vehicle is a white pickup."

Brad Oster answered him. "Did you say a white pickup?"

"That is affirmative."

He was about a block behind the truck when the driver spotted him; a moment later a spurt of black smoke came out the twin exhaust pipes and the truck, gathering speed, swung hard left around a corner.

Mudd hit the gas pedal and turned on the electronic siren. When he reached the corner, his hands on the wheel at three and nine o'clock position, he made a semi-high speed turn in pursuit. The white pickup was bounding away ahead of him, now visibly far above the legal limit.

Mudd grabbed the mike once more. "Pickup taking evasive action. I am in pursuit, west on Church. He's gaining speed; it looks heavy." He didn't ask for a backup, but that would get him one if it could be done.

The white truck spun into a severe left turn at high speed. As it barely managed to change direction ninety degrees, Wayne saw that the front end was down and that the rear had been raised; it had been hopped up for high performance. He had no chance to call in before he reached the corner; employing a technique he had just learned, he made the turn ten miles an hour faster than he had ever attempted before.

The truck was spurting ahead at very high speed for the city streets; as it made a crossing it bounced hard on its suspension, but it did not swerve. Mudd seized the mike, reported the new direction, and gave the speed. He had no time for any more. Ahead the truck turned again, and he knew that for at least several seconds it would be out of sight. The radio came on. "Mudd, this is Tallon. Keep calling the turns. ETA your area, two minutes."

Holding hard onto the wheel, Wayne Mudd risked a skid to try and save two or three seconds, and succeeded; his patrol car slid across the dry pavement, but it did not overturn. The moment his new heading had been established he hit the gas hard, but the truck was not visible ahead of his.

That meant it had to have turned off in one block, either left or right. Left led to the outskirts; when he reached the corner he gambled and spun right at high speed. He skidded successfully again and the precious seconds he saved allowed him to glimpse the rear end of the truck vanishing left into one of the few alleys in Whitewater.

Wayne barked the turn into the radio, then spun his car once more in pursuit. He did it even better; the third try was a shade more skillful and his vehicle responded as he hadn't known that it could. With the siren going he couldn't hear anything outside the car, but he had to warn other traffic to keep out of his way.

Ahead the truck turned again, this time to the right. For a sick instant Mudd thought that it wouldn't make it and that it would turn over, but it held the road somehow and sped off in the new direction. He had never seen a truck, or anything else, driven like that in his life.

"White One, give your position." He barely caught that above the noise of the siren. He answered, then spun the car once more almost recklessly and made it obey him, but he knew that he could push it no farther. He had probably taken ten thousand miles off the tires as it was. A block ahead another racing car spun across the corner in pursuit, lights on. That would be the chief, and he was welcome. Down the hill toward Main Street the speed was dangerously high, but

Wayne kept up his pursuit with total determination. No man would drive like that just to get away from a traffic .ticket; the risk was too great. It wasn't a fine any more—it was jail, if he knew the judge.

Almost in horror he saw the chief spin his car around a corner at what had to be the very edge of maximum performance. The black tire tracks covered most of the intersection. When it was his turn, Wayne skidded hard himself, but at less speed—it was all that he dared.

He glimpsed the truck again as it was turning right and remembered the lesson. He was a block and a half behind it; as the chief held tight pursuit he turned his own car a block early, paralleling the pursuit path. If the white truck turned right again, he would be in an ideal position. He thanked God that he had fastened his seat belt, then took his right hand off the wheel for two or three seconds to loosen the top of his holster.

As he approached Main he slowed up; he had to because of the likelihood of cross traffic and because he would have to decide in a split second which way to go. His blood was racing through his veins, but he kept his head. Because the light was against him, he slowed still more to protect motorists who might be crossing the intersection, confident because the green light was in their favor.

As he entered the intersection his siren had done its work and it was clear. A quick glance to the left told him that the white truck was not coming at him. He skidded mildly to the left and hit the gas pedal once more. He saw the truck, still a block and a half ahead or a little more, the chief behind it. The truck hit a hard left; without hesitation he did the same at the next corner and was running parallel once more.

Then he heard the radio. "Good work, Mudd, keep it up." A stab of pride came with that; the chief's voice had been cool and precise. It was a team effort now. Oster came on. "Position, please. I'm in unit three."

Great, that meant they could run two parallels, one on each side, and they would get him! The driver of the truck knew where his pursuit was, he turned hard right again, away from both patrol cars. Mudd followed the chief, holding his pursuit, wondering how much longer it would last.

Another right turn, back down toward Main and no chance this time to run a parallel. The tires of the truck were smoking now and it was no frightened boy driving it; it was far too expert a job. At the bottom of the hill the truck skidded hard left and there was a loud smashing of metal against metal as it slid into a standing car, waiting in a double-parked position while it was letting someone out.

Mudd spun and hit the brakes; as he slid into the intersection he saw that he was the third car to arrive; Oster in unit three was stopping in the middle of the street. Already the sergeant was leaning out the window and holding a gun on the cab of the truck.

Wayne pulled up, released his belt, and sprang out with his weapon in his hand. Without being told he covered the chief, crouching behind his engine hood as he had been taught. He saw Tallon run to the truck door on the driver's side and yank it open. He seized the driver's left arm, pulled it hard back against the car frame in the Koga technique and literally levered the driver out of the cab. Mudd saw at once that he was a big fellow and then a stab of wild realization hit him—the rapist!!

Tallon had his man down on the street, and held in an Aikido arm lock. Wayne ran up, his weapon still at the ready.

The chief looked up. "Check the other car," he ordered. "Possible injuries." Mudd jumped to obey, saw the condition of the woman driver, and radioed at once for the ambulance. Then the chief looked down at the man who had just been cuffed and he was flooded by a burst of pride: pride in his profession and in his own men. It had been one hell of a chase, better than anything he had ever seen on TV.

He bent down and along with Oster helped the man to his feet. He was perhaps thirty, heavy-featured, and his eyes were like a serpent's. Mudd knew that this was a human animal that had been captured, and he did not relax his guard.

Tallon marched the prisoner over to his own car and put him in the cage back. When the man was secure inside, he turned to Mudd. "Take charge," he directed. "Take care of the people in the other car, get names and addresses. I'll take the prisoner in."

As Mudd turned to obey, he heard the siren of the approaching ambulance. Someone tapped him on the shoulder and he turned quickly. "What's the man wanted for?" he was asked.

He knew that he shouldn't answer that, but the realization came a half second too late. His own emotions were so fired up, he was almost anxious to tell. "Rape," he said, and regretted it instantly.

But it was out; a crowd had gathered and the word spread like prairie fire. Shaking because of his indiscretion, Wayne hurried to help the driver of the sideswiped car.

Literally within minutes, it was all over town.

Chapter Sixteen

On the way back to his headquarters Tallon drove in a sane and careful manner, in part to counteract the emotions that were boiling within him. During his career as a policeman he had made many arrests, some of them easy and some of them close to impossible. He had had desperate chases on foot through back yards and over fences in neighborhoods where the police were hated. Once he had almost had his hand torn off when he had had to make a blind jump in the dark; another time a suspect had fought so fiercely he had ended up with two cracked ribs and a broken nose by the time he had his man in custody. Never before, however, had he ever transported a prisoner with the same raw acid feelings that were trying to consume him as he pulled up to the curb before his small domain.

As he got out, he noted that Oster was already back inside, busy on the telephone. Francie was just leaving, but lingering to see the suspect being brought in. With Oster in support he took his man inside and put him without ceremony into a cell; the booking process could wait for a few minutes.

"Get some help in here," he told his duty sergeant.

"Already sent for," Oster answered.

Tallon went back out to his car and drove to the scene on Main Street where the capture had taken place. There was still a considerable crowd and Wayne Mudd obviously had his hands full trying to keep everything under control.

The ambulance had already left with the injured woman driver. The tow truck had arrived and was hooking onto her vehicle. Since the left side of the car was badly smashed, he hoped that the insurance company wouldn't quibble. He waited until the wrecker pulled away with the sedan in tow behind it.

"Has anyone been in or near the truck?" he asked Mudd.

Wayne shook his head. "No, sir, I kept everyone away."

"You can swear to that if you have to?"

"Absolutely."

"Good. Call the fire department and tell them that we'd like to use the spare bay they have. Can the truck be driven?"

"I think so."

Tallon looked up and saw Bill Albrecht approaching him. "Can I help?" the councilman asked.

Tallon gestured toward the truck. "I'd appreciate your taking that to the fire station. Keep watch over it until I get there. I may need you to testify that it was moved intact with nothing added or taken away."

"Right." Albrecht climbed into the white pickup, started the engine, and drove away.

With the last evidence of the accident and capture removed, except for the two remaining police cars, the small crowd dissipated. Tallon turned to Mudd. "Wayne, that was very good work; we'll talk about it later. If you and your unit are both O.K., you can go back on patrol."

Mudd actually grinned. "As far as I know, we're both fine," he answered. "I'd better check the safe house; it's been uncovered for some time." He got back into his car, turned off the overhead lights, and rolled down the street.

There was a little broken glass, but it was being swept away. With nothing more to do at the scene, Tallon got into his own unit and headed back to his office. When he got there, he found Ned Asher, Ralph Hillman, Gary Mason, and Walt Cooper all on hand. That gave him a little burst of satisfaction; he did not have many troops, but when he needed them, they responded. He filled them in on what had happened and then issued some orders. He sent Ned, his detective, along with Walt Cooper up to the fire station to go over the truck in detail. "We've got plenty of probable cause," he added, "so an all-out search is in order. If you find either that Halloween mask, or a knife with a homemade wooden handle, call me immediately."

"You can depend on that," Asher said.

He turned to his remaining men. "Ralph, I want you and Gary to stay here for a little while. I'm not expecting any trouble, but if we have got the rapist and word leaks out, we might need some added security. Meanwhile, I want the door from the lobby into the back kept locked at all times while the prisoner is here. If anyone phones, we have a suspect in custody—nothing more. If a member of the city council calls, or Judge Howell, you can give them a little more, but don't even suggest that we have a rape suspect."

Hillman and Mason looked at each other. Ralph cleared his throat a little self-consciously. "I think, Chief, that some of the people who were at the scene of the arrest may have jumped to that conclusion. I've already heard some talk."

"Damn!" Tallon said. "I guess it can't be helped, but the instructions stand."

"Yes, sir."

"Brad," he said to Oster, "book the prisoner. For the time being the charge is flight to avoid arrest plus reckless driving. That's enough to hold him. If you can make an ID, see what Spokane has on him."

Oster got up. "Right away, Chief. I'd like to have Mason with me, he may get ugly."

"Good idea, do that. After he's booked, let him make one phone call. And for God's sake, don't forget to give him his rights; I don't want to lose this one."

"Not a chance, Chief. Come on, Gary." As the two men went in back, Hillman took over the switchboard. He did so just in time to handle an incoming call; as soon as he had it he pointed to Tallon. "Ned Asher," he said.

Tallon went into his office trying to look cool and not at all sure that he was succeeding. He picked up his phone and spoke his name with tense expectation.

Obviously Asher was trying to control himself too. "Chief, I think we've got something. Can you come up here?"

"On the way," Tallon answered.

At the time that the fire station had been built, the Whitewater city council had done some forward thinking. Construction cost had been going up with no end in sight and no one had doubted that the city was going to continue to grow. So the plans had been drawn with two spare bays to allow for the future acquisition of equipment. One of them had since been filled by a new pumper, the other was still vacant. When Tallon pulled up at the side of the firehouse, he saw that there was considerable activity in the extra bay and it was hard for him to control his tension.

He went inside prepared to learn that the long hunt for the rapist was at last over. When Ned met him something in his detective's face conveyed a different message. Walt Cooper looked excited and Bill Albrecht, the councilman, apparently had no desire to leave.

"We may have something big, Chief," Asher told him, pride written all over his face. Officially he had been a detective for almost a year without ever having discovered anything of moment. At last, apparently, he had.

"We went through the truck thoroughly with Mr. Albrecht as a witness," Ned said. "We didn't find any mask or knife, but we did find something else." As he finished, Walt Cooper held up a glassine bag. It contained what might have been almost a quarter pound of white powder.

"Our guess is that it's heroin." Asher's words were unnecessary, but he was entitled to his triumph. "No wonder the guy tried to get away!"

"And what a damn fool he was to run the light," Cooper added.

Tallon turned the packet over in his hands. "It's very white, so it isn't Mexican stuff. My guess would be China white and assuming that it is, you and Mudd have done a fine piece of work." That was an overstatement, but he was glad to make it.

"Can you smell it?" Albrecht asked.

Tallon turned toward the councilman. "That would be very hazardous. When dealers or distributors cut it, they usually wear masks or handkerchiefs over their faces to guard against inhaling any of the powder. And whenever you see anyone on TV wet his finger and then pretend to taste the stuff, remember that that's preposterous. You might as well try to taste arsenic or strychnine."

"I'm glad you told me," Albrecht said.

"Just remember: heroin is dangerous." He spoke to Asher. "Did you finish your work on the truck?"

"The search part is over; do you want anything more?"

"No," Tallon answered. "Leave it here with orders to the fire department that it isn't to be disturbed in any way."

With the glassine bag in his possession, Tallon drove back to his office with the doors of his car locked and the windows up. By the time he arrived he had put aside his disappointment that no proof had been found that he had the rapist in custody. The man certainly looked the part, but that was the old Lombroso theory of criminal man that had been exploded years ago. At least he had something else that could be of major importance.

In the day room he opened a cupboard and took out a small test kit; it was one of the few pieces of equipment he had added when he had taken over as chief. Very carefully he put a minute quantity of the suspect powder into a homeopathic glass container, then he broke a tiny vial of liquid that was contained inside and let the two mix. When he shook the test tube, a deep purple color appeared.

"It's heroin all right," he declared to Mason, who was watching him intently. "And reasonably good quality as well. It hasn't been cut to street strength, so someone is a substantial dealer."

He labeled the test set as evidence and set it aside. After that he sealed the glassine envelope tightly inside a much larger one and stored it, together with the test kit, in the department safe. "That evidence is worth a very large sum at street price," he said. "Rebook the suspect on a charge of possession of heroin in quantity for sale, then have Hillman notify the dorm troopers what we have. The dealer has to be on campus, I'm almost sure of that. Meanwhile I'll call the Feds and put them in the picture."

Gary Mason responded with his natural enthusiasm. "What happens next, Chief?" he asked.

"I'm going to interrogate the suspect," Tallon answered.

Fifteen minutes later he was back in his office after what had proven to be an exercise in futility. The prisoner had chosen to remain substantially mute and Tallon could not force him to talk against his will. "I want to see my lawyer" was all that he would say. Obviously, he was a professional who had been questioned before. He had refused to answer such simple opening questions as whether or not he had eaten; he had had no intention whatever of giving the Whitewater police the least crumb of information. After he had made his call he had sat still as though his release was only a matter of time. Jack had ordered him put back into his cell.

He glanced at his watch, calculated the likely events of the next two hours, then called Jennifer and told her not to expect him until much later. While he was out having a quick bite to eat he deliberately shifted his mental gears into a calmer mood, and thought hard. He was not concerned that an attorney would arrive with a document that would force him to release his prisoner: the evidence against him was too good and too well nailed down. Then he remembered that Liza Heilberg was still at the hospital; he had heard something about complications.

She was propped up in bed when he walked in; her hair was neatly arranged and for the first moment or two he thought that she looked healthy and well. Then he sensed that her appearance of good health was synthetic and that she was almost visibly under some sort of medication. There was an older couple in the room as well; he assumed that it was her parents.

"Good evening," he said. "I hope that I'm not intruding."

Liza looked at him silently as the man sitting beside her got to his feet. "Yes?" he asked.

"I'm Chief Tallon of the Whitewater Police."

"I see. I assume that this is an official visit. I'm Mr. Heilberg, and this is my wife."

Tallon acknowledged the introductions. "I don't want to interrupt your visit," he said, "but I would very much like to talk with your daughter if I may."

Heilberg glanced sharply at the girl in the bed before he replied. "I think that will be all right."

"I'd like to ask you two questions first," Tallon began. "Are you and Mrs. Heilberg aware of the reason why your daughter is here?"

"We understand that someone gave her an overdose of a dangerous drug."

"I'd like to know also if she has talked with legal counsel, or would like to do so."

"She has, Chief Tallon. I'm an attorney."

There was an empty chair; Tallon took it and sat down without further invitation. "Since you are both her father and her legal adviser, I'm very glad that I found you here. And Mrs. Heilberg too, of course."

"Excuse me, Chief Tallon, but do you have jurisdiction over campus matters? I understood that the college has its own police."

"That's true, Mr. Heilberg, but I have overriding jurisdiction, because the college is inside the city limits. And we work very closely with the campus authorities."

"I see. I presume, then, that you know which drug was involved in our daughter's illness."

"Yes, sir—heroin. And it wasn't prescribed; there is no medicinal use for it whatever and no legal source of supply."

Heilberg changed his tone a little. "I want you to understand that neither my wife nor I are in any way sympathetic with the drug traffic. We know what it can do to young people and if we can help you to control it here, of course we will co-operate."

Tallon took that calmly. "That's very fine, sir, and I appreciate it. I hope that you have advised your daughter to be as helpful as you are."

"You're welcome to question her if you like. I'm not sure how responsive she'll be."

Tallon shifted his chair to a more strategic position. He did not want to stand over the girl; an eye-level position would be much better. Also he wanted to make his visit appear as informal as he could. "Liza," he began, "I presume you know that as soon as you passed out, one of the campus policemen rushed you down here. If he hadn't, it might have been a lot more serious than it was."

"I know," Liza said. Her voice was distant, as though she were giving him only half of her attention. He understood the real cause of her detachment, and decided on a swift change of tactics. He turned to her father.

"Mr. Heilberg, since you're an officer of the court, I'm going to give you some information that hasn't been made public. We've known for some time that there was a drug problem on the campus and I've conferred with the president of the college about it. Earlier this evening we pursued and captured a man who was transporting a large quantity of heroin in his vehicle. He was headed toward the campus when we intercepted him."

"You have him in custody?"

"Yes—and on a very serious charge, as you realize."

"I certainly do."

"So now we have two ends of the problem: the source of supply and your daughter here, who, among others, represents the ultimate consumers."

"I'm not prepared to concede that," Heilberg declared. "I believe that someone, in some manner, administered the drug to Liza without her knowing what it was."

Tallon did not challenge that, because it was not the right time to do so. "Let me put it this way, sir," he said. "However the drug was administered, it nearly cost her her life. I want to learn who has been trafficking in it: who is responsible for supplying the heroin that put her in here."

Heilberg pondered for a moment. "As a responsible citizen," he said at last, "and, as you pointed out, an officer of the court, I am advising my daughter to co-operate with you fully. I hope that you'll take that into consideration."

"Of course." With that behind him, Tallon felt that he was in a much better position to talk with the girl, who had been listening, but who had shown no reaction whatever. He turned toward her and gave her his full attention.

"Liza, you heard what I said about capturing the man who was supplying the smack on campus."

"I heard, but I don't believe it."

"It's true, Liza, and there's going to be a small panic when the hypes find that their source has dried up. You know that you had a very narrow escape, don't you?"

"Yes, I know."

He was deliberately repeating himself in order to keep that idea uppermost in her mind. "Please tell me; who did this to you?" Perhaps that was too direct, but with her parents there, he wanted to be brief and straightforward.

Liza rolled her head sideways on the pillow, as though it were a ritual. "No," she said. "I won't blow my connection."

"Liza!" her father exclaimed. He could no longer pretend, after that, that she had had no knowledge of what she was being given.

Tallon kept his attention focused on the girl. "He isn't your connection any more," he said, sharply and clearly. "He's finished. He's a user too, isn't he?"

Weakly she nodded her head.

"Then very soon he's going to be cold turkey, and you have no idea how bad that is. He can't get any more; no one is going to take a chance on running any in—not for a long while."

Tears came into the girl's eyes. "I can't blow my connection," she repeated.

Her father got up and bent over her. "Liza, you've got to tell him. If you don't, others like you are going to be in terrible trouble. It's all over, he isn't your connection any more."

"But he . . ." She let it trail off.

"Look," Tallon said. "I know why you're worried; you don't want it known that you told us. On that you're safe; we've got the courier in jail and right now he'll spill his guts to get off. You know that, don't you?"

"I guess so."

"Everyone will be sure that it was him. You won't be blamed."

"Tell us, Liza," her father urged.

The resistance had run out of her; she was on the verge of sleep. "All right," she murmured. "All right . . ."

"What's his name?" Tallon pressed.

"Al. Al Steinglass."

Tallon stood up and turned to the lawyer. "Thank you very much, Mr. Heilberg," he said. "I'll make it a point to mention to Judge Howell how very co-operative you and Liza were. I'm certain that he will take note of that fact." He nodded to the girl's mother, who had not spoken once during his visit, and got out while he was ahead.

From the hospital he drove directly to the college police office and checked in with the man who was on duty. "I think I've ID'ed your heroin dealer on campus," he announced.

The patrolman was all attention. "God, that's good! We haven't been able to get a thing. Who is it?"

"Someone named Al Steinglass."

The man pressed his lips together in no surprise and shook his head. "I might have known. Do you want him now?"

"Right now. He's been fingered and I want to grab him before he finds out."

The college policeman got up. "It may be a little hairy; he isn't a gentle kind of guy."

That didn't call for a reply and Tallon didn't offer one. Instead he followed his guide into a nearby dorm and up to the third floor. They went down a corridor together and into one of the rooms where the open door was an invitation.

The walls were covered with a clashing display of posters. A blow-up of Mao Tse-tung dominated a confusion of nudes, psychedelic patterns, and sunsets. The two cots that were set in opposite corners looked as though they had not been changed for a month. Two males were in the room and one very pregnant female. She was lying next to a man who was dressed in a pair of cut-off shorts and hard sandals. His black hair, unwashed and matted, hung below his shoulders. An untended beard covered half of his face.

As soon as the campus patrolman nodded toward him, Tallon spoke. "Please ·get dressed, Mr. Steinglass. We'd like to talk with you downtown."

Slowly, the man got to his feet, ignoring the girl who had been cradled against him. "Shove it," he said.

Tallon ignored him.

"Put on some clothes and let's go."

For a moment Steinglass stood still, then he jerked his body sideways and aimed a hard, vicious groin kick at the campus. policeman. The heavy, studded sandal smashed home with shattering force; a sharp cry burst from the lips of the patrolman. At the same instant Tallon knew that his man was deadly fast. He spun ninety degrees to his left and shot a hard side thrust kick straight at Steinglass's abdomen.

It didn't land; Steinglass saw it coming and jerked backward, then he lunged forward to attack.

Tallon timed it; at precisely the right moment he snapped his forearm up and delivered an elbow smash with stunning force under his opponent's jaw. With an *osotagari* foot sweep he knocked Steinglass's legs from under him and flipped him as he fell. With his knees on the suspect's back, he brought his man's arms down and cuffed them in the proper manner.

Despite the obvious fact that he was in great pain, the campus policeman managed to get to his feet. He was dead game and Tallon was forced to admire him for it. "Rest awhile," Tallon suggested.

The patrolman shook his head. "I'll help you with your prisoner."

The girl spoke for the first time. "You didn't have to knock him down like that, pig."

Tallon ignored her. "Get to your feet," he directed.

The bearded man got up. "These cuffs are killing me, you son of a bitch," he barked. "Loosen them!"

Tallon took him by the arm and shoved him through the doorway into the corridor. To the accompaniment of stares from every room that he passed, he took his man outside with the campus patrolman close behind him. Tallon put the prisoner in the back of his police unit and then turned to his colleague. "That was a helluva shot you took," he said. "Let me drop you at the hospital; you may need some treatment."

"I can't; there's no one else on duty."

"I'll send someone to cover. Get in the front."

Reluctantly the man did so, sitting carefully and holding the area of his injured groin. His position drew a short, harsh laugh from the prisoner in back. "He isn't going to screw anybody for a month," Steinglass jeered.

"You aren't going to screw anybody for years," Tallon answered him.

"You wanna bet, pig?"

Without wasting any more time, Tallon drove to the hospital and dropped the patrolman at the entrance to the emergency ward. Once more the heavyset, thoroughly efficient nurse was on hand. "He's been hurt in the groin," he advised. "I'll call you in a few minutes."

"Thank you, Chief Tallon."

As he drove away, he wished that everyone could be as capable as the night emergency nurse had proven herself to be. At headquarters he unloaded his prisoner and took him inside for booking. "Assaulting a police officer," he told Ralph Hillman. "Also suspicion of dealing in illicit drugs. He just put a dorm trooper in the hospital."

"Yes, sir!"

The suspect grinned, apparently delighted with what he had done. When he had been taken down to the day room for processing, Tallon was agreeably surprised to see Frank Smallins coming in in civilian clothes. He promptly drew his sergeant aside. "Frank," he said, "will you take on something for me?"

"You name it, Chief."

"First, get someone to cover for the trooper in the hospital, he was the only man on watch. Then go up to the college to room three seventeen in the south dorm. The suspect I just brought in has a roommate who was there when we left. If Steinglass was dealing, and I'm confident of that, his roommate has to know."

"Of course."

"From the looks of things, I don't think that the roommate will want any part of this flap. Go up and talk to him. Since it's likely that the roommate wasn't dealing himself, you can offer him a release in exchange for the recovery of whatever stuff Steinglass has on hand. He'll probably know where it is. See what you can get out of him."

"I'll give it my best shot," Smallins promised.

Steinglass himself refused to co-operate. He would not make his allowed phone call, and claimed that the line was bugged. When he said anything at all, his language was as foul and abusive as anything Tallon had ever heard.

Jack went into his office and called Jim Morrison. He explained the situation, including the prisoner's total refusal to act, even in his own behalf. "I want to interrogate him," he concluded. "I think I can needle him into some admissions; I've handled that type before. But I can't until he's had the advice of counsel. Since he won't call anyone himself, will you consent to advise him—for tonight only?"

"If it will help you out, Jack, of course I will, but you understand that I'm duty bound to give him the best counsel that I can."

"Come on in."

In less than half an hour Morrison appeared. Tallon took him back to the one small private room that his headquarters had available, showed him inside, and then had the prisoner brought to him. "This is Mr. Morrison, an attorney," Tallon said. "After you've conferred with him, I'm going to talk with you."

The suspect spat on the floor.

More than an hour and a half later it was still no go. Two units from the sheriff's department had come in and were standing by to transport the prisoners into Spokane, where they would be held in the county jail. In the day room Tallon sat with the suspected dope dealer, Ralph Hillman, who had been relieved at the front desk, and Jim Morrison, who remained with his client.

Steinglass simply wouldn't talk. "You've got nothing on me," was all that he would say. He repeated the same phrase until it began to wear Tallon down. It was a standoff, and the prisoner knew it. Once again Morrison advised him to co-operate, and pointed out that he was gaining nothing. To that the prisoner had an answer. "Sure I am. I'm making this pig sweat, and that's what I wanted to do."

At that point the door opened and Sergeant Smallins came in. He did not speak; he simply stopped for a moment in the middle of the small room. Then he opened his hand and dropped several brightly colored tiny rubber balloons, each one fastened with a rubber band, onto the table. After that he left.

With a flash of insight Tallon saw his game plan and kept totally still himself. Presently Smallins returned, carrying another heroin field test kit. With a pocketknife he slit open one of the balloons, dumped the tiny bit of powder it contained into the test vial, broke the self-contained globule of liquid, and shook. The purple appeared, fainter and paler, but it was clearly there.

Then Smallins spoke. "The test is definite, sir. It's heroin; about four per cent. I found it in his room."

"Like shit you did," the suspect said. "There was nothing in my room."

"That's right," Smallins agreed. "I should have been more exact. It was in his luggage in the storage room. Under a false bottom in a suitcase. I wouldn't have known, except for that case in Seattle."

There had been no case in Seattle that Jack could recall, but he understood completely. "Right you are," he said to his sergeant. "The same thing precisely; they're probably connected."

"Before I came back, I had the luggage formally identified as his." He nodded toward the suspect. "Absolute proof of possession for sale."

Steinglass recrossed his legs. "All right," he said. "What kind of deal can I get?"

"Tell me about the rapes," Tallon said. "That's your best bet."

"Shit, man, I screw my own woman—and others that ask for it. But don't try to hang those rapes on me; I'll make a monkey of you if you try it."

"I know you're not the rapist," Tallon said quietly. "But you might have a lead."

"I've got nothing," the prisoner answered.

Three quarters of an hour later a sudden quiet had descended once more over the small headquarters facility. The deputies had taken the two prisoners away and the jail was again empty. The extra troops had gone home. Sergeant Oster had taken over the watch and Jerry Quigley was out on patrol. The radio was still.

Tallon knew that he was entitled to feel some sense of triumph, but it would not come. After he got a report from the hospital on the injured dorm trooper he should have gone home, but he didn't. He still sat in his office, once more studying the four sheets of paper he had lined up side by side.

The inspiration that he needed simply would not come. The facts were still all there, row by row, but if they held any clue at all to the identity of the rapist, or to the thing that motivated his crimes, he still could not discover it.

Chapter Seventeen

By the time that it was half eaten, Mavis Collins knew that her dinner was not a success—and that it was not her fault. By the light of the two candles that decorated her table she could see that Jack Tallon was too preoccupied to pay proper attention either to what was on his plate, or to the other three persons who were present. Occasionally she had seen Dick that way, when some particular city problem was bugging him; at such times she could have fed him ambrosia and he would have thought that it was meat loaf.

Tallon toyed with her excellent stroganoff and left his glass of wine almost untasted. When she spoke to him he perked up and quickly ate a mouthful or two, but it was only to please her; he had no appetite.

Dick came to her rescue. "Jack," he said. "Last night you and your men pulled off the most important and successful piece of police work we've seen here in years. You should be damn proud."

Tallon did his best to respond. "I'm certainly proud of my crew. According to the sheriff's lab, the comparatively small quantity of heroin that we recovered is worth, at street price, almost a hundred thousand dollars. That's hard to believe, but it's true."

"Tell us about the pursuit," Mavis prompted.

Tallon reacted to her question as she had hoped he would. "The full credit for that should go to Wayne Mudd. He spotted the truck, and when the driver took off, he did an expert pursuit job at very high speed through the streets. The suspect drove like a madman, but Wayne stayed right with him and made the capture."

"With a little help, I hear," Dick interjected.

"Yes, Oster was in on it and so was I to a small degree, but it was Wayne's show. If the council is going to hand out a commendation, it should certainly go to him."

"That's likely," the city manager said. "Now, with a triumph like that right behind you, what the hell is eating you? Something is."

Tallon flushed. "All right, I'll admit it. I can't get the rapist out of my mind."

Mavis spoke unexpectedly. "I understand. I grew up in Boston. We moved away before it happened, but when I read about the strangler, it gave me a sick feeling in the bottom of my stomach and I could feel for every woman still in the city. It must have driven the police there crazy."

Collins backed up his wife. "Look, Jack, you can't make bricks without straw and you can't catch someone with the luck this man has had so far. Now, here's a tiny crumb. I should have given it to you before, but it seemed too trivial to take up your time. You remember the last rape—the sixteen-year-old girl."

"Vividly."

"I passed a car that evening that was stopped by the side of the road, facing the opposite way. I slowed up to see if someone was in trouble and I noted the make: it was an old Buick with four round dummy portholes on the side. It was either black or else a very dark blue. Then I saw that a man was out changing the left rear tire. He seemed to be alone, but he had the job well along; as I passed him he waved me on, refusing the offer of any help. One thing I noticed about him: he was a pretty husky guy."

Tallon tried to be patient, but it was hard. "Dick, why in hell didn't you tell me this before tonight?"

"It didn't seem important enough to mention. All that I had to report was that a big man was out changing a tire, and that he was headed away from Whitewater. And remember that at the time I didn't know that another rape had taken place."

"But you did find it out shortly after you got here. And there would be damn few cars on the road at that hour." Tallon stopped and forced himself to speak more calmly. "I'm sorry, but I'm not normal where that rapist is concerned, and I won't be until we nail him. It's a good lead and with the exact car description, I should be able to trace it down first thing in the morning. There can't be too many of those old Buicks still on the road up here."

The phone rang. Collins picked it up, spoke briefly, and then listened. "I'll tell him," he said, and hung up. As Tallon looked at him, Collins kept his voice under control. "That man who was driving the white pickup: he has a number of priors."

"I expected that," Tallon said.

"Including two indictments and one conviction—for rape."

"Oh, my God!" Jennifer cried.

"Jack, you did get him," Mavis echoed. "You'll prove it, I know you will!"

At that moment the party was over. Tallon's first impulse was to go immediately to his office, but he knew that would accomplish nothing. The man was in custody and he was going to stay there for a long time. It would wait until morning, and his head would be clearer by then. He drove Jennifer home with his fingers almost white as he gripped the wheel. Once inside, and with the door locked behind him, he went into the kitchen and raided the refrigerator for a substantial late night snack. He seemed hungry enough to eat everything in sight.

Because he knew the advantages of being thorough, he still checked out the Buick in the morning. Oddly enough, the Spokane police reported that no black or dark blue Buick of the right vintage was registered anywhere in the city or its surrounding area. He already knew that no such car was known in Whitewater.

At his request, the SPD agreed to spread a wider net to try and locate the suspect vehicle. A statewide teletype went out.

As Gary Mason chauffeured Tallon to the Spokane airport, there was a sharp hint of autumn in the air. The leaves were beginning to turn and the air was extraordinarily clear. Because he was carrying the chief, Mason held his speed down to a conservative sixty and had the radio at low volume; if there were any calls, the other guys on duty could handle them. As Gary guided the police unit into the entrance roadway, Tallon wished once more that he could have driven to Seattle, but the several hours that the trip would consume each way were a luxury he felt that he could not afford.

He found himself begrudging even the limited time he would have to be away from his desk and his responsibilities. As he entered the terminal and checked his bag, he was comforted by the thought that Frank Smallins could be relied upon to keep things going well in his absence.

From his seat on the left side of the Northwest Orient plane he watched the snow-capped magnificence of Mount Rainier and reflected on how much in the way of natural beauty and genuinely spectacular scenery had been bestowed on the Pacific Northwest. He had invested his own minute personal stake in this vast region, and it was not a bad place to be.

When the taxi he had taken from the airport pulled up in the driveway of the big motel where the conference was to be held, he noted a dozen different police units parking in various slots. There were also a number of other vehicles that he recognized as unmarked official cars. In combination they gave him a certain renewed sense of satisfaction in his profession and the realization that it placed him, to some degree, in a privileged position. He was glad of that for Jennifer's sake.

When the first session was called to order, the chairman began by introducing Tallon to the others present. "In case you haven't heard," he said, "Chief Tallon and his department made a major dope bust a few days ago and recovered a substantial quantity of uncut heroin. There were warrants out in four states for the suspect he took into custody, including two for armed robbery and one for an assault on a police officer. So congratulations, Jack, from us all."

Tallon stood very briefly to acknowledge the applause, then he made himself inconspicuous again as quickly as he was able. Midway through the afternoon, he was given the floor to discuss the rapes.

"We don't know whether our man is a local, or someone from the outside who is using Whitewater as a happy hunting ground," he admitted. "We have some slender evidence that points to an outsider, but someone who is keeping close tabs on our community. We realize that this kind of hit-and-run MO is a standard technique that's been used a great deal in the past. To date we can't discover any pattern whatever to this man's attacks. Any help you can give us would be appreciated."

He sat down to an understanding silence. There was hardly a man present who hadn't been faced with a police problem that he had not been able to resolve, and they all knew the feeling. No one, however, had anything to offer; no one had had any cases that involved a similar MO.

The one bright spot of the day was the tacit, but unreserved acceptance of Tallon as the police chief of a respectable city. The fact that his department was small was not held against him; rather he was welcomed as an equal by men who had much more responsible jurisdictions. This was an encouragement that he badly needed.

It was past midnight when the meeting finally adjourned. A great deal of ground had been covered, much confidential information had been exchanged, and the existing problems of law enforcement had been reviewed in detail. Despite some fatigue, Tallon was in a good frame of mind when he had at last relinquished a chair that had been designed more to be stackable than comfortable, flexed his muscles, and prepared to go to his room for what he hoped would be a good night's rest. As he walked through the lobby he noted the attractive coffee shop and went in.

There were not many customers, so, despite the fact that he was alone, the hostess put him in one of her best window booths that looked out over a small area of lawn and shrubbery. A few colored lights provided enough illumination to make it visible at night and to add a touch of glamour. As he sat and looked out, he thought of the weary decorations at the Hawaiian Gardens in Whitewater and wondered with what original enthusiasm they had been put up.

It was an old story: the eternal desire of people to go somewhere they had not been. He often felt it himself, and once he and Jennifer had talked about the day when they might walk together, hand in hand, through the Gardens of Shalimar.

A waitress came and, despite the hour, she gave him a pleasant smile. He drank half of the glass of ice water that she provided and then studied the menu. Prudence told him to go light, but he had not enjoyed his dinner and he was honestly hungry. He compromised by ordering bacon and eggs, toast, and coffee.

When it came, the food was good and there were fried potatoes he had not expected on his plate. The girl poured him more coffee and was so cheerful he made a mental note to reward her with a better than average tip. She was attractive and appealing, and earning her living at an hour when most young women like her would much prefer to be out on dates, or home with their husbands if they had them.

He was forcefully reminded of the rapist once more because he knew all too well that there were some men who could not look on any girl without thinking of her as an anatomical specimen rather than as a person. He was glad that the waitress lived far from Whitewater.

As he drank his coffee he decided that they raised them well in the Pacific Northwest. Happily that was true almost everywhere. And people moved around so much. Many of the residents of Whitewater had not been born there; they had moved in from all parts of the country.

Then he saw it.

It came like a mental explosion; he held his fork halfway to his mouth while the shock of realization went through him like a current. He saw again the four sheets of data about the victims that he had studied until his eyes had ached, and the thing that had been there all the time, and that he had seen and seen and had never grasped, jumped out at him like a bright, flashing red light.

Right then he knew that he was going to catch the rapist and exactly how he was going to do it.

Normal men did not become rapists. Often these deviates were triggered by weird and irrational motives, but this man was methodical and systematic. He was following a plan that was suddenly as clear as burning sunlight. The rapist was "collecting" women from the major cities of the country.

Betty Weber was from Houston, Texas.

Janet Edelmann was from Cleveland, Ohio.

Diane Jones was a native of Denver, Colorado.

Ruth Clay, the teen-age baby-sitter, came from San Francisco.

If they had all been from one place, he would have seen it at once. It had never dawned on him that the fact that they had all come from different places had been the connecting link.

As he relaxed and began to resume normal breathing, he had a sudden urge to phone his department and tell the man on duty what he had discovered. He quickly discarded that idea; it would only make him look like an impulsive fool. His flight back would depart at nine-thirty in the morning; he would be in Whitewater before noon and then he could get to work with a vengeance.

At that moment a second mental bombshell burst. A sudden sense of terror gripped him until his body almost shook. *Mavis Collins had just told him that she came from Boston.* And Dick had gone to Portland on city business.

Jennifer, thank God, was safe; she had been born and raised in a small town. For a few seconds he debated, because he didn't want to be an alarmist; then he went to the cashier and asked, "Where is there a telephone?"

He was hurrying across the lobby when he suddenly remembered the number of times reference had been made to the fact that he had a big city background. Everyone knew it. *And they would therefore presume that Jennifer came from Los Angeles or Pasadena.*

Jennifer!!

He burned with the delay while the operator carefully took his credit card number, then he heard the phone ringing. After seconds of exquisite agony he heard her voice, sleepy, but otherwise normal. "Are you all right?" he asked.

"Yes, of course, is something wrong?"

"No, I just wanted to be sure. Love."

He hung up before she could say another word and swiftly dialed Dick Collins's home number. Now that he knew the pattern of the rapist's attacks, he was not going to hold the knowledge back, even for an hour, while Mavis was also a possible target.

He knew that it was an indecent hour to be calling, but his message was pressing enough to justify it. He gave his card number again and waited.

On the fourth ring the phone was answered with the words, "Collins residence. Who is calling, please?"

He almost had a heart seizure as he recognized the voice of Sergeant Frank Smallins.

Chapter Eighteen

From the airport Tallon went directly to his office. He was greeted there with the news that the heroin runner in the white pickup truck had a firm alibi for the night that Janet Edelmann had been attacked. He almost brushed that aside; and he had never really considered the man as a class A suspect to be the rapist.

He called Dick Collins, not knowing what he was going to say, and found the city manager embittered, but reasonable. "It happened, Jack, and there's no doubt that it was the same man. That is, unless someone is imitating him exactly, and I very much doubt that."

"So do I," Tallon agreed.

"Mavis is all right; there was no physical harm done to her in the pathological sense. Arnold gave her immediate attention and then told us that we shouldn't have to worry about a thing. I can't really say that that helped too much, but we understood what he meant."

"How is Mavis holding up?"

"As well as you could expect. I know that you have to go and talk with her; in fact she's expecting you, but we gave the whole story to Frank Smallins. We both thought that he did a fine job, by the way. He was considerate and thoughtful, but just as thorough as we knew he had to be."

"I'm glad to hear that much good news. Suppose I defer the call on Mavis until after I've had a chance to confer with Frank and she has had a little more time to recover. Say, this afternoon about three."

"Good, Jack, I'll be there too if you don't mind."

"By all means."

When that was over he called in his senior sergeant and got a full report. It was exactly what he had expected to hear: the man in the Frankenstein mask, his sudden appearance in her bedroom when she had been asleep, his forcing her to disrobe, the menacing knife, the forced oral sex, and then the rape. It was a grim story and the fact that it was all too familiar did not make it any easier to accept. And, as in the cases of the other victims, there had been no new clues: no fingerprints, no vehicle sighted—nothing. The man's luck was phenomenal.

"By any chance did Mrs. Collins recognize anything about him? Did she even feel that she might have seen him somewhere before?"

"That's odd: I asked her precisely that question. She told me that to the best of her knowledge he was a complete stranger."

"Frank, was there anything new at all to go on? Anything whatsoever?"

"The only thing different was that this time you were positively out of town, but Mrs. Hope is dead now and I believe that her rumor about you died with her."

The call on Mavis Collins was not quite as painful as it might have been. For one thing, there was no need to question her about the details of the crime. Tallon was received as an expected friend and clearly Mavis had recovered her composure enough to be reasonably calm.

"Physically I wasn't seriously injured," she told him, "and mentally I think I'll be able to adjust after a few more days have passed. I'm just trying to block it out of my mind for the present. The girl I feel sorry for is the sixteen-year-old; it must have been hell on earth for her. And the Edelmann girl had a rough time too, I understand. I sometimes think that if we didn't have so many sexual hang-ups left over from the Puritans, we wouldn't have all of the sordid stuff that goes on today, but that's another matter."

"When we get him, will you testify?" Tallon asked.

"Damn right I will. And if you need a blow by blow account for the jury, I'll supply it right out loud in public. Ask me anything else that you want."

Tallon turned to his host. "You've got one hell of a wife, in case you didn't know it," he said.

Collins nodded. "I do know it—why else would I go to all the expense of keeping her?"

Tallon looked at them both. "I'm going to tell you something: I know how to catch the man now. For weeks I've been looking for the key; now I've got it. Keep that strictly to yourselves. I'm holding a small meeting tomorrow. Dick, if you'll go along with something, I'm almost certain that we can bag him."

"I'll do anything that will help," Collins said.

"You may have to," Tallon told him.

The meeting was held in a little-used room in the civic building, where absolute privacy was guaranteed and where it was masked by the normal flow of people in and out of the building. To outline his plan

Tallon had summoned Collins, Harry Gilroy, the newspaper publisher, Arnold Petersen, and Mary Clancy from the hospital. As soon as they were assembled, Tallon impressed on the other four the absolute need for complete secrecy. When that had been agreed to, he told them of his discovery.

As soon as he finished, Collins nodded. "That answers the question that was in my mind: how in the hell did you know to call my home from Seattle? Jack, even though it was too late, thank you very much. I can't tell you how much I appreciate it."

"My job," Tallon answered. "Now, with the help of the four of you, we're going to nail this son of a bitch. It's going to take some stretching of journalistic ethics, Harry, but after it's all over you can print the whole story and run any corrections that you want to."

The publisher pulled a sheaf of folded blank sheets from his pocket and extracted a pen. "Tell me exactly what you want," he invited.

"I want an article about Mary in the next issue of the paper. Announce that she has been selected for a special nursing scholarship back East; she has been chosen from a whole field of candidates. She will be leaving in a short time, something like next month. It mustn't be immediate, but imply that she won't be around too long."

"I know just how to do that," Gilroy said. "Shall I run a picture of her?"

"Yes, please—and make it a good one that shows how attractive she is."

"That's no problem."

"Fine. Now, in the article I want one very important thing." He turned to Mary. "How many people in town know the details of your background?" he asked.

"Not very many. My roommate does, but she's about the only one."

"Good. Now, without giving her any reason, tell your roommate to keep her mouth shut about anything she might see in the paper; we're only going to get one shot at this."

"She'll keep still; I guarantee it."

"Where were you born?" he asked.

"Mitchell, South Dakota."

Tallon turned back to the publisher. "In your article, Harry, I want you to state that she was born and grew up in Washington, D.C. Add a phrase about the nation's capital having something of which to be proud."

The newspaper owner smiled. "It will be just prominent enough," he promised.

"All right. Now I'm going to let you in on something else." He explained about the alarm system that had been installed in Mary's apartment. "We've been using her for bait and she's been co-operating completely," he added. "She even wore a yellow dress until she was sick of it. Incidently, she's been officially sworn in as a policewoman."

"There's a problem," Mary said. "I've never been to Washington."

Tallon answered that. "I very much doubt that anyone will ask for details. If it does happen, say that you were actually only five when your family left there and you don't remember anything except the Lincoln Memorial and the Washington Monument."

Mary nodded.

"By putting a time limit on her remaining here, I hope to provoke the rapist to move quickly," Tallon explained. "On the day that the story appears, I'm going to begin intensive coverage of Mary's apartment. I won't divert the patrol cars, because that might be noticed, but at the cost of some overtime, I'm going to have a man watching her apartment every night that she's there. And I'm going to arrange to have her roommate away on some pretext."

"How about a newspaper item on that?" Harry suggested. "Something to let it be known that she's gone."

Tallon thought quickly. "That could help," he agreed. "However, it would have to be subtle, so that our man doesn't catch on."

"Leave that to me," Harry said. "The main thing is not to let the two items appear together; I can set it so that they will be two entirely different stories. Your job will be to arrange for the girl's absence."

"I'll authorize any extra costs right now," Collins said. "I'm sure that Arnold backs me up on that."

The mayor nodded. "All the way."

"Then the stage is set," Tallon concluded. "When this is all over, Harry, I want you to run another piece and tell everyone what a heroine Mary was in this operation. She's as gutsy as any policewoman I've ever met."

"Forget it," Mary said. "We're all in this together and I know that Jack will have me covered. I can ring the alarm from almost anywhere in my apartment; I've been practicing. I've always wanted to be where the action was, this time I'm getting my wish."

"This is a pretty dangerous guy," Tallon warned.

Mary shrugged. "No more so than some we get at the hospital. I hear that he likes to look at his victims nude before he attacks them. If it comes down to that, I can probably keep him drooling long enough for you to get there."

"I wish to hell that you'd been around when I was younger," Gilroy told her.

When the newspaper came out, Tallon read it in his office with a faint sense of disbelief. It was that good. He discovered that he had un-consciously put Harry Gilroy down in his mind as a man a little past his peak, and he was ashamed of himself.

The article was beautifully written, and as he reread it for the third time, he found himself believing it completely. It explained that some months before Miss Clancy had responded to a questionnaire that had been mailed at random to a limited number of registered nurses. That simple device neatly covered the possible question of why none of the other nurses in the vicinity had heard of the competition.

It was impossible, after reading what had been printed, not to believe that Mary had been born in Washington; the point was even made that most of the government workers lived across the line in either Maryland or Virginia. It was cunningly designed to whet the rapist's unnatural appetite, and so effective that Tallon almost shuddered.

Bert Ziegler's picture of Mary was also better than he had hoped for. He had turned her slightly sideways and with her head tilted at just the right angle, she looked stunning.

On the inside, in the *Comings and Goings* column, the sixth item down reported that the young woman who was Mary's roommate would be gone for two weeks visiting her parents. Nothing even remotely suggested that the small paragraph buried inside the paper was in any way related to the front page story on Mary Clancy.

Francie, her hands fluttering as usual, appeared in the doorway. "Mr. Crawford to see you," she announced.

"Show him in." He didn't know any Crawford, but it was part of his job to be available to the citizens.

Francie returned with a big, bluff man who was in no way hesitant. He shook hands with gusto and then sat down as if he were prepared to sell insurance. Then he passed across a card which bore the city seal of River Falls and the legend: *Melvin R. Crawford*. Below, in smaller letters, was *mayor*.

"What can I do for you?" Tallon asked.

"Chief Tallon, have you ever been to our city?"

"No, not yet."

"We like to think that we have one of the best communities in the whole of the Northwest. We have some light industry, but we keep our air clean and our percentage of homeowners is one of the highest."

Tallon nodded, but withheld comment until he had heard more.

"In about six months our police chief will be retiring. He's earned it, the whole city is grateful to him, and he's been voted a hundred per cent pension."

"That's very generous," Tallon said.

"Fortunately, Chief Tallon, our financial structure is very sound.

We don't have the welfare load, for example, that burdens so many eastern cities. At the present time we're conducting a search for a replacement. Do you find what I'm saying at all interesting?"

"Very interesting, of course, Mr. Crawford, but if you're thinking of me, please don't. I have commitments here and I plan to stay awhile."

Crawford pushed his lips together for a moment. "I was afraid that would be your answer. Since you're not available, could you help us with a suggestion? It occurs to me that you may know someone back in your old department who might be interested."

Tallon got up and shut the door. "Since you put it that way," he said, "I can offer a suggestion. I recommend that you consider my senior sergeant, Frank Smallins. I'd hate like hell to lose him, but he's fully ready for more responsibility than I can offer him here. He's mature, capable, experienced, and thoroughly reliable. You can see his personnel file if you'd like."

"One question: in your opinion is he ready for the top job in a twenty-man department?"

"Definitely, or I wouldn't have recommended him."

Crawford was not the kind of man to delay action. "I'd like to talk with him," he declared. "Obviously I'm not going to offer him the job immediately, but I'd certainly like to see how he comes across."

Tallon got to his feet. "You can use the judge's office," he said. "He's out of town today."

That afternoon at four-thirty Tallon called a meeting of his whole department. Since the schoolchildren were already home, he ordered in the lone patrol car so that Walt Cooper, who was driving it, could be present. Francie was left to cover the switchboard with authority to interrupt the meeting if any significant calls came in.

Jack surveyed his men proudly: they were good, every one of them, and they had crossed the invisible line that had put them in the category of professionals.

"Gentlemen," he began, "this is totally confidential; nothing that I'm going to say is to be mentioned to anyone, even to your wives. Don't even discuss it amongst yourselves unless it is necessary.

"I'm sure that you all saw the story about Mary Clancy in the paper this morning. It's a fake—all of it. I'm setting a trap for the rapist and it was planted there for him to read." He then told them of his discovery of the rapist's pattern and of his further plans to use Mary Clancy for bait. "If I had tumbled to what motivates this man a little sooner, I could have spared Mrs. Collins a terrifying and horrible experience. Now you know why we planted the information that Mary Clancy comes from Washington, D.C.; actually it isn't true."

"Obviously, we're going to have to keep a very close watch over Mary," Ralph Hillman said.

"From this moment on, it's going to be a major job. We're going to set up a stake-out, and to man it, everyone is going to have to put in some overtime. Or I can get some help from Spokane. How do you feel about that?"

After a few seconds, Brad Oster answered. "This is our case, and I think we ought to handle it ourselves. I'm sure that we can."

Tallon looked at the rest and read agreement on their faces. "All right, but we can't fall down on the job for a moment. If we do, you know what could happen to Mary. She lives on the ground floor of a small apartment building. After an open area there's another apartment house very much like it in design. And here we luck out: there's a vacant flat that overlooks the windows of Mary's apartment. They can't be seen from the street out front, and the rapist has used that means of entry three times before."

When he paused he saw that his men were listening intently.

"We'll use the vacant apartment for our stake-out. The telephone company installed a line in it this morning with a flashing light instead of a bell. Also the special alarm system in Mary's apartment will read out both here and at the stake-out. So we're all set up. Effective today, from ten in the evening until dawn, at least one of us is going to have to man the stake-out without interruption.

"About the patrol cars: they are not—repeat, not—to go past Mary's apartment any more frequently than usual. We're dealing with a man clever enough to have left us completely out in the cold after every one of his known attacks. It's not going to be an easy capture, and we can't risk a tip-off of any sort. All clear so far?"

There was no response.

"Now, we need a cover story. Tell your wives, and anyone else concerned, that we expect another attempt at a narcotics delivery to the college. To thwart that we are putting up some secret surveillance out on the highway. That will explain your absence while you're on your actual assignment. Otherwise, keep your mouth tight shut about this whole operation; don't even give out the cover story unless you have to. The more cautious you are, the more it will be believed."

Gary Mason put up his hand halfway. "How are we going to get in and out of the stake-out without being spotted?" he asked.

"A good point," Tallon told him. "There's a back entrance that's well screened by shrubbery and some parking slots for the tenants' cars. On the municipal parking lot I've got a brown Ford that's been loaned to us; Francie has the keys. It's only to be used for going back and forth to the stake-out, except in an emergency. Try not to drive it during daylight hours and never in uniform; not in a town of this size."

When he concluded his briefing, he gave out the overtime assignments and outlined the exact procedures he wanted followed. His men listened carefully and they all seemed satisfied with the plan he had drawn up.

When he was back in his office, Frank Smallins came in. "I had quite a talk with the mayor of River Falls," he said. He tried to make his voice as matter-of-fact as he could, but he did not entirely succeed. "He told me about the opening for a new police chief up there."

"Yes, I know."

"Chief, I'm a little bowled over that you recommended me for the job."

"Why?" Tallon asked. "You've got the experience, unofficially you've been second in command here for some time, and in my opinion you're ready for it."

Smallins was temporarily at a loss for words. "Anyhow," he said finally, "I wanted you to know how much I appreciate it."

"I'd hate very much to lose you, Frank, but I won't stand in the way of your taking a more responsible assignment. I hope you get it."

Smallins hesitated for a moment, then he held out his hand. "You're the best chief that we've ever had," he said. "We all know that. If I do get the job, I'll try to do half as well."

Tallon stood up and took his hand. He hadn't asked for any thanks and Smallins's gratitude embarrassed him. After all, he still hadn't caught the rapist.

That evening Ed Wyncott took the first shift at the stake-out apartment. He had dressed in outdoor type clothing that made him look even stockier than usual. He went equipped with a pair of binoculars, a couple of sandwiches, and a Thermos of hot coffee. He checked his sidearm and then left for his vigil. Walt Cooper was scheduled to relieve him later.

In the morning both men had done their jobs, but nothing whatever had happened. At an agreed upon time Mary had touched the alarm twice quickly, confirming that the system was still operating properly; that had been all.

It went like that for the rest of the week. No one could remember a time when it had been so quiet at the Whitewater Police Department. Hardly a call of any kind came in, not even a barking dog complaint.

On request, Frank Smallins sent a detailed résumé and a photograph of himself in uniform to Mayor Crawford at River Falls. Tallon dictated a letter to be enclosed recommending him for the vacancy.

The next issue of the paper appeared without a word in it about Mary Clancy or her roommate.

Tallon came in on Saturday morning as if by doing so he could somehow force a showdown. It was as quiet as a crypt. He went to the Barbecue Pit with Judge Howell and overate out of pure frustration. In accordance with the strict rule that he had laid down himself, he did not even tell the judge about the stake-out or the trap that had been set.

The judge sensed his mood and was careful not to pry. He was able to make an excellent guess as to what was the matter and kept the conversation as far away from the subject of the rapist as he was able.

When he returned to his office, Tallon reviewed the carefully hidden schedule of stake-out assignments and noted that Wayne Mudd had the second trick on Sunday night. Since Mudd had already stood three watches without complaint, Tallon crossed out his name and wrote in his own. In only a ten-man department his services as a working policeman were essential in any operation that called for manpower.

Feeling a little better, he went home to Jennifer. She met him at the door and kissed him. "How is the roadblock?" she asked.

"So far, nothing," he answered. "We have some intelligence reports that there may be a shipment coming in very soon. We know most of the cars that are in and around the college now, so we have a little better chance to spot the one that we're after."

"Have you any idea what it looks like?" Jennifer asked.

Tallon shook his head. "I'm sorry, I can't tell you that."

That reassured her; obviously he did know. Soon, she was confident, he would score another triumph.

After the last TV show that they watched together on Sunday night, Jack went into the kitchen and made himself a sandwich. "I'm going out to the roadblock," he told Jennifer when she came to see what he was doing. "I won't ask my men to do anything that I won't do myself."

Jennifer understood; she prepared a container of coffee and wrapped a doughnut in waxed paper. At a quarter to twelve Ed Wyncott picked him up in the patrol car and drove him to within three short blocks of the stake-out location. There he got out and completed his trip on foot. No one called the police station to report a strange man in their neighborhood and he met no one on the way. He went to the back door and let himself in.

The building was quiet. He climbed the few steps to the corridor level and then went quickly to the door of the apartment. He slipped inside, where Ned Asher was waiting for him. When the door had been carefully shut, they were able to talk in whispers.

"Anything?" Tallon asked.

"No, nothing at all. Mary's home and she's going to bed right now."

"Window unlocked?"

"Up three or four inches, as ordered."

"O.K., I'll take over. You know where to meet Wyncott."

"Right. Have a good night." The door opened and closed noiselessly; after that he was alone.

He sat down in the chair that had been placed where it gave a clear view of the side of Mary's apartment and her bedroom windows. There was a good hundred feet of open space between the buildings, but the high quality binoculars that were part of the stake-out equipment effectively took care of that. Under other circumstances he might have felt a little like a peeping Tom, but Mary knew that the stake-out was being maintained, and she had volunteered to be under surveillance.

He sat quietly for half an hour until his eyes had adjusted fully to night vision. After that, by means of what light leaked into the room, he was able to see quite clearly. He checked the location of the telephone and the various other equipment on hand. The room was otherwise empty and the light was too dim for him to be able to see what color the walls had been painted.

At the end of fifty minutes he got up and exercised his legs, being careful to make no noise—he had been on stake-outs many times before. He did two or three knee bends, rotated his arms in the air for a few seconds, and then sat down again. Opening the vacuum bottle, he poured himself a cup of coffee.

He burned his mouth a little on the first sip and grimaced, knowing that the tenderness would stay with him for the rest of the night—a minor irritation that went with the job. He finished the rest of his coffee more cautiously and then, unwrapping his sandwich, he picked up some of the butter on his fingertip and applied it to his tongue. It gave him a little relief that would last for a few minutes. After that he sat still, watched, and tried to think of things that would keep him awake.

He remained there, making sure that he did not doze, until he got up once more, poured a little more coffee, and then went into the bathroom.

He was standing in front of the toilet when a flash of red light painted his shadow on the wall. In a matter of five seconds, his heart already pounding, he was out of the bathroom and in one glance confirmed that the signal light was on.

As adrenaline pumped into his body, he took one second to look across at the apartment he had been watching; the bedroom window was wide open. The signal confirmed, he dashed for the door, yanked it open, and almost threw himself down the rear steps.

He collided hard with a man who was at that moment coming in: a powerful, burly man who grabbed him and slammed him down onto the concrete-floored entryway. "What the hell are you doing here?" he demanded.

Tallon had to fight for breath; the impact of his landing had forced most of the air out of his lungs. "Police," he managed to gasp. "Let me go!"

"I don't buy that," the man came back, hard and heavy. He literally yanked Tallon to his feet. "We'll call the cops and find out just who you really are."

It was no time for the niceties; in one quick solid movement Tallon freed himself and whipped out his badge. "Look!" he said.

"Then what in the hell . . . ?"

He did not hear the rest of the words. As he swung open the rear door his body protested violently; he had landed harder than he had realized. A sharp, stinging pain tore at his side as he dashed outside into the cold air.

He ran across the open area, his side crying for respite, toward the open window. His mind was fixed with total determination on his objective; his aches and pains were thrust aside. He got close to the window at last; just as he did so, he heard his patrol car scream to a halt at the front of the building, its overhead lights biting into the blackness of the night. He braced himself, took a short run, and launched himself into a flat dive through the open window.

He didn't actually feel it when he hit, he only knew that he did and then rolled with his head tucked close in and his arms protecting his neck. Then he was on his feet, legs apart, his weapon almost automatically in his hand.

There was a dim bedside lamp on and beside it stood Mary Clancy, naked, the pink glow dramatically outlining her body. And there was a man, a man with a mask over his face, and a knife held in his outstretched hand. The man whirled and the face of the Frankenstein monster was ghastly in the pale light.

"Freeze!" Tallon yelled, hurling his voice into the man's face.

The monster leapt at him, ignoring the gun. They went down together, the knife still in the man's hand. Tallon knew that the face he saw was only a mask, but its horrible realism made it seem alive. When he saw the arm come up, and the point of the knife, he reacted almost instantly. With a co-ordinated jerk of his body he rolled over, away from the knife, taking the other man with him. As soon as he saw the masked face below him, he smashed the heel of his right hand with all of his power onto the bridge of the nose. His own side burned with agony.

From behind the rubber mask he heard an agonized cry, then the knife hit him in the back.

The thrust was weak and somewhat blocked by his left arm, but he knew at once that it had drawn blood. He clamped his teeth and refused to let it handicap him.

The door burst open and tall Jerry Quigley was there with his gun drawn. As Quigley hit the light switch, Tallon thrust both of his thumbs into the front of his opponent's neck, just above the muscular V where it joined the breastbone.

The sound that came in response was almost a gurgling; the man under him could not draw breath. Tallon held the pressure hard, savagely, until he felt the man slacken off, then he released one hand and knocked the knife away.

While his own body screamed in protest, he rolled the man over, grabbed his left wrist, and locked on one side of a pair of steel handcuffs. He was not even conscious that he had reached for them.

Quigley seized the other arm and held it while Tallon finished locking on the cuffs. At that moment Brad Oster appeared at the window, leaning half inside with his gun drawn.

His side bursting with pain, and his body all but limp, Tallon picked up his own gun, put it away, and got to his feet. He could hardly stand. He turned to Mary, who was tying a robe about her, and asked, "Are you all right?"

She was astonishingly calm. "Yes, he never touched me. God, you guys got here in a hurry!"

He looked down at the suspect and then with Quigley's help turned him over. The hideous mask was twisted sideways so that the mouth appeared to be grotesquely at one side of the face. Without trying to be gentle, Tallon reached behind the man's head, pulled it off, and looked into the face of Bert Ziegler.

Chapter Nineteen

He should not have moved so quickly; the pain in his side ballooned into agony and for the first time he was conscious of additional pain in the middle of his back. Because he had to, he sat down on the corner of Mary's bed and tried to recover himself.

"Take him in," he told Quigley, and then allowed himself a few moments of motionless peace. He sat with his eyes closed, trying to block out the burning agony in his body.

The slamming throw he had taken in the hallway had done him more damage than he had realized. He remembered then that he had not landed flat, but onto something—he didn't know what. That had made things vastly worse. He was in so much pain for the next half minute, he did not think about the rapist at all.

Then he became conscious that Mary was dialing the telephone. "I want an ambulance," she said, and gave her address. "Chief Tallon has been hurt capturing a suspect."

Tallon managed to turn. "Don't bother," he said, but she had already hung up.

"Don't tell me, I'm a nurse—remember?" Mary retorted. "It won't be long."

He resigned himself because his side hurt like hell and he knew that something had to be wrong. Mary helped him to stretch out on her bed and to turn over so that he was lying on his stomach. The limited movements caused him additional pain, but he made no protest. He lay there as quietly as he could and tried to understand that the rapist had been captured. It was still surrounded with an aura of unreality in his mind. It was a nightmare—a bad dream that the throbbing pain in his body had forced into his brain.

Gary Mason came into the room and stood by, waiting to see if he could help. Jack had no idea how he had gotten there, and for the moment he didn't care. As the minutes ticked on, sleep began to overcome the stresses and strains that had been inflicted on his body. He was already half unconscious when the men came in with the ambulance cart to take him out.

It hurt, of course, when they moved him, but he didn't particularly care. There were a few people to observe as he was wheeled down the corridor and out into the street.

"Isn't that the police chief?"

"Yes, I think so."

"So he was the rapist after all! I heard . . ."

The short ride to the hospital was uncomfortable, but he was able to endure it by knowing that it would soon be over. Presently the ambulance stopped; when it went into reverse he tried to brace himself against the shock when it would hit the loading dock. The vehicle stopped, the doors were opened, and then he was being taken out. The cold air revived him momentarily and he saw that the driver had stopped inches short of making contact; he had worried about the jolt for nothing.

Then he was inside where it was warm again; he was being wheeled into a room where there was a massive bright light overhead and he wanted to cover his eyes. He glimpsed a heavyset, middle-aged nurse who gave him a fractional smile and then vanished from his view. A second or two later he felt his shoes being removed, and then his socks. Something partially shaded the light; he opened his eyes and saw the youthful face of Dr. Lindholm looking down into his.

"Where does it hurt?" Lindholm asked.

"My side," Tallon answered. "Left side. I had a fall."

He was lifted a few inches while his coat was expertly removed, then his tie was undone and his arms were lifted to free his shirt. That hurt enough to make him wince; a sound escaped from his lips that he tried to recall and failed. He felt probing fingers on his bare flesh, then a sudden stab of pain almost made him dizzy. Involuntarily his back arched and his teeth were set hard together.

He heard the young doctor's voice, calm and controlled. "I'll get the stab wound in the back first. Turn him over carefully; there's at least one rib fracture."

Immediately he felt better; if his ribs really were broken, then he wasn't such a fool coming to the hospital this way and crying out in pain when he was moved. He tried to relax and to take control of himself, at the same time fighting off sleep. He felt the sting of a needle in his back, but he could not tell when it was removed. He felt a second injection, not too bad this time, and then the agony that had been eating at him began to ease away. He deliberately relaxed the muscles in his neck and tried not to think of anything.

When he awoke he discovered that he was in bed, but the head end had been raised so that he was halfway up to a sitting position. A series of dull aches throbbed through his body, but he did not really mind. He looked about him, saw that it was daylight, and became conscious of the fact that he was in a hospital room. The next thing he experienced was an awareness of a massive amount of tape strapped to his side; it was a little difficult to breathe and it was as stiff as concrete.

The door opened and Mary Clancy came in, fresh and radiant in her white starched uniform. "Good morning," she greeted him. "You look a sight."

He raised his right hand and felt the stubble on his chin. Then he became aware that his mouth was full of morning aftertaste. Strands of his hair were dangling in front of his eyes. "You look great," he said. "Terrific. But not as good as you did last night."

"A girl is a girl just like every other girl," Mary said as she moved a small table on wheels up next to his bed. "That's something you've got to remember."

She fixed his pillows, carefully applied some pre-shave to his face, and then handed him an electric razor. "Go to it," she directed. "Incidently, you had a nice bath this morning. I gave it to you, so we're even."

"Why didn't I wake up?"

"Because we had you doped, silly. Jennifer is on her way; she was here most of last night until we sent her home. Also a Joe Hanley is here to see you."

"I don't know any Joe Hanley."

"He says that you do. Anyhow, shave."

Tallon obeyed. He brushed his teeth with the aid of a chin basin that Mary held for him and then with his own comb that had been taken from his jacket pocket he got his hair out of his eyes and back into something approaching its normal condition. When he had finished, Mary took the table away and tucked in the bedsheets. "How about some breakfast?" she asked.

"What time is it?"

"Daytime. Take it easy and I'll have something for you shortly. Shall I send in Hanley?"

"All right, whoever he is."

Mary went out and for a minute or two he was alone. Then the door opened once more and a muscular young man who could have been a professional football player came in. As he approached the bed, Tallon could not recall him.

"Chief Tallon, I'm Joe Hanley."

"What can I do for you?"

"I came by to tell you how sorry I am about last night. I had no idea who you were; I only saw a guy burst out of an apartment and try to leg it as fast as he could out the back door. I remembered the rapist, so I went after you. I threw you on top of the lawn mower that was parked in the rear hallway, and that's why you're here. You're welcome to prefer charges if you want to."

Tallon shook his head and held out his hand. "What do you do?" he asked.

"I'm a railroad foreman in Spokane. I was just coming off shift when I ran into you."

"Joe, you did exactly the right thing. A lot of people just stand by so that they won't get involved. I hate their Goddamn guts. You had every right to believe that I had no business there and you did something about it. Thank you."

"You're a damn good sport about it," Hanley said.

Tallon managed to gesture with his right hand. "Hell, back in Pasadena they give awards to citizens who respond to emergencies. Next time, do it again, unless you happen to know that it's a policeman."

Hanley had nothing to say after that. He shook hands again, and left the room. A few seconds later Jennifer came in and when he saw her, every ache and pain in his body seemed to disappear. She bent over and kissed him.

"I'll be out of here right away," he promised.

"I know; Mary briefed me. You'll be home in your own bed tonight. But no strenuous exercise for a little while."

"Damn it to hell," Tallon said.

He was released shortly before three that afternoon. Moving a little gingerly, because of the heavy taping on his side, he insisted on going to his office. Propped behind his desk, he read the reports of the previous night's activity. A warm, comforting glow took over his body as he realized that the rapist was lodged in a cell sixty feet from where he sat.

He sent for Frank Smallins, who came in promptly. "Have you talked to the suspect?" Tallon asked.

Smallins sat down without being asked. "Yes, at considerable length. He wanted to talk after we finished booking him last night. Since you weren't available, I did the best that I could."

"You gave him his rights, of course."

"Twice—once when we picked him up, again after he had been booked. He didn't want a lawyer and he did want to unburden himself. I got the feeling that in a way he was glad that he had been caught, and that it was all over."

"Obviously he read the cover story on Mary."

"Read it—hell, he set it. I blame myself, Chief, that I didn't think of one thing: Bert worked at the paper, where he had to read all of the little fill-in items, because it was his job to put them into type. It was doing that, week after week, that gave him the idea you figured out—about wanting to have women from all different cities. After he had been talking with me for a while, he broke down and cried like a baby. He kept insisting that he never really wanted to hurt anyone."

Tallon shook his head. "Frank, have you ever noticed that some of the most aggressive people become the most penitent when they get caught, or have to take the responsibilities for their actions? And they always have some kind of rationalization, some explanation that they feel gives them justification. I can't feel sorry for Bert. He had a good job; Harry Gilroy is close to retirement and Bert was in line to take over the whole operation. Now, no matter what, he can never amount to a damn for the rest of his life."

Smallins nodded. "There are times when I'm not too happy about being a cop, but this isn't one of them. Do you know what he said to me at one point? He said that he wasn't really doing any harm because those women he attacked were going to waste. By that he meant that they weren't properly appreciated and utilized. And I think he really believed it."

"He's sick, Frank, he has to be to think like that."

Smallins stood up. "Anyhow, it's over," he said. "Congratulations."

When Tallon arrived at the city council meeting a day later he was wearing a knit shirt because it was one of the few garments he owned that would stretch over the heavy taping on his side. It was beginning to itch badly and he would have given a week's pay for a good satisfying scratch. But that couldn't be, so he had to endure it. Arnold Petersen personally prepared a cup of coffee for him and then invited him to take the floor.

Tallon was prepared. He gave a concise résumé of the work that had been done on the rapist case prior to the time that he had had his flash of insight in Seattle. Then he explained how the trap had been set, giving particular praise to Harry Gilroy for his story about Mary Clancy. He spoke a good word for his men and then suggested that the council make some special recognition of Mary's co-operation and courage. "The rest of it I believe you know," he concluded. "We found a map in his room; on it he had drawn circles around certain cities—the ones from which his victims had come."

"Would you say that he was mentally ill?" Marion McNeil asked.

"With the obsession he had, I don't believe that he's normal. Whether he's legally responsible or not I can't say—that's for the court to decide. We do have a full confession, Sergeant Smallins got that, and it should save the state the cost of a trial."

Dick Collins sat quietly and said nothing.

Petersen spoke on behalf of the council. "Jack, we're all immensely grateful to you and your men for a great piece of work. I'll skip the platitudes, but we're glad that you're here."

"Thank you," Tallon responded.

When the meeting broke up, Harry Gilroy took a folded newspaper out of his pocket and handed it across without comment. Tallon opened it and saw the headline: RAPIST CAUGHT. He took time to read the story, which was brisk, lucid, and pulled no punches concerning Bert Ziegler's employment by the newspaper. There was a different picture of Mary Clancy, one of Ziegler, and one of himself. The credit line under Mary's photograph was "Bert Ziegler," perhaps an intentional comment on the potential opportunity that a horribly misdirected sex drive had killed forever.

It was a good account, although Tallon felt that his own role had been overplayed and it embarrassed him a little. Catching the rapist had been part of his job, something that he was paid to do.

When he returned to his office, Smallins met him with a piece of news. "While you were away, I got a call from River Falls," he said. "The job is mine if I want it."

Tallon shook hands with enthusiasm. "I'm delighted; congratulations. We'll be working together, I'm sure of that."

"I only hope I can hack it."

"Get that doubt out of your mind," Tallon advised. "You can, there's no doubt of it. How soon do they want you?"

"As soon as I'm ready. Fortunately, there's no great rush."

"Still, you'd better plan on going up there as soon as you can."

Smallins dropped his voice. "I'd like to put in a word for Wayne Mudd," he said. "He's a good candidate for a sergeant's job."

"I already had him in mind," Tallon told him. "Good luck, Chief Smallins."

"I hope to hell that I can live up to it the way you have," Smallins said. Then he turned quickly and left the office.

Francie appeared. "Marion is here—Marion McNeil. She wants to know if you're free."

Tallon went out to the front desk, where the councilwoman was waiting for him. "Could you get away for a few minutes?" she asked.

"I think so. Is anything wrong?"

"No, but I want to talk with you. Perhaps we could drive somewhere."

Although the air was crisp, he did not go back for his topcoat. The sun was bright and the heater in his official car worked very well. He told Francie that he would be out for a little while, then with Marion beside him he drove down toward Main Street. "Any particular place?" he asked.

"How about the north road."

Eight minutes later Whitewater was behind them and they were on the open highway. The Washington countryside was rich with fall colors. Where there were trees, intricate patterns of leaves lay under them. He set an even steady pace as he sat angled on the seat, his tender back fitted into the corner between the seat and the side door. In that position he was half facing his passenger. "How can I help you, Marion?" he asked.

His companion looked straight ahead through the windshield as she answered. "Jack, you remember when Lily Hope was spreading some malicious gossip—about us."

"Yes; of course."

"I said then that I had never been so furious in my life. That old bitch called me a public woman to my face, and her awful smugness made me want to tear her eyes out."

"But you didn't."

"No, I didn't, but the more I thought about it, the more I made up my mind to have it out with her."

Tallon continued his driving, keeping his eyes on the road.

"I knew that if I went to her front door, she wouldn't let me in. She always knew who was there, because she watched all the time. So when I drove over, I parked a block away and walked across to the back of her house. She was old and frail and I knew that I couldn't touch her, but I could threaten suit and tell her that I was going to take her house away from her. I knew that I shouldn't have gone, and I hated the very idea of seeing her, but I was blind with anger."

She waited for a moment, but Tallon offered no comment, waiting for her to continue.

Presently she did. "Up here most of us leave our back doors unlocked all the time. I knew that if I knocked on hers, she'd come and bolt it in my face, so I opened it and let myself into her kitchen. Legally that's probably breaking and entering, but we all do that a lot and no one thinks anything of it.

"As soon as I was inside, I realized that the house was dark. Since she never went out evenings, I knew what she must be doing. So I tiptoed into her living room to catch her in the act and there she was—up on the stepladder, using her binoculars to watch across the street. She was looking into your house."

"I know," Tallon said quietly.

"Seeing her spying like that was more than I could stand. I yelled at her, 'What are you doing!' She jumped as though she'd been shot, then she raised her arm to throw her binoculars at me. That was when she fell off. She let out a little yelp and then came down hard, with her head against the floor.

"I bent over her right away to try and help her. But her eyes were open and glassy, and she had stopped breathing. I felt over her heart and found that it wasn't beating. Then I knew she was dead. I should have called for an ambulance, but I didn't; I panicked instead. I was in a frenzy to get out of there as fast as I could and I didn't think of anything except escape. I got back to my car in the dark and went home. I was shaking so hard I almost couldn't drive."

She stopped and searched his face, fearful and afraid. Because he didn't even turn to look at her a tightness gripped her and she knew what she had done to herself. But she had to go on. "In the morning for the first time in my life I didn't know what I should do. Then—she was found." She stopped and discovered that sudden tears were running down her face. Her voice broke and she all but lost her composure completely. "I had to tell you," she said. "I couldn't keep it in any longer. Now you can take me back and do whatever you have to do."

Tallon turned the car around and then set up the same steady pace back toward Whitewater.

Finally he broke his silence. "Marion, police work is something that the public only understands to a limited degree. As a rule of thumb, policemen see life at five times the rate of ordinary citizens and we're privy to a great many things that are never made public. Also we cultivate the habit of being unusually observant, that's part of our job."

He guided the car around a lazy curve in the road and shifted a little to ease the continuing pain in his back. "The men driving our patrol cars are expected to keep their eyes open for any unusual occurrences. Being a councilwoman, you're very well known, of course. My man on patrol that night saw your car where it was parked and recognized it. After Mrs. Hope had been found dead in her home, he remembered the incident and told me about it."

"Oh, my God!" Marion said.

"Because I have a sworn duty to the community, I sent my detective, Ned Asher, out to the house with instructions to check thoroughly for any evidence of wrongdoing. He reported back that it was unquestionably a case of accidental death and his formal finding is in our official records."

He paused and waited until he judged that it was the right time to continue. "Frankly, Marion, I knew that you had been there, which is why I directed Ned to check everything out completely. And as you said, I knew your frame of mind at the time. But I couldn't see you making a felonious assault on a frail old woman, no matter what the provocation. The fact that there was no evidence whatever of any foul play supported my belief that her fall had been accidental."

"But I *was* there," Marion said.

"True, but Mrs. Hope put herself into a precarious position, and you had nothing to do with that."

"Are you sure that you're not just trying to whitewash me?" Marion asked.

Tallon shook his head. "Not at all. First of all, there was no deliberate malice on your part. I firmly believe that you did nothing intentional to make her fall off that ladder, and if you could have prevented it, you would have. You startled her, there's no doubt about that, but that isn't an indictable offense. If I did try to make a case against you, the DA would throw it out for lack of evidence. Even if it went to trial, there's no way you could be convicted, because the risk Mrs. Hope was exposed to was of her own making and no fault of yours."

The seconds passed silently after that for some time; the only sounds that intruded were made by the car as it rolled steadily down the road. Marion found a handkerchief and wiped underneath her eyes. Then she turned her face toward the man beside her. "Thank you," she said.

Tallon continued to drive, knowing that he had not allowed his friendship with Marion, or her official position, to influence his judgment.

The radio came on. "Whitewater One." Francie's voice was loud and clear.

Tallon reached for the microphone. "Whitewater One; go ahead."

"Chief, there's something up and you'd better come in."

That was good; she hadn't said any more over the air than was necessary.

"ETA ten minutes. Do you need me code three?"

"If you don't mind, Chief."

So it was something heavy. He flicked the switch that turned on the overhead lights as he picked up speed, and then activated the siren. Within seconds he was up to seventy. Blocking the presence of his passenger out of his mind, he held the wheel expertly, maintaining a sharp lookout for any possible cross traffic that might suddenly appear. In a semi-rural area that could happen. As he drove, he checked in his mind who he had on duty and who should be promptly available in case he needed more manpower on short notice.

But whatever it was, he would handle it. He would have to, because that was his job and his responsibility. He was the top man on the totem pole. Whitewater was depending on him, and he knew that he would not let his city down.

Manufactured by Amazon.ca
Bolton, ON